Anne Allen lives in Devon, by her beloved sea. She has three children and her daughter and two grandchildren live nearby. Her restless spirit has meant a number of moves, the longest stay being in Guernsey for fourteen years after falling in love with the island and the people. She contrived to leave one son behind to ensure a valid reason for frequent returns. By profession a psychotherapist, Anne has now written three novels, the first being Award-Winning *Dangerous Waters*.

Visit her website at www.anneallen.co.uk

Praise for Guernsey Retreat

'I enjoyed the descriptive tour while following the lives of strangers as their worlds collide, when the discovery of a body, and the death of a relative draw them into links with the past. A most pleasurable, intriguing read.' *Glynis Smy, author of Maggie's Child*

Praise for Finding Mother

'A sensitive, heart-felt novel about family relationships, identity, adoption, second chances at love… With romance, weddings, boat trips, lovely gardens and more, Finding Mother is a dazzle of a book, a perfect holiday read.' *Lindsay Townsend, author of The Snow Bride*

Praise for Dangerous Waters

'A wonderfully crafted story with a perfect balance of intrigue and romance.' *The Wishing Shelf Awards, 22 July 2013 – Dangerous Waters*

Also by Anne Allen

Dangerous Waters
Finding Mother

Anne Allen

GUERNSEY RETREAT

Sarnia Press
London

Sarnia Press
Unit 1, 1 Sans Walk
London EC1R 0LT

ISBN 9780992711214
Typeset in 12pt Aldine401 BT Roman by Sarnia Press

To my children, Louise, Craig and Grant, with love

"Whenever evil befalls us, we ought to ask ourselves,
after the first suffering, how we can turn it into good.
So shall we take occasion, from one bitter root, to raise
perhaps many flowers."

Leigh Hunt

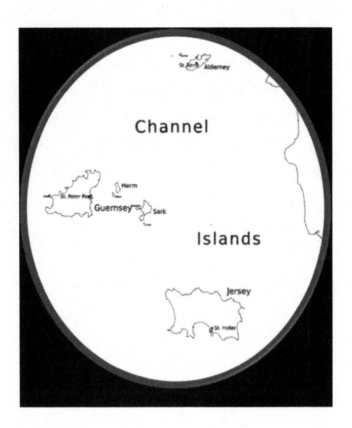

chapter 1

1939 – September – Guernsey

Betty woke with a start. For a moment she wondered what had disturbed her but then the sound of shouting cut across the silence of her bedroom. Groaning, she swung her legs out of bed, and grabbed the old, patched dressing gown that Roland insisted should be thrown out. But she hated throwing things away and pulled the belt tight around her thickening waist before tiptoeing out into the passage.

Darkness enveloped her but as she crept towards the stairs she could see lights in the hall, guiding the way. She trod softly downstairs, knowing that her appearance would only provoke the men further. Roland, her employer and now fiancé, and Archie, his nephew and her one-time lover. She could guess what they were fighting about – her. Their voices echoed around the expanse of the hall as Betty's bare feet hardly touched the granite-tiled floor as she headed for the library – Roland's domain and the source of the shouting.

Her heart pounded as she hesitated outside the door. She hated the thought the men were now at loggerheads and, from what she could hear through the slightly ajar oak door, close to blows. Peering through the gap, she could just make out their figures. Roland sat behind the imposing mahogany desk he'd inherited from his grandfather. He glared at Archie, who leaned over the desk, his fists thrust towards his uncle. With his back to the door Betty couldn't see his face, but guessed it would be red with anger. He'd always had a temper on him.

'I'll marry who I like! I won't be told what I can or can't do by some young whipper-snapper who doesn't know when he's well off.' Roland thumped the desk before standing up, looking down at Archie. 'I took you in out of duty after that benighted sister of mine died. And in spite of what you claim, I never promised to adopt you and make you my heir. Why would I, while there was still a chance I'd marry and have children of my own?' He marched around the desk to stand proud and tall in front of Archie. Betty's heart swelled with love as she squinted through the crack. *You tell him, Roland! Cocky braggart! He can't hold a candle to you.*

'And now I *am* marrying and about to become a father and count myself the luckiest of men. But I'll not see you homeless, boy–'

'You're damn right you won't!' Archie shouted, causing Betty to jump. 'You owe me, Uncle. I've worked hard for you these past seven years and been paid a pittance. I didn't complain, thinking I'd inherit one day. But now you tell me I'll get nothing and it's not right!' Archie's fists were now clenched by his side, his head thrust close up against Roland's. Betty's heart beat faster. *Oh, dear God! Don't let them start fighting, I couldn't bear it.*

'I paid you the going rate for the work you've done, such as it was. You're not exactly the hardest worker I've employed, boy. And as we don't even know who your father was, I'm not legally obliged to provide for you.' Roland paced around and Betty only caught a glimpse of him now and then.

'You can stay here at La Folie if you like, after Betty and I are wed and leave for Canada. I want us to be far away now war's been declared. Stay here as my steward until the fighting's over and we can return–'

'No!' Archie's voice, harsh and desperate, filled the air. Betty held her breath, her hands placed protectively on her stomach. She caught a glimpse of Archie as he grabbed something from the desk before lunging forward out of sight. A loud cracking sound, followed by a groan, propelled her through the door.

At the sight of her beloved Roland stretched out on the floor, blood pouring from an ugly gash on his head, she felt everything go black and crashed to the floor. The next thing she knew, strong arms lifted her up and sat her down roughly in a chair. As her head cleared, she looked up at Archie's face a few inches in front of her.

'Why did you come down, you daft woman! Thought you'd be asleep,' Archie growled.

'What have you done? Roland...?' Betty twisted her head to try and see her fiancé but Archie blocked her vision.

'I...I didn't mean to hit him that hard. He hit his head on the corner of the desk as he went down.' He screwed up his face and gripped Betty's arms. 'He's out cold. I–'

Betty drew on all her strength and managed to push Archie from her, before crawling across to where Roland lay.

'Oh, my God! Don't say you've killed him!' she cried, kneeling beside Roland's inert form. 'Here, help me turn him over.'

Archie knelt and rolled Roland onto his back. One look told them both that he was dead.

Tears splashed down as Betty hugged Roland's battered and bleeding head. She rocked back and forth, a keening sound escaped from her lips.

'He got me so mad about me not inheriting anything. I'm family! He owed me–'

Betty was hot with rage.

'He owed you nothing! Like he said. Why couldn't you have been satisfied with being steward? Thanks to your greed I've lost the man I love and my child is fatherless before it's born. Oh, Roland, Roland!'

She carried on rocking, as sobs racked her body. Roland's blooded face filled her with horror. They had planned to see the vicar about the banns that very day, wanting to marry at the end of the month. She had been so happy, so looking forward not only to marrying Roland, but to the adventure of sailing off to Canada. Away from the inevitable reality of war. Roland had often said that the Channel Islands were particularly vulnerable, with the islanders not standing a chance if Hitler decided to invade.

But now…Thanks to Archie and that temper of his, she was a widow before she was a wife. And carrying the child that had filled Roland with such joy and pride.

'We…we have to bury him, Betty. And then get away from here. I'm not going to hang for this…'

Betty looked up sharply. 'What do you mean "we"? This is all your doing, not mine. I've just seen you kill my…my love in cold blood! I'll have no part in your trying to cover it up. Once I tell the police–'

Archie grabbed her arms and shook her till her teeth rattled.

'You're not telling no police nothing! If you so much as start to spill the beans to anyone, I'll say you did it. A lover's tiff. It'll be your word against mine. Either way, you'd be an accessory and would hang as well.'

Betty's head reeled with grief and anger.

'You won't get away with that! Everyone knows how much we loved each other. And I'm carrying his child! Why would I…I kill him?'

'I wouldn't say you *meant* to. It was an accident. Just like it was with me. But they still might find you guilty of

4

murder and you'd hang. So,' he said, letting go of her bruised arms, 'we have to get away. And soon.'

Betty tried to focus on what Archie was saying. Was it true? They were alone in the house and there was no-one to support her. The rest of the staff lived out and wouldn't return until the morning. Her parents were dead and she had no other family. Although considered a bright pupil at the Girls' School, Betty had found it difficult to get a good job until Roland appointed her his housekeeper. It was Archie who'd got her the position, when they'd been sweet on each other, three years ago. That had not lasted long, not once she discovered his awful temper. And Archie hadn't reckoned with her falling in love with Roland. And he her.

'But where can we go? And what'll we do for money?' Betty sat dazed on the floor, still cradling Roland's head. Surely this was all a bad dream and she'd wake up and everything would be as it was. The two of them off to St Phillipe's to see the vicar…

Archie paced around, tugging at his hair, as if that would give him inspiration.

'We'll have to get away from the islands. Get to England somehow.'

'But I don't want to go to England! This is my home, where I belong–'

'Not anymore it isn't! It's not safe for either of us now. I just need to think…' He pulled up short. 'I know. That Ed Sarre owes me a favour. He can take us in his fishing boat. I'll make up some story that Roland wants us to leave quickly now that war's been declared and that he's flying out to join us once he's locked up the place. As for money, there's plenty here worth a bob or two and Roland always kept a wad of cash in the safe, so we'll be all right. But first we have to bury him. And quick, before it gets light.'

Betty found herself dragged roughly to her feet and forced to find a sheet in which to wrap Roland. She moved around as if in a trance, her mind shutting her off from the reality of what was happening. All she knew was that her life was about to change. And not for the better.

chapter 2

2008 – October – Guernsey

'Hold it there!' the foreman shouted to the digger driver, flagging him to stop. The giant arms stopped, poised over the hole in the ground, leaving the serrated metal jaws of the bucket swinging above Bill's head as he jumped down for a closer look. He'd been right, there *was* something sticking out of the soil. The driver joined him.

'What's up, Bill?'

'I'm not sure, but I think…Oh, God! It's an arm!' Bill had brushed some of the soil away from what had appeared to be a white stick. The skeletal remains of an arm and hand poked up from the surrounding earth.

'Better call the police, Ted, while I go and have a word with the boss.'

Ted nodded, peering uneasily over Bill's shoulder before pulling out his mobile phone. Bill strode off into the house, his pale face displayed his feelings of shock.

*

Malcolm Roget looked up from the plans spread over his desk as the foreman knocked on the library door.

'Sorry to disturb you, Mr Roget, but we've got a bit of a problem in the…pool.' Bill shuffled his feet before blurting out, 'Looks like there's a body down there and…'

Malcolm felt his heart pounding. His mother had told him…Could it be…?

7

'Right, thank you Bill. I'm coming. Have you called the police?'

They walked out of the back door as Bill confirmed the police had been informed. To their right lay a gate leading to what had been an area littered with defunct glasshouses, now cleared away in preparation for the new swimming pool and changing rooms. The bright orange arms of the unnaturally quiet digger hung over the hole meant for the pool: now apparently a grave. And what a grave! Malcolm thought, shrugging off Bill's proffered arm.

'I can manage, thank you. I'm not that old,' he grunted, not willing to give into his advancing years. But the jump down jarred his knees and he winced slightly, covering it up with a cough. Bill pointed to what looked like a bleached piece of wood.

'Over there. Lucky I spotted it before Ted reached it.' Bill nodded towards the digger where Ted sat crouched in the cabin, pulling on a cigarette. 'Nothing's been moved but I did brush away some soil so I could be sure...'

Malcolm nodded. 'You did the right thing. Make sure no-one comes near the area and let me know as soon as the police arrive. I'll be in the library.'

Fifteen minutes later Bill popped his head round the library door to say that the police were outside and Malcolm followed him to the excavation. Already the dug-out area looked like a crime scene: white-suited forensic officers loaded with bags were converging on the small white object highlighted against the brown soil. As Malcolm arrived, a man giving instructions broke off to meet him.

'Mr Roget? Inspector Ferguson. I understand that you're the owner of La Folie?'

'Yes, have been for some months now. As you can see, the men are digging out for the swimming pool and my foreman spotted the...arm and stopped the work.' Malcolm pulled the policeman to one side, saying, 'I may have some information that will be of use, Inspector. If we could talk in private?'

Ferguson, looking surprised, nodded his agreement, and told his men to tape off the area and erect the tent over the body.

Walking towards the house, Malcolm considered the best way of explaining what he knew – or rather, what he thought he knew.

He turned to face the inspector.

'My mother used to live here before the war. She worked for, and was engaged to, the owner, Roland Blake.' He pushed his hands in his pockets, feeling the inspector's eyes on him. As he continued, he remembered the pain on his mother Betty's face as she told him, tearfully, of the events of the night that had changed their lives forever. His own anger towards Archie had stayed with him ever since, bursting into the flame now coursing through him with the discovery of a body. His fists clenched as he finished, 'Apparently Archie buried the body in the adjoining field, not far from the house.' He pointed to where the digger's arm could be seen against the sky. 'Could have been there.'

'Mm. Right, thanks for that. Might be useful once we've got the body out and the forensics come back. Must have been about seventy years ago, then?'

Malcolm nodded. 'Yes, back in '39. I was born the following year.' He gazed at the inspector. 'Roland was my father, you see. He and my mother were due to be married but...'

Inspector Ferguson let out a long breath.

'I see. In that case I'm sorry that you've had to find him like this. But if it *is* your father's body over there, then we can prove it from the DNA. Could be a great help, Mr Roget.'

For a moment both men stood lost in thought as they watched the forensic team erect the tent before disappearing inside.

'Excuse me for asking, sir, but did you buy this property because it was connected to your family?'

Malcolm smiled.

'It was part of the reason. It felt right that I should own it as, after all, if my father had lived and married my mother, I would have inherited it anyway.' Adding softly, 'And my mother would have had a much easier life and perhaps lived longer.' Pulling himself upright, he went on, 'But the main reason I bought La Folie is because it's an ideal place for a natural health centre, or retreat.' He waved his arms around the walled garden and to the side where the pool had been dug out. 'Plenty of land around it and a path straight onto the cliffs. Idyllic, don't you think, Inspector?'

'Yes, sir, it is. A lovely spot. But getting back to your…father and what happened. You said that your mother's dead but what about the nephew, Archie? Could he still be alive?'

Malcolm shook his head.

'I've no idea. My mother managed to give him the slip when he was called up to fight shortly after their arrival in England. She took me with her to Canada. I was only a baby so remember nothing about it. She never returned to Guernsey or the UK and died in 1972. For obvious reasons neither of us wanted to meet up with him again and my mother changed her surname so he couldn't trace us.'

'Right. And did this Archie have any other family?'

'No, his mother died when he was a lad and no-one knew who his father was. He had his mother's surname, Blake.'

The inspector scribbled in his notebook before excusing himself to go and check on progress in the tent.

Malcolm stood, hands in pockets, watching the comings and goings. Buckets of soil were brought out of the tent and sifted before being emptied on the ground. He felt a shiver down his spine and the hairs on the back of his neck stood on end. 'Are you here, Ma? Is that my father buried over there?' he whispered. 'If it is, I'll make sure he's buried properly, don't you worry. And if that bastard Archie's still alive, I'll make sure he gets what's owing to him. Never fear.'

Several hours later Inspector Ferguson found Malcolm in the library.

'We've uncovered the body, Mr Roget. It's a complete skeleton of a man and the skull's badly crushed. So it could be your father.'

Malcolm wasn't sure whether to be relieved or not. At least he could honour his promise to his mother.

'Is there anything left on the…the body? Clothes, a watch?'

The inspector shook his head.

'No clothes, they must have gone long ago. And no watch. But there's a signet ring bearing the initials 'RB'. Which fits with it being Mr Blake. There's nothing else, which suggests his pockets were emptied before burial.' He cleared his throat. 'Did your mother mention a ring?'

Malcolm cast his mind back. It was so long ago…

'She said something about a family tradition, the men being given a gold signet ring on their twenty-first birthday. That was when I was twenty-one and she gave me this.'

He stretched out his left hand, displaying a gold ring on his little finger.

'Right. Well the evidence is stacking up, then. The pathologist will take a sample of DNA from the teeth and I'd be obliged if you'd allow us to take a sample from you, sir. That can be done now so as to save time.'

'By all means. I want this resolved as quickly as possible, Inspector.'

One of the forensic team was called for and the sample taken. Malcolm then asked a pressing question.

'Will the area be closed off for long, Inspector? Only we're due to open in three months and there's much to do...'

'I understand, sir. Once we're convinced the body's that of your father and nothing else turns up, we'll be out of your hair. I'll get the lab to fast-track the DNA result so we can finish the report for the coroner.' He gave Malcolm a quizzical look. 'You do realise there's bound to be some publicity about this, don't you? The local media are already on the case and we can't suppress it.'

Malcolm sighed. 'Yes, I thought that would happen. I know they say that all publicity is good publicity, but I'm not sure how a body turning up a few months before we open will be good for business.'

The inspector smiled.

'You'd be surprised, sir. A bit of scandal can build up interest and, if it proves to be your father buried there, people would be sympathetic and wish you well.'

'Hmm, not sure I want our family skeletons to be so literally on public show, but I take your point. You'll keep me posted, Inspector?'

'Yes, sir. As it happens, this is my last case before I retire, so I want to see it concluded as quickly and satisfactorily as you do.'

They shook hands and Malcolm was left staring at the plans strewn over his desk. He could only hope the inspector was right and the unwanted publicity would do more good than harm. His past experience as the owner of a hotel chain tended to confirm that idea. But he would still be glad when all the muck-raking was over and he could press on with the opening. And then, finally, sit back and let someone else do all the work.

chapter 3

2009 – January – London

Louisa Canning was late. She had promised her mother to be home by six and it was gone half past. Not too bad considering that her last physiotherapy patient had arrived late, causing her to miss her usual Tube connection. Consoling herself that her mother could not have long been home herself, and the dinner not likely to be spoiled, she hurried away from Angel station, clutching a bunch of red roses. Her mother's house was five minutes' walk away.

Slightly out of breath, she put her key in the lock, calling out, 'Mum, it's me! Sorry I'm late but–'

She got no further as a figure hurtled down the hall, knocking her off her feet, before continuing down the path.

Shocked and wondering who the hell he was, Louisa picked herself up and, after brushing the dirt off her coat, stared briefly after the retreating figure, trying to recognise him. Realising she had never seen him before, panic set in. Her mother! Quickly collecting the bruised-looking roses, she headed for the kitchen, calling, 'Mum! Where are you? Are you all right?' Finding the kitchen empty, she felt fear clutch her heart and ran back down the hall to the sitting room. Pushing the door open she saw her mother collapsed on the sofa, clutching her chest.

'Mum! What's happened? Who was that man?' She knelt down by her mother, frightened by how white she was. 'Is it your heart? Shall I phone for an ambulance?'

Her mother could only nod and as Louisa pulled out her mobile she saw for the first time that the room had been ransacked. *Oh, God, a burglar!* After alerting the police as well as the ambulance service, she tried to help her mother.

'It's okay, Mum, help is on the way. Where are your tablets? I'll get them for you.'

Her mother, Susan, managed to point in the direction of the kitchen and Louisa ran out and found her handbag. Fishing around she found the bottle of tablets and poured a glass of water before returning to her mother's side.

'Here you are. Just take it slowly.' Louisa offered the glass and two tablets.

Susan propped herself up and swallowed the tablets before sinking back onto the cushions. After a couple of minutes her breathing seemed to ease and she grabbed Louisa's arm.

'That...man...forced his way in when I opened the door. He...pushed me in here...became nasty, said wanted know where...jewels are. I said don't know what meant. He said...they'd seen a picture me wearing them. Then I knew what he wanted. Years ago, before you born your father let me wear jewels...charity ball.' Susan took a ragged breath and Louisa, scared, hoped the ambulance would hurry up. 'He asked where Malcolm was, wouldn't...believe me, said not know. Not heard years. He...he pushed me...around, threatened me, started pulling out drawers...cupboards.'

'It's all right, Mum. Save your strength. You can tell the police later, when you feel better.'

'No...no time, darling. Not sure...make...it. He said saw article about the business...last week. My picture...followed me home. Louisa, promise me...find Malcolm...your father, tell him...danger. He must look after...you.' Her mother's hand slipped from her arm and she lay still.

'No! No! Mum, stay with me! Stay with me, please! I can't lose you!'

Louisa sobbed over her mother's body as the sound of the doorbell echoed down the hall.

By the time the police finally left Louisa felt as if she had been in a pile-up. Although they had been kind, the persistent questions had made her feel dizzy. It was only the intervention of a paramedic that had brought proceedings to a halt and she'd been able to crawl upstairs to her own attic flat. She had been allowed to go up there as it was separate from the rest of the house, which was now out of bounds behind police tape. The doctor gave her a gentle sedative and advised her to get straight to bed, something she was only too willing to do. Louisa had been asked if there was anyone who could stay with her, but there was no-one. At least not in London.

The image of her beloved mother being taken off in an ambulance lay seared into her brain. Although it was obvious Susan was dead, out of respect for Louisa's feelings, the paramedics hadn't zipped her in one of those horrible black body bags, but laid her on a stretcher, covered in blankets, her head uncovered. That image of her mother's pale face accompanied Louisa up the stairs. Once in her own little space she undressed quickly and buried herself under the duvet, praying the sedative would give her the oblivion she craved. For the few moments before the drug kicked in, her head buzzed with questions – what was so important about the 'jewels' – who did they belong to – what had her mysterious father got to do with it – and, most importantly, who was the man who had killed her mother?

The next few days passed in a blur. Susan's sister, Margaret, came down from Yorkshire to offer Louisa much needed support. She organised the funeral director, although until the results of the post-mortem were ready, no funeral could take place. Once the police were satisfied that they'd scoured the house for prints, DNA and other clues, they allowed Louisa and Margaret access. Initially reluctant to enter the sitting room, Louisa was gently encouraged by her aunt.

'Come on, I've tidied up so it looks quite normal. Make yourself comfortable in the armchair and I'll make you a hot drink. What would you like?'

'Tea, please,' she muttered, curling into the embrace of the chair. She knew she looked a mess but didn't feel like washing her long, dirty-blonde hair which hung limply around her face. All she wanted was to sleep. With Margaret taking charge she had been free to spend most of the time in bed, but now her aunt seemed to feel that it was time to face the world. A world without her mother. As the memory took hold, Louisa struggled to hold back the tears. It was so unfair! Her mother never hurt anyone and went out of her way to help others with her charity work. Messages of condolence were pouring in but she couldn't face reading them: Margaret whisked them away to be dealt with later. At that moment she returned with a tray bearing two mugs and a plate of biscuits.

'Here you are. And how about a chocolate digestive? I remembered they're your favourite,' Margaret smiled warily as she held out the plate.

Louisa took a biscuit, nodding her thanks. She looked over the rim of the mug at her aunt. *Mm, she looks as shattered as me. Poor Margaret! First she loses her husband and now her sister. No wonder she's aged so much.* Margaret, the younger sister, was sixty-two, but her white hair and pinched face made her look more like seventy. Louisa felt a stab of remorse that she'd let Margaret take on so much when she'd only buried Charles six months ago. She gave herself a shake. *Perhaps I should do something...*

'I...I'm very grateful, Margaret, for your help. I'm not sure I could have survived the last few days if you hadn't been here. But you've got your own problems. After all, it's not long since Charles–'

Tears glistened in Margaret's eyes.

'It's not been easy, I admit, but I had to be here with you. Your mother would have expected me to help. Not that I could have foreseen the circumstances…' She wiped her eyes.

'No, neither of us could. Although we knew Mum's heart hadn't been strong for years, she seemed so well. So I suppose it…it might have happened at any time. But without that man threatening her she could still be alive. If I could get my hands on him I'd kill him!' Louisa cried, gripping her mug, anger bubbling to the surface and temporarily usurping the grief.

'Yes, well, I understand your feelings, but that won't bring your mother back will it? Let's concentrate on what needs to be done, shall we?' Margaret said briskly, forcing Louisa to focus on what she was saying. 'The police expect to get the post-mortem results today and then…then we can arrange the funeral. I've checked Susan's Filofax for her friends and colleagues so…'

Margaret made suggestions about the service and the necessary, but unwanted, get together at the house afterwards. Louisa began to switch off, not wanting to acknowledge the reality of a funeral. Until it happened she could pretend that her mother was away and due back any time soon. Perhaps Margaret sensed her detachment because she stood up, saying she needed to pop out to the shops before lunch and wouldn't be long. Louisa heard the front door bang and curled up into a ball again. *Oh Mum! Please come back! I miss you so much…*

chapter 4

2009 – January – Guernsey

'Can you tell us, Mr Roget, what made you decide to open La Folie Natural Health Centre? Was it something you'd always wanted to do?' The obviously pregnant reporter held a microphone to his face, her hazel eyes focused on his.

Malcolm had expected the question and carefully considered his answer. It would be almost the truth, he told himself.

'I've long held an interest in the natural approach to health and healing as practised in the East. I spent some time in India and that's where I met up with my manager, Paul England. He provided the inspiration for a centre and I provided the wherewithal and background experience.'

'Thank you. I understand that you used to be in the hotel business. Is that where you gained your experience?' She smiled at him as if it were just the two of them enjoying a cosy chat, rather than an island's worth of TV viewers watching and listening.

'Yes, I ran a small chain of hotels in Canada and I flatter myself I know what comfort and service guests require. Although La Folie is not a hotel, the principle is the same.' He waved his arms around the entrance hall where a discreet desk acted as reception, manned by an attractive young woman in a white uniform. 'I leave the therapy side of things to the experts, headed by Paul.'

Malcolm noticed the reporter – now, what was her name again? – ah, Nicole Tostevin, that was it, shift uncomfortably on her feet and invited her to sit down. Moving over to a pair of elegant armchairs by the desk, she flashed him a grateful smile.

'Thank you. I understand that you have a connection to Guernsey, Mr Roget. It's rumoured that the body that was found in the grounds a few months ago was that of your father, who once owned this house. Is that true?'

He kept his expression neutral, aware of the camera focusing on him.

'You know how it is with rumours! My mother was originally from Guernsey and that's the only connection I have. She told me stories about it when I was a lad and I promised to bring her back one day.' Sadness clutched at his heart as he remembered that time. His mother, worn out from building up her hotel business, had taken to her bed with what everyone thought was exhaustion, but proved to be a malicious form of cancer. In an effort to cheer her up he'd said that as soon as she was well enough to travel, they'd fly to Guernsey and stay in the best hotel the island possessed. Betty's face had lit up and for a few moments they were swept away by their plans. But days later she was dead.

'Mr Roget? Are you all right?'

Malcolm shook himself and forced a smile, the smile of the consummate businessman.

'Yes, I'm sorry. My mother died, you see, and never did return. So it was with mixed feelings that I considered coming here myself. But,' he waved his arm around the wood panelled hall, 'I'm very glad I did. And I have high hopes that the centre will be a great success.'

Nicole gave him a sympathetic look.

'I'm sorry to hear about your mother. I'm sure she would have been very impressed with what you're doing here, Mr Roget. As is everyone I've spoken to. So, you have no knowledge of the man whose body was found?' *Mm. I'll give Nicole her due, she doesn't give up easily! But I can't tell her the truth, not yet. Not until...*

He shook his head, warding off further questions by suggesting that he gave her the grand tour of La Folie and Nicole signalled the cameraman to follow them. By the time they had peered into lavish bedrooms, immaculate therapy rooms and the cosy dining room, Malcolm hoped that the subject of the body could be dropped. He liked the young woman, who seemed particularly keen to see what work had been done on the old place. It wasn't until they were standing in the garden and she dismissed the cameraman, that he found out why she was so interested.

'I have a confession to make, Mr Roget. My mother and I inherited this house from my grandmother in 2007. She and her husband bought it from the States of Guernsey after the war. So *I* certainly do have a connection to it!'

'Well, I wasn't expecting that!' He thought back to the negotiations to buy the house. He remembered that two women were involved but hadn't registered the name of Tostevin.

She must have seen his puzzled look as she went on, 'I wasn't married then so I signed under my previous name of Oxford. My mother's called Mrs Bourgaize and my grandmother was Mrs Ferbrache. It gets a bit complicated!' She gave him a hesitant smile.

'I see. How interesting. So it was your grandparents who tidied up the place and started a growing business after the war?' He buzzed with excitement as Nicole told him what she knew of her family's involvement in La Folie. They continued talking as Nicole led the way around the garden, explaining how much her grandmother had loved it. Malcolm had thought it perfect too, and only let his gardener carry out the minimum of remedial work.

Although little was in flower in the winter, the garden was full of the muted colours of green hedging and shrubs, with white hellebores peeping out alongside snowdrops and a few early crocuses. And of course, there was the sea, spread out beyond the hedges and the cliff path. His mother hadn't been one for gardens, but she had loved the sea, telling him how much she missed the view from La Folie.

As they retraced their steps toward the house, Malcolm laughed.

'What's so funny, Mr Roget?' Nicole asked, her hand resting lightly on her stomach.

'Please, call me Malcolm. It's occurred to me that you must be a very wealthy young woman, if this was your inheritance. So you don't need to work!' He smiled at her.

'You're right. Thanks to my grandmother's generosity I'm financially secure. My husband Ben's a doctor and we both keep pretty busy. I love my work and didn't want to give it up. But now…' she patted her bump and smiled.

'When's the baby due?'

'In April, in the spring. I can't wait!'

He nodded. 'Well, take it easy, my dear. And if you'd like a massage or some other pampering, please be my guest. It's the least I can do for a former owner!'

Nicole smiled. 'Thank you. I could always report on my experience in my programme and gain you more guests.'

'Now that is a good idea! By the way, I'm late registering with a doctor, would your husband take me on?'

Nicole said he would be happy to, explaining that he had been her grandmother's GP. Malcolm noted his contact details before saying, 'Now, I must introduce you to La Folie's manager, Paul. Without him, this centre would not exist…'

He was glad of this opportunity to earn good publicity for the centre. The digging up of his father's body had created a flurry of prurient prying, but Inspector Ferguson had managed to keep the identity secret. The police agreed that it was better not to alert Archie Blake, assuming he was still alive. And having invested millions in the project, Malcolm wanted it to be a success, untarnished by stories of murder. It wasn't for the money. He was financially secure, but the idea of failure was anathema to him. Something he'd learnt from his mother. He had to succeed – for *her* sake, not his.

Once the TV crew had left Malcolm was able to relax and decided to ask Paul to join him for a beer. As he waited for him to finish talking to one of the therapists, Malcolm recalled how they had first met. Not a propitious occasion.

'What a load of old codswallop! I can't believe people pay good money to hear such rubbish,' Malcolm muttered to his neighbour in the meditation group. The young man turned round, looking surprised.

'Oh! So why are you here if you think it's rubbish?' he asked, his blue eyes boring into his.

Malcolm shifted in his seat. 'I was talked into it by a friend who persuaded me it would do me good. But I can close my eyes and picture a flower without paying out good money for the privilege. Thought TM was more than that – supposed to be transcendental isn't it? I don't feel any different!' He stood up, disliking the pungent scent of incense clinging to the saffron-robed followers of the guru seated on the dais. The bearded man, for one, looked beatific. *And so he should, charging so much for nothing!*

The young man smiled. 'Well, it does take time, you know. Took me weeks to really let go when I started. This your first time?'

'Yes, and my last! I don't wish to be rude, but I'd like to go and get a drink. Could do with a whisky.' Malcolm moved towards the door, wanting to leave the ashram and head back to his hotel, but the man stayed by his side.

'You're not staying in the ashram?'

'No, I bought a daily pass so I wouldn't be stuck here with a load of weird...' He stopped, and then continued, 'I'm sorry, I didn't mean to imply that–'

The man laughed. 'Don't worry, I used to think that people who came here were weird too! But I assure you, they're not. Or at least most of them aren't! Look, I don't have any classes for a while, how about if I take you to a great place for a drink? My name's Paul England, by the way.' He held out his hand and Malcolm shook it, giving his own name and deciding that he hadn't anything to lose by joining him. Paul certainly looked normal; tall, slim with blue eyes and blonde hair, he could pass for Nordic but for his name and voice.

Moments later they sat outside in a whitewashed bar overflowing with tubs of olive trees and exotic flowers Malcolm did not recognise. The aroma of spices and fragrant flowers made a confusing mixture and Malcolm felt light-headed. The heat didn't help, either. Paul ordered a whisky on the rocks for Malcolm and a beer for himself.

'So, what brought you to Mumbai? Not the ashrams, I'm sure!' Paul said, grinning.

'No, you're right. I had some business to attend to and one evening got into a conversation with a fellow guest in the hotel. I happened to mention that my doc had told me to slow down, that my blood pressure was way too high. And this guy told me how he'd spent time at the ashram and how much good it did him. Had to admit he did look pretty good for his age. I'd put him at about sixty but he was seventy-five; a few years older than me.' Malcolm sipped his whisky. 'Gave me a shock and made me think I should try it, too. But, as you gathered, I wasn't much impressed.' He took another sip.

Paul laughed. 'So I noticed! But there's a lot more to it than one hour of TM, Malcolm. I've been involved in yoga and meditation for years and, believe me, it does work. But you have to be patient and not give up after the first attempt. Let me explain...'

He went on to give Malcolm a potted over-view of Eastern medicine, suggesting approaches that might be of benefit to him. It transpired that he'd been working in natural health centres in the UK for years and came out to India for what he referred to as a field trip every year or so, picking up new ideas along the way. A qualified yoga teacher, Reiki Master and herbal practitioner, he now managed a centre in London. But he really wanted to get out of the city and live by the sea.

'Although I'm a Londoner by birth, I've always preferred to be near the sea. My artist parents were archetypal hippies, travelling whenever possible, and they brought me with them to India when I was quite small. They often headed to the coast to pitch camp and I thought it was magical.' He sighed and took a sip of beer. 'Unfortunately, I have to go where the work is. But if the chance to run a health centre by the sea came up, I'd grab it.'

'Is there good money to be made in that business? I'd always seen it as a bit fey, all sandals and brown rice.'

Paul grinned. 'You'd be surprised! Things have moved on apace since the '70s. As long as the facilities are top rate then people are prepared to pay thousands for a week's stay. Personally, I'm not keen on the financial aspect; I like to focus on getting people well, on all levels, mind, body and spirit. There's so much dis-ease nowadays...'

Malcolm felt the familiar tingle of an exciting idea. Is this something he could be involved in? He needed a project to occupy him now that the business was sold. He'd felt so empty these past months but this young man, with his beliefs and enthusiasm, bubbling with vibrant health, seemed like the answer to his prayers. He wanted to ask more questions.

'Sorry, I've got to shoot or I'll miss my next class. Perhaps another time?'

'Of course. When are you free?'

Several meetings later and they were firm, if unlikely, friends. Paul agreed to help Malcolm improve his health – providing Reiki healing, personal meditation sessions and a foul-tasting herbal concoction, all of which left him feeling better than he'd done for years. He became a firm believer in what he'd once thought to be codswallop and had nothing but respect for Paul. He could understand why people might want to visit a centre that offered such healing and asked Paul if he'd be interested in working for him if he were to invest in a centre. Paul agreed instantly, on condition that he found a place near the sea. Malcolm smiled his agreement and shook on it. And his quest for the ideal place began.

That had been two years ago and now here they were, about to open their centre. Right by the sea, as agreed. Malcolm smiled inwardly at the journey that had brought him full circle, back to the place where he was conceived. And if it hadn't been for the hand of fate – or in this case, Archie's – where he would have been born and grown up to inherit from his father. That thought made him scowl. *I still have unfinished business to attend to. I haven't forgotten, Ma.*

chapter 5

2009 – March – London

Somehow Louisa muddled through the months since her mother's death. Margaret stayed until after the funeral and then suggested that she return with her to Yorkshire for as long as she needed. Although tempted by the offer, Louisa declined. In her heart she knew that leaving London would only delay her recovery. She needed to get on with her life, hard as it was to imagine without her mother by her side. Having inherited both her mother's house and business, money wasn't an immediate issue, so Louisa gave in her notice at the hospital, glad to escape her stressful job. She intended to find something else when she felt stronger. At thirty-four it was time to be an adult, she told herself, and follow her mother's example. As a single mother in her thirties, Susan had kept working, eventually opening her own successful, upmarket travel agency. Louisa couldn't recall her mother ever moaning about the difficulties of bringing up a child on her own, always willing to spend as much time with her as possible. She worked long hours, employing a mix of au pairs and mother's helps to ensure that Louisa was well cared for. Susan's parents, now dead, had lived in Surrey and she only saw them in the school holidays. But they had helped Susan financially until her business took off.

After her mother's death, Louisa had tried to recall everything she had said about Malcolm, the father she had never known. Susan had seemed reluctant to say much, only telling her that they had met when he worked in London for a couple of years. A Canadian, though born in England, he worked in his mother's hotel business, and came to London to gain more experience. Although her mother hadn't said so, Louisa got the impression that Malcolm was the love of her life. Susan only dated occasionally and never, as far as Louisa knew, became seriously involved with any man. Her life revolved around her business and her daughter.

One cold, blustery day in early March, Louisa paced around the sitting room excited by what she'd just discovered. For weeks she had tried to trace Malcolm Roget on the internet without success. But this day, she was flicking through the latest edition of a natural health magazine, when her attention was caught by a feature about a new residential centre, *La Folie Retreat & Health Centre*, in Guernsey. While admiring the photos and descriptions of stunning rooms she noticed a reference to the owner, Mr Malcolm Roget. Stunned, she read it again to be sure. Yes, she'd read it right. The reference was short, mentioning that Mr Roget, a retired Canadian hotelier with an interest in natural health, had invested in the centre after being impressed by the man who would become his manager, Mr Paul England. The rest of the article went on to extol the virtues of spending time as a guest at the centre.

Louisa's emotions were mixed. Excited that Malcolm was only a short plane hop away, but sad that he and her mother could not now reconnect. *I wonder how long he's been back in Britain? Mum seemed to think he'd be unlikely to return. So what happened? And what's it going to be like meeting him after all these years and…and without Mum?* Tears welled in her eyes as the pain hit her in force. For a brief moment her only thought had been about finally meeting her father, a man who had been lying in wait at the back of her mind for years. Everyone wanted to know who their father was. What he looked like, how he spoke, laughed. Was he funny or serious? But it seemed so cruel that just as she might now have a chance to meet him, her mother was no longer there by her side. As the tears flowed Louisa reached for the only photo she had of Malcolm. The one with her mother wearing fabulous looking rubies and diamonds. Assuming they were real. But that horrible burglar seemed to think they were or why threaten her mother? Brushing away the tears, she studied the photo for the umpteenth time. Malcolm, in full black tie gear, stared straight ahead, a frown creasing his forehead. He didn't look as if he wanted to be photographed, his hand close to his face, as if to shield it from view. Tall, dark haired, a little overweight, he looked a serious kind of guy. She wondered what her bubbly mother had seen in him. *I guess he does look sexy, in a broody way. Oh, Mum! Why aren't you here? There's so much I want to ask you. I know I must go and see this man, my...father. But will it only bring more heartache? What if he's married, with his own family? He might not be best pleased to have me arrive on the doorstep.*

The questions skittered around her head until it ached. There was only one way to find the answers. Picking up the phone Louisa dialled her mother's assistant manager, now running the business while she decided whether or not to sell.

'Hi, Glenn. Could you book me a trip to Guernsey, please? With an open-ended return.'

Louisa, not one to act on impulse and, she would be the first to admit, a tad unadventurous, found it difficult to travel anywhere on her own. She'd always been able to rely on either her mother, a girlfriend or boyfriend for company. The advantage of having a mother with her own travel agency was a constant supply of cheap holidays and Louisa had taken full advantage of that. Susan had often asked her to go somewhere new for a recce, taking a friend along for company. Louisa had loved it, knowing her mother would be able to sort out any problems that arose with a phone call. But now she was on her own, and somehow even flying the few miles to Guernsey seemed a step too far. As she prepared for take-off at Gatwick, anxious thoughts gnawed at her mind. The first problem was not even knowing how long she would be away. A couple of days? A week? Or more? A lot depended on Malcolm's reaction to finding he had a daughter. With a woman he hadn't seen for thirty-five years. When Louisa had told Margaret that she was going to see Malcolm, her aunt had suggested it would be better to write to him first. But she didn't want to do that in case he didn't reply, or wrote and said he wanted nothing to do with her. This way he wouldn't have any choice but to at least see her.

Louisa's self-confidence had not been great since she'd been unceremoniously dumped the previous year by Jack, her erstwhile live-in boyfriend. Telling her "you're no longer fun to be with and anyway, I've found a new girlfriend", Jack had simply packed his bags and left. Unable to afford the rent on her own, she had crawled home, devastated, to Susan's comforting embrace. Her mother suggested she move in to the attic converted by the previous owner, and providing a large bed/sitting room, kitchenette and shower. Previously only used for guests, Louisa was only too happy to have her own space and still be near her mother. The downside was the long journey to the south London hospital where she worked, but she could cope with that. As the hurt began to heal, Louisa felt more settled in herself, socialising with her friends, but unwilling to risk further heartbreak by dating.

Her fear of rejection had grown from the seed planted by the lack of a father. Logically, she knew Malcolm had not rejected her. He hadn't even been aware of her existence. But logic did not enter into it where her emotions were concerned. Particularly after Jack's self-confessed betrayal. Sitting in the airplane, braced for take-off, Louisa sent up a silent prayer that her father would accept her and, perhaps, might even come to love her. If not she was truly an orphan. Glenn had booked her into La Trelade Hotel, a short drive from the airport and en route to St Peter Port, the capital. He had also arranged a hire car, giving her the freedom to explore the island if she wished. Louisa had visited Jersey with her mother as a teenager and remembered it as a pretty island with lovely beaches and a bustling shopping centre in St Helier, but this was her first trip to Guernsey. From the air she could see it possessed great beaches but looked more built up than its larger sister island. Her hotel booking was for a week so, at the least, she could use the time to have a break. Not that March was the ideal time, she thought, buttoning up her jacket against the brisk wind accompanying her walk to the car park. Glenn, efficient as ever, had provided a map showing the directions to the hotel and to La Folie. She had told him that she had business at the centre and asked Glenn to choose a hotel within reasonable reach.

Pulling into the drive, she thought La Trelade a good choice. Smart, but not ostentatious. All she really needed was a comfortable room and good food at reasonable cost, but was pleased to find that the facilities included a health suite with indoor pool. The double room having met with her approval, she changed into her swimsuit and went downstairs to the pool. Louisa joined a solitary swimmer, and as she struck out in a strong, smooth crawl, her tight muscles began to relax. She hadn't been near a pool for months, unheard of for her. Swimming was her go-to exercise of choice, enabling her to keep fit while freeing her mind. Bliss! But since her mother's death, she hadn't felt in the mood. Like so many things, it had seemed too much effort to get out of the house and down to Ironmonger Row Baths for a good workout in the pool.

The thirteen metre long pool gave her ample opportunity to stretch her body and after a few lengths her mood began to lift. With a nod to the other swimmer, still crawling slowly up the pool, Louisa pulled herself out in the shallow end and shrugged into her towelling robe. Glancing out of the French windows, she noted the terrace and lawns. Hmm, pity it wasn't warm enough to sit outside. Shivering, she wrapped a towel around her hair before returning to her room and a welcome hot shower.

Dressed, she found her way to the bar for a snack lunch. While waiting for her soup to arrive, Louisa gave some thought to her next step. She decided to turn up at La Folie and ask if Mr Roget was available. She knew it was unlikely that he would be and planned to make an appointment. From the article in the magazine it was clear that the manager, Paul, ran the place and that Malcolm took a back seat. She could only hope that he wasn't off the island. In that case she was back to square one. Trying not to think about that eventuality, Louisa enjoyed her meal, allowing herself a small glass of wine. Feeling as if she were about to enter the lion's den, she grabbed her bag and made her way to the car park.

The wind buffeted her car, forcing her to grip the steering wheel hard as she negotiated round broken tree branches littering the road. The wintery weather sent a chill through her body and Louisa prayed that spring would soon return. She hated being cold and this winter, since her mother's death, had seemed to go on for ever. Concentrating on the road, she could only catch glimpses of her surroundings; noting a few cows quietly grazing in the fields and roadside stalls selling flowers and vegetables. It was only a matter of minutes before she took the left turn towards Torteval in the south-west of the island. After passing rows of greenhouses, some clearly disused, Louisa came to a narrow lane on the left, marked by an impressive, new-looking sign: *La Folie Retreat and Health Centre.* 'Right, looks like this is it,' she muttered to herself, steering the car sharply left. As she bumped along the lane Louisa glanced around with interest. Open fields, some sporting the remains of greenhouses, gave way to what looked like newly landscaped gardens and a large glazed building that she guessed was the swimming pool. Turning a tree-bordered bend, Louisa gasped at the gothic structure looming up in front of her. She had seen the photos and knew about the towers, but the reality still took her breath away. Pulling the car to a stop on the gravel, she switched off the engine. She stepped out of the car and gazed at the forbidding grey granite building; the round towers, gargoyle embellished parapets and mullioned windows reminding her of old horror movies. In an obvious attempt to brighten and lighten the effect, giant terracotta urns planted with olive trees, date palms and rhododendrons edged the area in front of the house. Smaller pots brimming with colourful spring flowers helped to create a warmer welcome than the scowls of the gargoyles.

Taking a deep breath, Louisa headed to the front door, sheltered by a portico. To the side of the panelled oak door was an old-fashioned bell pull, but the door stood ajar and she walked through into the hall. Her eyes were immediately drawn towards the imposing oak staircase, bathed in a thin wintry light filtering through a tall window on the landing.

'Good afternoon. May I help you?'

Louisa jumped. She hadn't noticed the desk in a corner and the young woman in white now offering her a bright smile.

'Oh, right. I…I was wondering if it would be possible to see Mr Roget, please?'

'I'm sorry, but Mr Roget isn't here at the moment. Can I help?'

Louisa pushed down the feeling of disappointment. Tinged with an edge of relief. Wanting, needing to meet him. But also scared. Scared of rejection. It made for an uncomfortable feeling in her solar plexus, as if her stomach muscles were being squeezed.

'Thank you, but I really only want to see Mr Roget. Is he away?'

The young woman, glowing with health and in possession of shiny brown curls, looked at her intently.

'I believe he had to fly over to London on business but will be back tomorrow. But Mr Roget isn't here much, anyway. He leaves everything to Paul, the manager. Is he expecting you?'

Back tomorrow! So, not long to wait…

'No, he…he isn't. It's a…personal matter but I don't have his home address. Could you let me have it, please?'

The curls bounced as the girl shook her head.

'I don't think I should. He might not like that.' She frowned, as if trying to decide how much she should disclose.

Louisa thought quickly. 'Look, I do understand and I don't want to get you into trouble. Do you know if and when he might call in? Then I could pop in on the off-chance and you won't be involved. It is *very* important I speak to him. I…I have a message I can only give to him in person. Please!'

The receptionist chewed her lip. 'Well, I don't see any harm in that. At least you don't look like a murderer or anything!' She laughed.

Louisa felt the blood drain from her face as the image of the man knocking her to the ground filled her mind.

'Are you all right? Have I said something...?' The receptionist looked at her with concern.

'No, it's okay. I...I recently lost someone very dear to me.' Louisa forced a smile, not wanting to scare the poor girl. She needed her help.

'Oh, I'm so sorry!' The girl, whose name badge identified her as 'Nadine', frowned. 'I do put my foot in it sometimes. Look, Mr Roget is booked in for a session with our physio tomorrow afternoon at three. If you were to drop in about three thirty you should catch him as he usually stays for a swim afterwards.'

'Thanks, I'll do that. I, er, understand that you've only recently opened.'

Nadine nodded. 'Yes, in January and we've had quite a few bookings so far. We expect to be busiest in the summer, of course.' She grinned at Louisa. 'Do you fancy a few days here? We're offering weekend packages.'

Louisa shook her head, laughing. 'No thanks, I couldn't afford it! But I'm sure you'll do well. Will you be on reception tomorrow when I call?'

The brown curls bobbed up and down. 'Yes, I'll look out for you.'

Louisa said goodbye and returned to her car, lost in thought. *So, tomorrow I might finally meet my father! Will I look like him? Mum never said. But her eyes were grey and mine are blue so...*Sliding into the car, she glanced back at the front door. With a sigh, she revved the engine and drove off, the tyres squealing on the gravel.

chapter 6

Feeling at a loose end, Louisa drove past the hotel and on towards St Peter Port. Glenn's easy to follow instructions took her through a village-like area called St Martins, which boasted a few shops along the main street. She drove on, passing large, expensive looking properties set back from the road sweeping down to St Peter Port. In the winter light the sea looked grey, melding with the cloud-heavy sky. As she steered carefully down the steep winding hill, she could see marinas separated by breakwaters and parking areas. Small boats and yachts bobbed uneasily at their moorings as, in the distance, white caps signalled the height of the waves. Glad she wasn't on a boat in this weather, Louisa pulled into the nearest car park. Wrapping a scarf around her neck, she stood for a moment, taking in the sights.

The waterfront area was composed of shops and restaurants and she smiled when she noted the familiar Marks and Spencer sign. Something English among many French names. Standing with her back to the shops, Louisa looked towards the sea. Blurry outlines of islands peeped through the gloom and a fort-like castle stood guard at the entrance to the port. She could taste and smell the sea in the air. Pushing her hands deep into her pockets, she headed for the shopping area and warmth.

It didn't take her long to realise how compact St Peter Port was. Hilly, but small. Narrow streets, lined with tiny shops, wound up from the seafront, jostling with the newer, larger buildings housing familiar UK stores. Louisa felt at ease, seduced by the smallness of the town after the noise and bustle of London. She passed groups of people chatting animatedly in the street; some dressed casually for shopping, others wearing smart suits and carrying briefcases. After mooching around a few shops, Louisa needed a break and nipped into a café. She found an empty table in the window with a clear view of the street and passers-by. Louisa felt alone, but somehow the sight of people nearby, going about their daily business, was of some comfort. She may not be part of their world but at least she was *there*, finally trying to get her life back on track. As she sipped her coffee, she couldn't help thinking of what her mother would say, if she were there. "Chin up, Louisa! You'll get there in the end, I know you will. You're not my daughter for nothing. Focus on the future and being happy." Echoes of her mother's loving voice floated in her head, and for a moment her sense of loss caused her hands to shake and she gripped her cup tightly. *Oh, Mum! I wish you were here with me now. Then we could both meet my…father. Perhaps we could have been a proper family at last…*

Her unseeing eyes stared out of the window as a daydream of what might have been played in her mind. With a shake of her head, she pushed the fantasy aside and drained her coffee. Retracing, with leaden steps, her way back down the high street, Louisa noticed the church at the bottom of the hill and walked towards it. *Perhaps I can find some peace of mind in there.* Although not religious, she had become more interested in spirituality since her mother's death, wanting to believe that life had a deeper meaning than the mere physical. One of her fellow physios was a Buddhist and Louisa admired her calm approach to life. Something she needed to cultivate herself. Pushing open the main door to the church she stepped into a space larger than she'd imagined from the outside. White painted walls and granite arches and pillars offered a sense of solitude after the bustle of the street. Louisa tip-toed across the wooden floor, slipping into a pew near the back. Scattered among the pews, a handful of people sat in quiet contemplation of their surroundings or in prayer. The beautiful colours of the main stained glass window behind the altar shone out in spite of the poor daylight. Still feeling heavy-hearted with her profound sense of loss, Louisa took a deep breath, closed her eyes and sat in silent communion with her mother: asking for help. Initially the sadness blotted out everything until she sensed someone sit beside her; opening her eyes she saw the pew remained empty. *Mum, are you there? Please let me know!* She felt a feather-like touch on her face and smiled. *Thanks, Mum! I can be strong knowing you're beside me.* A feeling of peace and warmth flowed through her mind and body as she sat, eyes closed, as if wrapped in her mother's embrace.

When she finally opened her eyes, Louisa felt energised as if a burden had been lifted. Gazing around the now empty church she noticed the light fading through the windows. Checking her watch she was shocked to see that more than an hour had passed since she had entered the church. She stood up, squared her shoulders, and strode out towards the car park. Once back in the car she saw the lights of the church emblazoned against its granite walls and smiled, before heading up the hill and back to the hotel.

The next morning spring returned to the island. As Louisa opened the bedroom curtains the room was flooded with sunlight that reflected off the conservatory windows below. The wind had dropped and as she opened the window, she could hear birdsong from the nearby trees. Breathing in deeply, Louisa noted how much warmer it was than the previous day and decided to go for a walk that morning.

After the waitress had taken her order for breakfast, Louisa asked about the best places for walking.

'If you're up for a long walk then you could follow the cliff path from near here and go as far as St Peter Port. It's about nine miles so if you don't want to walk back you could get a bus or a taxi. Lots of our guests have done that. Lovely views of the bays and the islands.' The waitress, her uniform strained tight over her stomach and hips, not looking as if she walked anywhere, gave a big smile.

'Thanks, that sounds just what I need. Where will I find the path?'

The girl suggested she ask at the reception desk for directions before she went off to the kitchen with Louisa's order. Left nursing a cup of strong coffee, Louisa felt a spark of enthusiasm for something for the first time in ages. A long walk with sea views would be bound to set her up for the meeting that afternoon. She might even have time for a swim on her return.

Armed with the directions, Louisa set off towards the cliff path, clearly marked on the local map provided by the hotel. The walk to St Peter Port – or "Town" as known by the locals – would be just right for a stretch, she thought. Access to the path started above a pretty sandy bay, known, according to the map, as Petit Bôt. It boasted an ancient defence tower and café and Louisa thought she'd explore it further another time. The path wound along the jagged cliffs, initially giving her limited views ahead. But she did have a clear view of another island on the horizon, guessing it must be Jersey. The warm spring air brought out the scents of the wild flowers and the damp grass and gorse. Striding along, Louisa met an occasional walker and smiles and hellos were exchanged. It dawned on her how she had cut herself off from humanity these past weeks and vowed to stop living like a hermit. Since being dumped by Jack and then losing her mother, Louisa had become a real loner. Perhaps I can find healing here in Guernsey, she mused, taking deep breaths of the tangy air. It was certainly time.

Small sandy bays lay below her feet as she headed towards a high cliff point. Taking a breather she gazed in delight at the vista spread out before her. A small harbour held a few leisure boats adjoining the beach, proclaimed by the map as Saint's Bay. Further around the headland she saw a rocky cove leading to a large sandy bay. A glance at the map told her it was Moulin Huet Bay, made famous by the paintings of Renoir. She sat down for a few moments, drinking it all in. Beautiful! Regardless of what might happen between her and Malcolm, she was glad she had come here. She couldn't help smiling at the view and felt keen to explore further.

It was a tired, but happy, Louisa who finally arrived near the hill leading into St Peter Port. Resting on the path, she gazed down at bathing pools filled with sea water and in which, even now, some brave souls were swimming. Rather them than me, she thought, as her gaze moved upwards and out to sea. The islands which had been barely visible in yesterday's greyness, now appeared clearly before her. Her map named the nearest as Jethou, a tiny off-shoot of neighbouring Herm, then Sark. Louisa realised there was plenty to explore if she stayed for a while, but wasn't sure. It all depended on her meeting with Malcolm. Her father. A quick glance at her watch prompted her to continue quickly down the hill and on towards the taxi rank. Time to get back.

By three o'clock, Louisa had lost all the calmness and happy feelings of the morning. Her stomach churned and her palms felt moist. She was awash with mixed emotions, excitement at meeting her father, tempered by feelings of anger on her mother's behalf for his walking out on her. Wishing she could emulate her Buddhist friend, she closed her eyes and took deep breaths, trying to focus on something cheerful. Unbidden, an image of Moulin Huet

Bay popped into her mind. It looked so calm, waves gently lapping against the sand. It helped. Moments later, she opened her eyes and stood up, checking her appearance in the bedroom mirror. Her long blonde hair was pulled back into a ponytail, emphasising her pale, freckled face. Light blue eyes stared back at her and she quickly glanced over her chosen outfit of jeans, a long-sleeved T-shirt and leather bomber jacket. She preferred casual dress and had driven her mother to distraction with her lack of interest in dressing up. 'Okay, you'll do,' she muttered to herself, before picking up her keys and bag.

After parking her car, Louisa checked her watch yet again. Three twenty-five. Perfect. She pushed open the front door and was pleased to see Nadine on the desk. They exchanged smiles.

'Hi, again. You're in luck, Mr Roget will be heading for the pool shortly and has to come past us. If you sit on that sofa you can't fail to see him,' Nadine said, nodding towards a black leather designer sofa near the staircase. Her face creased in thought. 'You do know what he looks like, don't you?'

Louisa felt her face redden. 'Not exactly. I've…I've not seen him for some years.'

'Okay. I'll give you a quick nod as soon as I see him.'

Louisa sat down, willing herself to stay calm as she rehearsed what to say to this man who was a stranger, yet not a stranger. A man, she was convinced, who had been dearly loved by her mother. But had he loved *her?* She might soon find out. As she waited, several people walked past. Some appeared to be staff, wearing white uniforms like Nadine, walking noiselessly down the corridors. A man and a woman, who she judged to be guests, and wearing white fluffy bathrobes, came laughing down the stairs, giving Nadine a quick nod before disappearing into a nearby room.

Just as Louisa was beginning to feel she had wasted her time she noticed a tall man come out of a room, heading in her direction. A glance towards the desk was rewarded with a nod from Nadine, who smiled warmly at the man as he approached.

'Mr Roget? May I speak to you for a moment, please?' Louisa felt her throat constrict and the words came out in little more than a whisper. She had a brief impression of a fit-looking man with greying hair, tanned face and light blue eyes.

He stared at her. 'Sorry, do I know you? I don't remember...'

She shook her head. 'No, we...we haven't met.' At this Nadine's head swivelled towards her, her mouth open in a large O. Louisa rushed on, 'I...have a message from someone you do know. Susan Canning.'

It was as if she had slapped him. He took a step back, his eyes opened wide with surprise and...was it pleasure?

'Susan? A message from Susan? I can hardly believe...' Malcolm seemed to pull himself together, aware of Nadine's listening ears. 'Look, we can't talk here. Follow me, please.' He strode off down a corridor, leaving Louisa to follow behind. Giving the wide-eyed Nadine a quick grin, she set off. Malcolm held open the door to what looked like a study, furnished with a large mahogany desk and a pair of armchairs.

'Please, take a seat.' He gave her a searching look as she sat down.

'Who are you? And how did Susan know I was here? It must be more than thirty years since I last saw her. And what's her message?' He looked eager to know more.

'My name's Louisa Canning and it's thirty-five years ago to be exact. She...doesn't know you're here. Because...because she's...dead. She died in January.' Suddenly the dam burst and Louisa felt the hot tears pouring down her face and was powerless to stop them. Through blurred eyes she saw his face registering shock and what looked like sadness. She searched in her bag for a tissue and dabbed at her face, blowing her nose.

'Sorry,' she muttered, 'I thought I'd be all right, but saying those words…'

His face softened. 'I understand. I presume Susan was your mother?'

She nodded. Then, suddenly swamped by anger towards the man who had left her mother in the lurch, she virtually spat out, 'And you…you're my father.'

chapter 7

The silence was palpable. Louisa forced herself to calm down. Anger was not going to achieve anything, even if it was justified. Malcolm sat like a stone in the big armchair, mere touching distance away. He seemed to be in a trance, his eyes unfocussed. She told herself that it must be shock which held him silent, and not the dreaded rejection.

He let out a shuddering breath and his eyes – so like hers! – gazed at her face, drinking in her features.

'I…I don't know what to say! I never knew. Susan never told me. How…?'

'Mum told me that she only found she was pregnant after you'd had to return to Canada. Something about your mother being ill? She…she thought you'd write or phone but you didn't. Nothing.' Her voice took on an edge when she thought how awful it must have been for her mother and the anger still hovered around her heart.

He seemed to pale under the tan. 'I…had meant to get in touch, of course I did. But my mother was gravely ill and somehow the time passed in a blur and I…I was devastated when she died. For a while I was too depressed to think straight. When I finally recovered I told myself that Susan would have got over me and met someone else. That it was for the best.' He shifted in the chair. 'Susan knew I wasn't keen on commitment and seemed to accept that. We'd agreed no ties.'

'Well, you should have made sure she couldn't get pregnant then, shouldn't you?' Louisa felt tears welling up again. *Oh, Mum! How it must have hurt!* 'So you didn't love my mother?'

Malcolm bit his lip. 'That's the awful bit. I did, very much. But I managed to convince myself that I was better off not being tied down. To be free to live as I wished.' He let out a harsh laugh. 'How wrong could you be! I missed your mother so much, and learnt that being on my own was the opposite of being free. But it was too late. Or so I thought.'

Louisa didn't know what to think. Which was worse, her mother being on her own but reasonably happy, or her knowing that Malcolm really did love her but hadn't had the guts to admit it?

'Would it have made any difference to you if you'd known Mum was pregnant?'

His eyebrows shot up. 'Of course! I'd have married her and looked after you both. I'm not a monster!' He took a deep breath. 'Did…Susan marry someone else?'

'No. She had the odd boyfriend but no-one serious. It was just the two of us. Until now.' She fought down her grief, not wanting to fall apart in front of this man. Her father.

'I see. That must have been tough on both of you. I'm so sorry. I should have been there. If only I'd known!' He punched his fists together and Louisa saw the pain in his eyes. *Yes, if only you had known, our lives would have been so different. And Mum would still be alive!*

'How did Susan die? Had she been ill?'

She shook her head. 'No, she wasn't ill, although she did have a dickey heart. Some…bastard broke in and threatened her and she…she had a heart attack. She died in my arms.' Tears glistened in her eyes and she quickly brushed them away.

Malcolm looked at her in horror. 'Oh, my God! How awful for you! Did the police catch him?'

'No, and I don't think they will. Mum died before she could describe him and I only caught a brief glimpse.'

She went on to tell him all that had happened, including the bit about the jewels.

At the mention of the cause of the robbery, Malcolm sprang up from the chair and paced around the room. 'My mother said those jewels would bring bad luck but I didn't believe her. I'd never have let Susan wear them if I'd thought she would come to harm.'

'But who would have known about them? Who did they belong to?' Louisa had been driving herself mad with those questions.

He sat down again, looking uncomfortable. 'That's a long story. In the meantime, I'm sorry, but I have to ask: do you have anything to prove who you are?'

'Of course.' Louisa opened her bag and pulled out various pieces of paper. 'Here's my birth certificate, the photo of you and Mum and my passport.' She pushed them across the table, glad she had anticipated his asking. After all, from his point of view she could be anyone.

Malcolm studied everything carefully, hesitating over the photo. She saw the pain in his face but it did little to assuage her own.

He looked up and their identical blue eyes locked.

'Would you mind if I hold onto these for a day? I'm sure you are who you say you are, but I need to be absolutely certain. Do you understand?'

She was hurt. Of course she was telling the truth! She had the photo and everything to prove it. Why...Then it hit her. He must be an extremely wealthy man. Anyone claiming to be his daughter could be after his money. She flushed at the thought and for a moment was tempted to grab her papers and leave. Then she realised she would be the loser if she did. Still fatherless and not knowing who was after those bloody jewels.

She nodded, not trusting herself to speak.

'Good. Thank you, Louisa. Look,' He glanced quickly at his watch, 'I have an appointment shortly. How about if we meet up tomorrow? I assume you're staying on the island?'

'Yes, I flew over yesterday and I'm booked into a hotel for a few days.' She could not help but feel she was being treated like a potential employee instead of a daughter, but had no choice but to go along with him. It was hard, because she knew with all her heart that she *was* his daughter.

As she drove away, unshed tears glistened in her eyes. She had been a sentimental idiot, hoping to be welcomed with open arms by her father. Her head told her Malcolm had to be sure, may even want DNA proof, but her heart had hoped he would just *know* she was his daughter. Even though she was angry with him for not contacting her mother again, she wanted him to accept her. To want her as his daughter. She sped back to the hotel and dashed up to her room, wanting to hide her hurt from the world. They were meeting again at three the following afternoon. Until then she had to deal with her old enemy: rejection.

Louisa managed to drag herself down to dinner that night, before returning to her room to watch television in an attempt at distraction. It was partly successful, but she still felt a heaviness in her heart as she prepared for bed. She lay awake for ages before finally drifting off to sleep, her dreams pervaded by mixed-up images of both her new-found father and her mother.

With several hours to kill before the next meeting, Louisa forced herself to go for a lengthy swim before taking to the cliffs. The exercise and the bracing air worked their usual magic and she felt decidedly better by lunchtime. Not entirely optimistic, but more sanguine. What will be, will be.

She arrived at La Folie shortly before three and, straightening her shoulders, walked into the entrance hall. Nadine looked up and smiled.

'Hi, there. Mr Roget said to expect you. If you'll follow me?'

Louisa followed her to the same room as before. Nadine knocked and opened the door, gesturing for her to enter. Malcolm was busy writing something when she went in but looked up and smiled.

'Louisa! Good to see you again.' He came round the desk and stood in front of her. She searched his face for clues. He *did* look pleased to see her, his eyes were smiling, and he looked far more relaxed than he had yesterday.

'You'll be pleased to know you are who you say you are,' he said, his smile broadening.

'That's good to know. You…you've had me checked out?'

He nodded. 'I would have been an idiot not to. Although, to be honest I knew you were genuine. You knew too much not to be. Let's sit down, shall we?'

She sat down, wondering what would be the next step.

'Do you need a DNA sample? I might be genuine, but that doesn't prove I'm your…your daughter, does it?'

'No, it doesn't. At least not in the eyes of the law. But I knew your mother well. Susan was the most honest woman I've ever met and if she said I was your father then that's good enough for me. And you've inherited my eyes.' For a moment they both stared at each other and Louisa felt her body loosen. He wasn't going to reject her! Whether or not she would warm to him, as a daughter to a father, remained to be seen, but at least he accepted *her*. She felt a smile tug at the corners of her mouth and gave into it.

Malcolm gripped her hand. 'We've got a lot of catching up to do, haven't we? I still don't know how you found me.'

'I saw an article...' Louisa explained about the magazine feature.

'I see. You've been very brave in coming here alone. I think you must take after your mother. She had lots of guts, too.' He sighed, looking at her sorrowfully. 'We should all have been together, shouldn't we? But we can't turn the clock back.' He shook his head and then went on, 'I think we both need a cup of tea, don't you?'

She nodded her agreement and Malcolm phoned for a tray of tea.

'May I ask you something?' Louisa said.

'Sure, go ahead.'

'Did you ever...marry? Have children?' Her heart jumped into her mouth as she awaited his answer.

He looked at her steadily. 'No, I never did. To both your questions. I think after Susan...' he shrugged.

She couldn't help feeling a huge sense of relief. It would have been too awful for her mother to have been supplanted by another.

'Okay. There's one other question. Mum mentioned your mother, but said nothing about your father. Was he not in your life?'

Malcolm frowned. 'Strange you should ask that. He was...killed before I was born and only days before he was due to marry my mother.' He spread out his arms. 'This was his house.'

'Oh! So is it a coincidence that you've bought this place?'

'Hard to answer that. I only knew that he had lived on a cliff in Guernsey and my mother referred to it as a 'folly'. When I met Paul, my manager, a few years ago, we started looking for a prospective health centre near the sea. We received details from realtors around the world. Nothing really clicked. Then one day Paul forwarded me the details for La Folie and, from the description, I guessed it must have been my father's house and it piqued my curiosity. Until then I'd not thought about it. My mother had loved Guernsey but had mixed feelings about this house.' He shifted in his chair. 'She saw him killed here.'

Louisa gasped. 'What! Murdered?'

Before Malcolm could answer, there was a knock at the door and Nadine, grinning broadly, brought in a tray laden with the accoutrements of tea and a plate piled with a variety of cakes. As Malcolm took the tray from her she turned and winked at Louisa before leaving.

He must have noted the wink and said, 'I'd wondered how you knew when I'd be here yesterday. Did Nadine tell you?'

'Yes, I told her it was very important I saw you. I hope she isn't in trouble, she was only trying to help.'

'No, I'm glad she told you. As long as she doesn't make a habit of telling strangers where I am!' He smiled as he handed her a cup of tea and offered her a cake. She took some buttered fruit bread.

'Your father? Was he…?'

His face darkened. 'Yes, he was. Or rather, it might legally have been manslaughter, either way he was struck deliberately and in anger.' He looked at her thoughtfully a moment, before adding, 'His body was found recently when we were digging out the pool. The police and I have kept it quiet that it was my father's body, in case we can still trace the killer. As this happened in 1939, he'd be an old man now, assuming he's still alive.' He took a sip of tea as Louisa took in his words.

'You know who he is, then?'

'Oh, yes, my father's nephew.'

Louisa was horrified. 'His own nephew! That's awful. But why?'

'It's not something I'd like to go into just yet, my dear. I'd rather we talk more about you and your mother. Tell me something of your childhood.'

The time sped by while she talked about her upbringing and her small family. Malcolm seemed genuinely interested, continuing to ask questions as if he needed to know everything. He must have realised that it was turning into a mini-inquisition as he suddenly stopped and smiled.

'This isn't fair, is it? How about I take you out to dinner tonight and you can be the one asking questions. Okay?'

'Thanks. I'd like that.'

'Good. Now, tell me where you're staying…'

After agreeing a time, Louisa got up to leave. Unsure of how to part, she hesitated. Malcolm resolved the issue by embracing her warmly.

'Until this evening, my dear.'

She smiled and walked down the hall, feeling that she was no longer the "reject".

chapter 8

Louisa swam up and down the pool trying to calm her jumbled thoughts. What a day it had turned out to be! Not only had Malcolm accepted her as his daughter, but he seemed keen to establish a relationship with her. She'd been glad that she was his only child. Selfish, she knew, but the thought of him being a proper father to others would have been painful. She'd never had to share her mother with anyone either, although there were times when she would have liked some siblings. A brother or sister to spend time with when her mother was busy working, someone to chat to about problems at school or the latest boyfriend. At times she'd envied friends with a father, someone to share her love of sport and the outdoors. Her mother hadn't been that keen on either. Looking back she recognised how solitary her childhood had been, with few friends at school and her only relations her grandparents and aunt and uncle. As the lengths of the pool mounted, her thoughts turned to Malcolm, the new – and only – man in her life. Physically, he was quite attractive for an old guy pushing seventy, she decided. His thick head of grey hair gave him an air of distinction and his light blue eyes shone out brightly against the tanned, lined, face. He bore the look of a man who had lived life well, reminding her a little of the actor Donald Sutherland, minus the beard. It looked as if he kept himself in trim, too; no paunch threatened his shirt buttons. It occurred to Louisa that his love of swimming may have been passed down to her, as her mother never enjoyed a swim unless it was in warm, shallow tropical waters. *I wonder what other traits I've inherited?* With that question bouncing around her mind she pulled herself out of the pool, reaching for her robe. Malcolm was picking her up at seven and it was nearly six.

Forty-five minutes later, Louisa checked herself in the mirror. In honour of a restaurant meal, she discarding her beloved jeans for a pair of black tailored trousers, teamed with a cream and black polka-dot slinky blouse, topped by the ubiquitous bomber jacket. Her choice was limited, having grabbed clothes haphazardly to pack for the trip, not thinking beyond the need for something suitable for a short hotel stay. A quick slick of deep pink lipstick and she was ready.

Once in the reception area she seated herself near the window, keeping an eye out for Malcolm. Moments later she saw a dark blue BMW convertible pull up outside and he emerged. Malcolm came round and opened the door for her, smiling broadly.

'Hi, there. I'm glad to see you're not one of those women who keep a man waiting.'

She grinned and slid into the passenger seat. He drove off back towards the main road.

'I've reserved a table at one of my favourite restaurants, La Fregate. It's near my home in St Peter Port and I eat there several times a week. I'm not much of a cook, I'm afraid. What about you?' He glanced towards her before pulling out onto the road heading east.

'Not too bad. Mum taught me the basics and I became quite a keen cook at uni. One of the students in our shared house was studying nutrition and she encouraged me to eat healthily. So no burgers and chips or pizzas for us!'

'Glad to hear it! I truly believe that we are what we eat.'

Louisa sat lost in thought as she recalled her conversations with her mother on that subject. Susan had enjoyed rich food, particularly creamy sauces and red meat. Although not overweight, her doctor had said her cholesterol level was too high and she had blocked arteries. An ideal candidate for a heart attack. Louisa had nagged her, but to no avail.

'Darling, I know you mean well, but I do enjoy my food and my glass of vino. It's my way of relaxing after a stressful day at the office. Doctors are such doom merchants! I'll be fine,' Susan said to her on one occasion. So Louisa stopped nagging, and a few months later Susan had suffered her first, albeit minor, heart attack. Her mother was shaken and made a big effort to eat more healthily. But within a year she was dead, thanks to that bloody burglar, Louisa thought angrily.

She dug her nails hard into her hands to keep calm as the memories buzzed around her brain. *I have to focus on Malcolm tonight, can't be a moping minnie or he'll not want to spend time with me. And I want to know the story of those damn jewels.*

'Are you all right, Louisa? You look pale.'

She turned to face him. He was frowning.

'Yes, I'm fine, thanks. You know, I've just realised that I don't know what to call you. 'Dad' doesn't sound right, somehow. What do *you* think?'

'I'm okay with Malcolm. I could hardly expect you to call me Dad. Although, perhaps one day…' He gave her a tentative smile.

'Perhaps.' That seemed a step too far…

The restaurant had views to die for, Louisa thought, gazing over the rooftops towards the marina, the sea and the castle guarding the harbour entrance. There was still enough light to see outlines of the other islands and the overall effect was magical.

'Quite something, isn't it? In the summer I enjoy having an aperitif outside on the terrace, but I think we'll agree to forego that pleasure tonight,' Malcolm said, standing close by her side in the bar.

'Yep, let's!'

They settled into the velvety chairs while the Italian manager offered them menus. He had greeted Malcolm with a hug, then turned to bow to Louisa.

'Signorina,' he said, smiling.

'Luca, may I introduce my…daughter. I expect you to pull out all the stops tonight. I want to impress her!' Malcolm joked.

Luca's eyes arched in surprise, but he only smiled and asked what they would like to drink.

'I think champagne is called for, don't you?' Malcolm asked Louisa and she nodded, pleased at the compliment but unsure if it was justified. Who was to say they would get on?

Within moments two flutes and a bottle of what looked to her like a particularly expensive champagne arrived at their side and was poured with a flourish.

They clinked glasses, calling out 'Cheers!'

She let the bubbles tickle her nose and took a sip. It had been ages since she'd tasted champagne, not the usual fare of a low-paid physio.

'Delicious, thanks. What would you recommend on the menu? You probably know it backwards!'

He chuckled. 'Sure do. Fortunately they change it monthly or I might have to consider going elsewhere. Fish is always good here and my favourite's the Dover sole.'

Sipping her bubbly Louisa scanned the menu, finally making her choice of duck to start, followed by the Dover sole. Malcolm placed their order and sat back in his chair, nursing his glass.

'You know, never in a million years did I expect to be in the company of my own daughter. I still haven't taken it all in. After we parted yesterday I couldn't get you out of my head. Found it hard to concentrate on my meeting, I can tell you! Haven't a clue what I said to the guy. All I could think of was you – and your mother.' He leant forward, patting her hand. 'I'm really, really sorry about what happened to Susan. If we could go back in time, I would have done things so differently.' He shook his head sorrowfully. 'But the good thing to come out of this awful business is that we've now met. Something that may not have happened otherwise.'

'Yes. As far as I know Mum hadn't tried to find you for years. I got the impression she imagined you settled somewhere, just as you said about her. We'll never know if you two *could* have got back together. I guess you'd both changed a lot since…' She trailed off, feeling shy of the thought of them together. As a couple.

Malcolm tapped his fingers on the arm of the chair, a far-away look in his eyes. He turned his head, finally focusing on her again. 'I would have loved the chance to find out,' he said softly. 'I was a stupid, bloody idiot…but,' he said, sitting up straight. 'Let's not go there, shall we? We both need to focus on the now, not "what if". No mileage in that.' He smiled and she noticed again how his eyes crinkled up at the corners. At that moment Luca came up to take them to their table, nestling in a corner by the window.

The aroma from their starters of duck and pheasant set her gastric juices flowing and Louisa tucked in with relish. In between mouthfuls she sipped the champagne, stealing glances at the other diners. Their table was set apart from other tables and she wondered why.

'Is this your special table, Malcolm? It seems placed to give a good view of the room but be apart from everyone.'

He chuckled. 'You've guessed right. I love people-watching, it's in the blood of any decent hotelier. But I like my space, too. Starter okay for you?'

She nodded, savouring a mouthful of duck spring-roll. *Mm, must be nice to be able to afford to eat regularly in a restaurant like this instead of cooking. Could get used to the lifestyle!* When she had finished she asked the question uppermost in her mind.

'Are you going to tell me about the jewellery and why that…horrible man wanted it?'

Malcolm rested his knife and fork, his face clouding. 'I will tell you, but here isn't the right place. It's…sensitive and not for other ears. If you like, we could have coffee at my apartment after dinner and I'll explain everything. Okay?'

'Yes, I can go with that. Perhaps for now you could tell me a bit more about yourself and how you ended up in Canada?'

Malcolm allowed the waiter to clear away their plates before answering. 'It's quite a long story so I'll give you the short version for now.' He took a sip of champagne before continuing, 'My mother, Betty, was forced to flee Guernsey with Archie after my father, Roland, was killed…' he described what had happened.

The waiter returned with their main courses and after he left Louisa asked, 'Your mother must have hated Archie for what he'd done. How on earth did she cope living with him?'

He grimaced. 'It was awful for her. She didn't tell me everything, but hinted that he threatened her with violence if she tried to leave or go to the police. Remember, she was pregnant with me, had no money of her own and no-one to turn to. But she did insist on separate bedrooms and he reluctantly agreed. They passed themselves off as brother and sister, my mother claiming to be a widow. Which in a way she was. Fortunately for her, it was only a few months later that Archie was called up to fight, just after I was born. Ma told me he tried to get out of it, but he passed the medical and was sent off for training.' Malcolm's face split into a grin. 'It was the best thing that could have happened. Once he'd gone, Ma used her savings to obtain berths for us on a ship evacuating children to Canada. My father had a distant cousin in southern Ontario where they had planned to go after their wedding. She never saw or heard from Archie again.'

'Wow! That's some story. Your mother was some brave lady! What happened after you arrived in Canada?'

'We were taken in initially by my father's cousin, but apparently he made it clear that it was only until my mother could find her own place. I don't remember him, as Ma moved a few months later to Sarnia as housekeeper in a hotel. The cousin had put in a word with the owner, a friend of his.'

'Sarnia? That name rings a bell.'

Malcolm smiled. 'It's the old Roman name for Guernsey and Ma chose to live there as a way of being closer to her old home. It's near the Great Lakes and had a huge petroleum industry so hotels were busy. My mother eventually opened up her own hotel, using savings and her canny eye for a bargain, the first of several over the years, all in Ontario.'

'So that's how you became involved in the hotel business?'

'Yep. I learnt at Ma's knee, you might say. All my growing up was in hotels, either ones where Ma was the housekeeper or, later, ones she owned. It seemed like the natural career for me.'

As Louisa enjoyed the tasty sole she mulled over what Malcolm had told her about his early start in life, and in particular his enterprising mother. With a shock she realised

Betty was her grandmother. *Oh, I would have loved to meet her! What an interesting life she had.* Although her maternal grandmother had loved her, she was not what would be termed warm hearted, as Malcolm's mother seemed to have been. Betty sounded the sort of grandmother who would have spoilt her. She sighed. She would have loved to be part of a bigger family.

'Something wrong with your fish?' Malcolm's voice cut into her thoughts.

She shook her head. 'No, it's perfect, thanks. I was just thinking what a pity it was I never knew your mother. My grandmother. My maternal grandmother's also dead.'

'I'm sure you would both have got on well. But...' he spread his hands. '*C'est la vie!* I promise to tell you more about her and show you some photos. We both have her eyes. Now, can you manage some dessert? They conjure up one of the best crêpe Suzettes I've ever tasted, but it's for two,' he said, smiling. 'As I'm usually eating on my own it's a rare treat to be able to order it. Would you indulge an old man's whim and join me?'

She laughed. 'I'd be happy to. You can't eat healthily all the time!'

There was an element of theatre in the production of the crêpes, culminating with the final flourish of the addition of flamed brandy. The taste lived up to expectations and she felt pleasantly replete after the last mouthful.

'Delicious, thanks.' She patted her flat stomach. 'I'll swim a few extra lengths tomorrow to burn it off.'

'Me too! Sounds like we share a love of swimming. That's good. I always stay in hotels with swimming pools so I can have a daily swim. For me it was a priority to build one for the centre, not just for the guests but for me as well.' He called the waiter for the bill and Louisa thanked him for the meal. He brushed aside her thanks.

'It's been a great pleasure, my dear. I trust it will be the first of many such evenings.' He smiled broadly, patting her arm.

Luca's goodbyes were as profuse as his greetings earlier and it seemed to take forever to leave the restaurant. As Louisa settled into the comfort of his car, Malcolm asked if she still wanted to go back for coffee.

'Sure.' *I want to know why those jewels were so important that they cost my mother her life.*

chapter 9

Malcolm's apartment was literally two minutes from the restaurant. Within easy walking distance, normally he didn't need to drive. He liked living in Town, he could walk to any part of it within fifteen minutes. The walk home was uphill and it was a measure of his fitness that he never returned out of breath.

After parking in the underground car park, he escorted Louisa to the lift for his penthouse. He still couldn't quite believe that he was about to invite *his daughter* into the apartment. Until yesterday he'd had no idea that she even existed, whereas Louisa had known for years about him. Or at least the idea of him. As the lift purred its way to the top, he thought of Susan, the lovely woman who'd had his child. If only his mother had not fallen ill at that time…Although he'd had a good life, he often felt the lack of something, someone. Initially, he'd thought it was the loss of his mother in her fifties. Too young. Their bond had been close, but not claustrophobic. It was her idea for him to spend time working in London.

'You need to breathe your own air, son. Do things and learn things that I can't teach you. You're thirty now, time to come out of my shadow and try a different path. You might decide you don't want to be an hotelier…'

'Don't be daft, Ma. I can't think of anything better. I've loved every minute of working by your side. You've taught me the business too well for me to want to try something different.'

His mother nodded, a pleased look on her face. At fifty she was still a very attractive woman, her blue eyes and fair hair drew admiring glances from much younger men. But she didn't seem to notice. She had an on–off relationship with a guy from out of town who "visited" at irregular intervals, but it seemed to suit her. Malcolm guessed that Betty liked being independent too much to settle permanently with a man.

They were eating dinner together in her private suite and his mother looked thoughtful as she sipped her wine. 'If you're serious about staying in the hotel business, then why not go to London and get a managerial position in a top-notch hotel. Just for a couple of years. When you return we'll open a luxury hotel or two ourselves.' She fixed him with her penetrating gaze. 'Could be fun.'

'What, going to London or opening luxury hotels?' he replied, laughing.

'Both, of course!'

Betty hadn't lived to see him open his first luxury hotel in Toronto. When he'd rushed back from London she was in the final, debilitating stages of ovarian cancer. Although they'd been in regular contact by phone while he was away, she had never once told him about her illness. His shock soon turned to despair when he discovered there was nothing to be done. His wonderful, loving, hard-working mother died weeks later.

As the lift reached its destination, Malcolm smiled at the woman he knew his mother would have adored. Louisa's answering smile was guarded, as if she wasn't quite sure about him. He sighed inwardly, it might take time but he was determined to make their relationship work. There had to be some good come out of Susan's untimely death.

'Right. Please come in.' He pushed open the maple wood door, switching on an array of lights from a central control.

Louisa's eyes opened wide as she gazed at the marble flooring and pale wood panelling of the hallway. He strode ahead into the softly-lit enormous, open-plan living/dining area, beckoning her to join him by one of the floor to ceiling windows. She followed his gaze and gasped.

'Oh, how beautiful! What a fantastic view of the marina and the islands. If I lived here I'd spend all day just gazing out of the window.'

Malcolm grinned. 'That's what I did when I first moved in. There's a terrace too, see? Too cold now, but great when it's warm.'

She nodded, staring out at the terrace bordered with glass and stainless steel and furnished with tables and chairs. Huge pots, filled with date palms and lit from inside, glowed with a soft blue light. It was enchanting.

'This is some place you have here. It looks pretty new. Is it?'

'Yes, I was lucky. These apartments were being built at the time I bought La Folie and was looking for my own place in Town. I bought this off-plan so I could choose the finishes. Made life a bit hectic once we started upgrading La Folie, but I found a great interior designer to work on both projects.'

After guiding Louisa to one of the two enormous sofas, he headed into the kitchen to make coffee. He hadn't used half of the fancy appliances his designer insisted he absolutely needed, but the jazzy coffee machine was a constant joy. Moments later he joined Louisa on the sofa, bearing two cups of aromatic coffee.

'Thanks.' She took an appreciative sip and grinned. 'You may not be much of a cook, but you sure make a mean cup of coffee.' Putting her cup down on an intricately carved wooden coffee table she asked, 'Ready to tell me about those jewels?'

'Not only will I tell you, I can show them to you if you like.'

Louisa's eyes opened wide. 'They're here? I assumed they'd be in a bank.'

Malcolm got up and headed towards the hall. 'I have a safe in my study. Back in a minute.' His study, originally planned as a bedroom, adjoined the master suite and the walls were lined with shelves crammed with books. A lifetime's collection, they had been shipped over from Canada when he moved in. But his pride and joy was the massive mahogany partner's desk that had originally belonged in La Folie. The previous owner, Hélène Ferbrache, had included it in the sale, not knowing it had once belonged to his father. It was part of the furniture that came with the house when her parents bought it after the war. A bit battered, Malcolm had restored it himself and now the wood glowed against the old leather top. Walking over to one of the bookshelves he pressed a concealed button. A shelf swung out, revealing the safe. Controlled by iris recognition and guaranteed bomb-proof, it offered him total security. He removed two velvet bags, closed the safe and returned to the sitting room.

He found Louisa sitting mesmerised by the flickering flames of the floating fireplace set in the wall.

Malcolm opened one of the bags and pulled out a necklace. Louisa gasped as the firelight reflected sparks off rubies and diamonds, creating the illusion that it, too, was on fire. Two pear-shaped rubies the size of walnuts formed a central drop pendant hanging from a collar of smaller diamonds and rubies.

'May I?'

'Of course.'

She picked it up cautiously, as if it would break in her hands. Looking up, she said, 'I recognise it from the photo, but it looks much more beautiful in the flesh. Is it very old? The setting seems a bit old-fashioned.'

He chuckled. 'You could say it's old. Late eighteenth century, actually. And it was from India, belonged to a Maharani, wife of a Maharaja.' Catching her look of amazement, he continued, 'I'll explain. It's a bit of a long story and, I'm afraid, doesn't reflect too well on my – our – ancestors.'

Bending over the table he took a matching pair of earrings from the first bag and then opened the second. He lifted out two gold objects, heavily encrusted with emeralds, diamonds and rubies. 'This is the turban ornament belonging to the Maharaja. Here, have a look.'

Louisa held the larger one first. Shaped like a peacock's feather, it was studded with "veins" of emeralds against the white of the diamonds. Pear drop emeralds hung from two golden hooks at each end. Picking up the second, looking like a pin brooch, she stroked the enormous central emerald, surrounded by diamonds, and hung with a large drop pearl.

'I can't believe this! If these are real they must be worth an absolute fortune.'

Malcolm leaned back with his cup of coffee. 'Oh, they're real all right. Had them checked out by an expert in London. One who didn't ask too many questions,' he replied, tapping his nose. 'That's why I had them with me when I was dating Susan. My great-grandfather was working for the British East India Company when a number of Indian rulers rose up in revolt in 1857. At that time the East India Company weren't just traders, they were political rulers and the princes, understandably, didn't like having their power usurped. Most of the old Mughal empire had been annexed by that time, hence the massed revolt.' He took a long sip of his coffee as Louisa sat wide-eyed on the sofa. 'The jewellery and artefacts belonging to the defeated Maharajas were sent to Britain and presented to Queen Victoria. However, some found its way into the pockets of the Nabobs, the high-ups in the East India Company, one of whom was my great-grandfather. Roland told my mother the story, passed down the family, that great-grandfather, Albert Blake, amassed quite a fortune while out in India. He scuttled back to England when the British government took control in 1858, kicking out the East India Company.'

'Wow! That's some story. So what happened to my great-great grandfather Albert?'

'Apparently he stayed in England long enough to find a bride and then came over here and built La Folie. With his ill-gotten gains. I gather there'd been rumblings about officials lining their pockets and old Albert thought it was best to be out of sight, but didn't fancy the tropics. My father was born in La Folie in '99 and the family still lived very well off Albert's shrewd investments.'

'Mm, this is all very interesting, but how does this connect with that…man and my mother?'

Malcolm sighed heavily. 'I suspect that he was linked in some way to Archie, who killed my father. He's the only one who knew about the jewels. You see,' He got up and walked around, stretching his legs, 'before Archie and my mother left Guernsey, he took the jewels and cash from the safe. Everything would have been inherited by her anyway, if she and Roland had married, as planned. But Archie knew he stood to inherit nothing, hence the row with Roland. So in effect *he* stole the money and jewels.' He stopped walking around and sat down next to Louisa.

Taking her hand, he said, 'There were no other relatives who stood to inherit, Roland was the last of the line and if my parents had married, I'd have been the heir. Although neither my mother nor I had a legal right to Roland's fortune, it could be argued we had a moral right.'

Louisa nodded in apparent agreement.

Malcolm continued, 'Archie hid the jewels and any unspent money in their new home in England but, unknown to him, Ma knew the hiding-place. After he was called up she used some of the cash to buy our passage to Canada. I'd imagine Archie was pretty steamed up about it when he got back on leave and found it all gone. Ma changed our surname to avoid being traced. He was probably looking for us for years. And then one day, perhaps he saw the photo of Susan wearing the jewels in the report of the charity ball and...' He shrugged, gripping her hand tighter. He could only guess this is what happened, but it fitted with what Louisa had said about Susan's last words – the man said they had seen the photo of her wearing the jewels and he asked about Malcolm. Archie knew Betty's son was named Malcolm so it would have been logical to assume he had inherited or borrowed them from her. He may have assumed that he had married Susan and she now had the jewels. At the moment he could not think of any other reason why someone would target Susan for the jewels.

Louisa chewed her lip and Malcolm's feelings of guilt and remorse rose up from where he'd pushed them since she'd told him about Susan. *Dear God, my family's robbed this poor girl of her mother, all for the sake of stolen jewels. I'm going to find the bastard who did this, if it's the last thing I do.*

'The man I saw wasn't that old. Late middle-aged, I'd guess. He didn't run like a young man. Could Archie have a son?' She looked up at him, her eyes glistening with unshed tears.

'I've no idea. We've been trying to track Archie down these past few months, so far without success. But I'm even more determined now. The police investigation was led by a local inspector, and he's since retired so I'd like him to act for me privately. He'll have access to useful sources and we have more to go on now.'

Louisa, appearing mesmerised by the bright, garish jewels, yawned. 'Sorry, I'm so tired. Any chance of a lift home? Or I can get a taxi.'

'Of course I'll run you home. Let me put these baubles away first.'

He came back bearing their jackets and jangling his car keys. Minutes later they were in the car and heading back into Les Canichers on the way to the sea front. A tired stillness filled the car, only broken by the purr of the powerful engine as Malcolm throttled up the steep Val des Terres. Louisa's head rested on the back of the seat, her eyes closed. Not wanting to disturb her he remained quiet, his mind full of the events of the past two days. His nightly ritual was to review the day, creating a virtual balance sheet of positive and negative experiences or events. Two entries in the balance sheet for the previous day stood out, one negative, one potentially positive. The negative was Susan's death, robbing him of the chance to make amends to the woman he now acknowledged was the love of his life. The positive was the arrival of Louisa, apparently a daughter he never knew he had. Initially, he was wary. After all, he was wealthy, an easy target for a con artist or the genuine article looking for money. In his heart he knew Louisa was his flesh and blood so that was okay. He still wanted her checked out and the London private eye had done a thorough job. It seemed that, not only was Louisa who she said she was, but that she had been well provided for by Susan. So not a gold-digger. It was a huge relief as Malcolm believed strongly in getting second chances in life, his mother being a prime example. As he negotiated the winding lanes out to St Martins and La Trelade, he fervently wished for a second chance at love. But this time

around, sharing the love between a father and daughter –
not a lover.

chapter 10

Louisa stretched her long limbs, her toes curling up under the duvet. She had slept more soundly than for a long while and was amazed to see the green flickering lights of the digital clock registering eight thirty. The memory of the previous evening floated into her consciousness and she re-lived it as if in slow motion. It was too early to form a definite opinion about Malcolm, but so far she thought he seemed a decent bloke, if a tad selfish. Probably spoiled rotten by his mother, she brooded; then the memory of her own upbringing brought her up sharp. Some would say she had been spoiled by *her* mother. Lying cocooned in the warmth of her bed, she could see the similarities between the pairings of herself and Susan and Malcolm and Betty. Two single mothers, never married, but with a child to raise. Susan had at least received some support from her parents, and had been brave enough to start her own business rather than settle for a secure job. Betty had no family support but did have some money, although Louisa had no idea how much it had been – and had not only moved to a strange country but started an hotel business on her own. She guessed that Susan and Betty, with so much in common, would have got on like the proverbial house on fire.

There was so much to learn about her father. It felt strange to be embarking on this journey of discovery at her age. The thought popped in that it must be even stranger for Malcolm who had had no idea that she even existed. As he dropped her off he had suggested that they met at La

Folie for lunch and he would show her around. The green digits now flashed eight forty-five and she swung her legs out of bed, heading into the bathroom for a quick shower.

The morning sped by: after a light breakfast Louisa went along to the health suite for a protracted swim, followed by a session in the steam room. Energised, she took a walk along the cliffs for an hour, the fine weather having held. After being cooped up in London for weeks, too depressed to go out, it was a joy to breathe the clear island air. At one point Louisa had stood and watched a group of seagulls ducking and diving over the sea, calling out to each other with high-pitched cries. One of her favourite books, given to her by Susan, was *Jonathan Livingston Seagull* and ever since, while watching seagulls, she had wondered if one of them was a *Jonathan*. An Outcast gull who became a free-thinking leader and teacher of other Outcasts. After the death of her mother, Louisa had felt like an outcast. To all intents and purposes an orphan. Someone to tip-toe around, not sure how to deal with. But she was no longer an orphan, an Outcast, she had a father. The thought made her smile as she made her way back to the hotel to change for lunch.

Louisa pushed open La Folie's front door and immediately was pounced on by Nadine, who rushed over from the reception desk.

'You're a dark horse, aren't you? Fancy being the boss's daughter and not saying a word!'

Louisa grinned sheepishly. 'It wasn't public knowledge so I couldn't say anything. Has my…father told everyone?'

Nadine nodded. 'I guess. He said you'd be coming here for lunch and a grand tour and that we were to be on our best behaviour.'

'What? He said that? That's a bit…'

Nadine giggled. 'He didn't use those words exactly, but I think he wants you to have a good impression of the centre and what we do here. I'm to take you through to the dining room and he'll join you as soon as he can. He's in a meeting with Paul at the moment.'

Nadine led the way down a corridor towards the back and opened a door leading into a long, narrow room with fully-glazed walls on three sides. Hazy March sun lit up the space, highlighting the collection of cosy dining tables. Louisa clocked about eight diners scattered around the room, before Nadine steered her to a window table set for two. Flashing a cheeky smile, Nadine left and was soon replaced by a waitress.

'Good afternoon, what would you like to drink? Our speciality's a choice of fresh juices but if you'd prefer a glass of wine…'

'A juice would be great, thanks. What's on offer?'

After making her choice from the list of exotic combinations, Louisa gazed out of the window. The garden was flanked by hedging, with a gate at the far end for access to the cliff path. The sea sparkled in the distance. She worked out that it was probably about a thirty minute walk from here to the point near her hotel. The garden itself looked immaculate; the beds abundant with tulips, hyacinth, daffodils and narcissi; all nestled among shrubs of camellia and rhododendron. Little paths cut across the flowerbeds and a couple of guests strolled round, stopping occasionally to sniff fragrant flowers. A paved terrace adjoining the sun room provided an outside seating area, with tables and chairs ready for warmer weather. *Heavenly. Malcolm's chosen a brilliant spot for his centre, regardless of its connection to his father.*

Her bright green juice, a mix which included spinach, kiwi and apple, arrived and she took a cautious sip. It tasted delicious and she was taking a longer sip when Malcolm appeared at her side. He patted her arm, saying, 'Sorry to keep you waiting. Something cropped up that couldn't wait,' before settling into the chair opposite. A waitress bustled up to ask if he wanted a drink. After ordering a juice, Malcolm turned to face Louisa and she found herself smiling at him. He looked genuinely pleased to see her again, if a little unsure of his reception.

'No problem. I've been enjoying the view of the wonderful garden. I imagine it'll look even more stunning by summer.'

'Yes, it will. The previous owner worked hard on it and we've changed very little. We'll walk round later. Now, what do you want to eat? I can, of course, recommend everything on the menu.' They shared a grin before Louisa perused the list.

The same waitress returned to take their order and after she had left there was an awkward silence.

'I...'

'What...'

They both laughed.

'You go first,' Malcolm said, patting her hand.

'I was going to say how much I enjoyed dinner last night. Although it still feels strange to be sitting talking to you. For years I'd imagined how it would be if we ever met, but I'd always assumed that Mum would be there too...' The hard ball of grief tightened in her solar plexus and she gritted her teeth.

'Of course. It can't be easy for you, my dear. But I hope in time you'll see me as an important part of your life, though I can never replace your mother.' He sighed. 'And although it's too late for me to be a proper father, I'll do my best to be there for you. I want you to know you're no longer alone.'

He certainly looked sincere, she thought, not doubting his words.

'Thanks. That's good to know.' She sipped her juice before continuing, 'There's still so much we don't know about each other…'

He nodded. 'Fire away.'

The waitress arrived at that moment with their food and Louisa waited until she'd left.

'Would you mind telling me what happened after you lost your mother? What you did, where you went?'

Malcolm picked at his salad. 'That's a long story. Initially I oversaw the running of Ma's hotels while the legal stuff was sorted, then I moved to Toronto and opened my first, luxury hotel. I'd gained a lot of experience in London and made some useful contacts too, so raising the finance wasn't difficult. Five years later I opened another one; eventually I owned four in the city. I upgraded Ma's original hotels, so it became a quality chain, with a good reputation.' He took a sip of his juice. 'It was hard work, I never took a day off and had no private life. A true workaholic. It was as if I needed to prove something.' He shrugged.

Louisa could picture him, being driven to succeed, to be the best. She said softly, 'Who were you trying to prove something to?'

He tapped his fingers on the table. 'Myself, mainly. Ma had suggested that we open luxury hotels at some point and I wanted to prove I could do it without her help. I'd always had the need to be the best, at whatever I did. Compensating for not having a father, perhaps.'

She pursed her lips. 'Makes sense, I guess. Although I don't share your high ambitions, I did work hard at school and university to get top results. I never wanted to go into business like Mum, looked far too stressful for my taste, but liked the idea of being able to help those with injuries or illness.'

'What attracted you to physiotherapy?'

'As a teenager I was into sport in a big way and I liked to push myself to the limit.' She gave a short laugh. 'Typical teenage arrogance, thinking I was invincible! It was school sports day and I'd entered in several events. I didn't bother to warm up properly or pace myself, and while jumping over the hurdles I twisted my knee badly and couldn't walk. Fortunately for me, a watching parent was a physio and took charge. I needed several sessions with her before my knee recovered, and without her help I could have ended up with a limp.'

'Are you still sport mad?' Malcolm asked, smiling.

'Not really. I tend to stick to swimming and walking these days. And this place is ideal for both.'

They continued their meal in companionable silence before Malcolm suggested he show Louisa around.

'Let's start outside with the gardens and the swimming pool. This way,' he said, opening the door onto the terrace. The air was a little warmer as they began walking towards the bottom of the garden, the bright flowers looking particularly cheerful under the spring sun. At one point Malcolm stopped and, taking her arm, turned her to look back at the house.

'Oh! Isn't it lovely. So different to the front. A house with a split personality!' she joked, gazing at the big bay windows on the upper floors, between which spread the branches of a wisteria still in bud. The sun room, clearly a recent addition, spread across most of the ground floor, finishing just shy of a bay window at the further end. Even with the round towers visible, the effect was much more English country house than gothic castle.

As they walked, Malcolm stopped to say hello to the guests strolling around the grounds. Louisa stood to one side, listening as he asked if they were enjoying their stay and if there was anything they were unhappy with. From what she heard, everyone was perfectly content, complimenting both the therapists and the accommodation. She felt a tiny frisson of pride that her father was the mastermind of this centre, able to please the kind of people who could afford to stay wherever they chose. Malcolm then moved off in the direction of the swimming pool, to the side of the house and set in the middle of what appeared to be a nascent kitchen garden, with small shoots of herbs and vegetables peeping through the soil.

'We started planting at the end of October, once the pool was near completion. The plan is to be self-sufficient in vegetables, herbs and fruit, all organically grown. This area was once an overgrown field with the remains of a greenhouse in the middle. It's where my father…'

He looked grim as he stared ahead. Louisa squeezed his arm and he turned and attempted a smile.

'At least something good's coming out of what happened, Malcolm. I'm sure your father would have been proud of what you've achieved.'

'Thank you. I'd like to think so. Let's check out the pool, shall we?'

Louisa was intrigued by the pool's glazed enclosure. 'Does it slide back in summer?' She asked, noticing how it was made up of sections like sliding doors.

'Yes, it's quite ingenious. Each section slides under the next, ending up at each end. It's all electronically controlled; on a dry day, as the outside temperature increases, the sections start telescoping back from the middle. Neat, huh?' he said, grinning.

'Yep, sure is.' They stepped inside and a wall of heat hit her, prompting a swift removal of her jacket. She guessed the pool to be about fifteen metres long and eight metres wide; a good size for proper exercising. Two women and a man swam up and down and others lay stretched out on loungers. With the sun pouring through the clear panels, the impression was of swimming outside on a summer's day. A door at one end led into a wooden lodge holding changing rooms.

'I think you've done a great job. And once the kitchen garden's matured guests will be able to look out and choose their veg for dinner,' she said, laughing.

'That's the idea. The only thing missing is a Guernsey cow,' Malcolm replied. 'But that seemed a step too far! But we've leased out another field to a local farmer so there are cows nearby.'

'Quite a bucolic picture you're painting,' Louisa said, looking out over the neighbouring fields. 'It's so peaceful here, too. No sounds of traffic: nothing. Your guests must sleep like babies. Heaven, after the noise of London.'

'That was the aim. To provide somewhere that's easy to get to, but in its own world. Most of the guests lead full on, stressful lives, and need to escape every few months. We've already had some re-book for later in the year.'

Louisa was suitably impressed. 'That's good. Have you, er, had any celebs staying?'

He tapped his nose, smiling. 'Can't mention any names, but we are expecting an A list film star next month.'

'Cool! Male or female?'

'Female. And not another word. Now, let me show you around inside; you've hardly seen anything yet.'

They retraced their steps to the sun room, walking through from there to the hall.

'Right, along this passage are a couple of therapy rooms and over there is the library, used by anyone as a place to relax and read or chat. Other therapy rooms are in the next passage.'

'What therapies are on offer?'

'Massage, physio, hypnotherapy, counselling, reflexology, Reiki, aromatherapy and some others a little more exotic. We also provide group sessions of yoga, meditation, nutritional guidance and Pilates. Oh, and a beauty therapist is on call if needed.'

'Sounds wonderful! I'd book in like a shot if I had the money,' she teased.

Malcolm frowned. 'Well, I guess we could offer a discount. Under the circumstances…'

Louisa was miffed, until he smiled broadly, saying, 'Only kidding. You'd be welcome to stay any time you wish, my dear. Just say when.'

'Mm, might well take you up on that. In the meantime, can I see some of the rooms?'

As he showed her around, Malcolm pointed out the areas that had needed most improvement. 'It was all rather dark and cold and I wanted a bright, but homely country house feel…'

They were coming down the stairs when a man about her own age and dressed in the white staff uniform, appeared in the hall.

'Oh, Paul. Just the guy I wanted. I'd like to introduce you to my daughter, Louisa.'

'Hi, Louisa, pleased to meet you. What do you think of our little retreat?' he said, reaching out to shake her hand.

'I'm very impressed. Um, are you a therapist as well as the manager?' She found herself gazing at him shyly. A young Peter O'Toole, she thought, taking in his fair hair and deep blue eyes set above high cheekbones. Tall with an athletic body, he was the epitome of brimming health. What an advert for the centre!

He smiled, displaying white even teeth. 'I teach yoga and nutrition as well as practising Reiki. So I'm kept pretty busy, aren't I, Malc?'

Louisa was surprised at the diminutive. It implied a close friendship and yet Malcolm came across as a loner.

Her father smiled. 'I certainly hope so! It was your idea, after all.'

He must have seen Louisa's look of surprise and told her how they had met in India, leading to the decision to open a natural health centre.

'I see. Sounds like one of those life-changing moments that happen when you least expect it. How weird, that you two meeting in India should lead to you coming back here, of all places. The family history...' She spread out her arms, looking around.

'Yes, you're right. But sometimes Fate plays a part in our lives that we can't explain. I'm just happy that we're here now. And with you, my dear.' Malcolm squeezed her hand and she smiled in return.

'Malc tells me you're a trained physio. Are you working at the moment?'

'No, I've taken some time off since...'

Paul looked stricken. 'Oh, God, how crass of me! I'm so sorry about your mother. I should have offered you my condolences immediately but–'

'No problem,' Louisa said, not wanting him to feel bad about it. 'I've worked as a hospital physio since qualifying but, to be honest, was glad to take a break. Cutbacks were putting us all under pressure and we couldn't think outside the box. Frustrating.'

Paul nodded in sympathy. 'I heard that a lot when I worked in the UK. I've been lucky to be involved with natural health centres for a few years now, and enjoy being able to put the patient – or client – first. Speaking of which, I must shoot as I've someone waiting for me.' He shook her hand saying, 'Nice to have met you. I guess I'll see you around.'

'And you.'

Paul nodded at Malcolm before heading off down the hall. Louisa was left thinking what a very attractive man he was. Very attractive indeed.

chapter 11

'Inspector Ferguson? Oh, of course. Thought you'd be allowed to keep the title...It's Malcolm Roget. Fine thanks, and yourself? Good. Look, Ferguson, I'm in need of your help. Something else has happened and...'

Malcolm finished the call and glanced at his watch. Ferguson had promised to meet him in his apartment in half an hour and it was now eleven. Briefly he wondered if he should have asked Louisa to join him, but decided that perhaps it was better if he talked to the detective first. Feeling restless, he strode around the living area before venturing out onto the terrace. He felt caged in, like an animal in a zoo, but genetically wired to roam free. He knew it was stupid, nothing and no-one had entrapped him, but the feeling persisted. Leaning on the balustrade, he began to calm down as he focused on the view below. Watching boats, large and small, gin palaces and hardy dinghies, upping anchor and heading out to sea was soothing, signalling the idea of freedom. Of being able to travel at a moment's notice. Which, until recently, he was free to do himself. But now...he frowned. Coming to Guernsey and opening the centre had given him a much needed *raison d'être* after the sale of the hotels. But at a price. The shock of seeing his father's remains, hastily dumped in that hole in the ground, brought back all his repressed feelings of inferiority; of not being as good as anyone else. A bastard. And all thanks to a greedy, good for nothing who was himself illegitimate.

Gazing with unseeing eyes towards Herm, Malcolm was brought up short by the knowledge that he'd also fathered an illegitimate child. Talk about history repeating itself! He slowly breathed out his anger towards Archie. The image of his child, Louisa, stood bright in front of his vision, blocking out the real view. It was wonderful, truly wonderful to find himself a father at his age; but the news was bittersweet, tempered by the awful death of Susan. He wouldn't be free to up anchor until the man responsible for her death – and that of his father – were found. Dead or alive.

The clear sound of the intercom cut through his thoughts and he walked inside to answer the call. Hearing Ferguson's voice, he pressed the buzzer.

'Inspector! Sorry, Ferguson. Please come in.' He ushered the man into the living area, asking him if he'd like a coffee. Ferguson thanked him and Malcolm went into the kitchen to press a few buttons on the espresso machine.

'So, how's retirement? It's been a couple of months hasn't it?' he asked, handing the coffee mug to his visitor.

'Thanks. Yes, I left the beginning of January. It's okay, this retirement lark, but it's boring. Hence my decision to offer my services in a private capacity. Not that there's much call for a private investigator in Guernsey, apart from divorce cases.' He sighed, 'Staking out unfaithful spouses is not my idea of detective work, I can tell you.'

Malcolm nodded in sympathy. 'I'm sure. You would be too good for that sort of work, Insp…Ferguson. Look, I'm not keen on using surnames. What's your first name?'

'John.'

'Right, John. Please call me Malcolm.' He settled himself on the sofa, drubbing his fingers on the arm. 'You know how I still want to find the man who killed my father?' John nodded. 'Well, there's been another death, a few months ago in London. And there's a connection…' Malcolm told him about Susan, their daughter and the burglar.

John sipped his coffee, looking thoughtful as he mulled over the few facts Malcolm had told him.

'Let's see if I've got this right; the necklace Susan was wearing in that magazine photo was the one taken by Archie, among other things, after he killed your father and scarpered to England. And it appears that either he, or someone else who knew about it, then saw a recent photo of her in an article about her travel business. And tracked her down and tried to get her to tell him where either the jewels or you were now. With a fatal result.' He looked across to Malcolm. 'And now the daughter's turned up, probably wondering if it's your fault her mother's dead.'

Malcolm winced. 'I hope not, but I take your point. I *do* feel responsible for Susan's death. If it wasn't for that blasted necklace she'd still be alive. That's why I want you to help me find that slime ball and get him banged up,' he said, clenching his fist.

'Right. I'm happy to come on board. Am I right in assuming the necklace is very valuable?'

'It is. I had it valued in 1972 and it was worth a couple of million then, so God knows how much it's worth now.'

John whistled. 'Weren't you tempted to sell it?'

Malcolm stood up and paced around, mug in hand. 'Never gave it much thought. It was a family heirloom, given by the eldest son to their bride. Perhaps I thought that one day...' He shrugged. 'My mother only ever wore it once: at a ball for the leading businessmen in the city. I was her escort but it was her name on the invite; it was her business, not mine.' He turned to face John. 'You know what she said afterwards? That all the women had blanked her once they saw the size of the rubies she wore. Jealousy. Pure jealousy.' He sat down. 'Ma called the necklace unlucky, refusing to wear it again. I thought she was being over-sensitive but now...I'm not so sure.'

'Where is it now?'

'Here, in my safe. Do you want to see it?'

'Please. I'll take a photo. Might come in useful.'

Malcolm returned moments later with the velvet bags, noticing that the detective had been writing in a little notebook. He emptied the contents onto the table.

The detective's eyebrows shot up. 'Those rubies are *huge*. No wonder those women were jealous. And what's this?' he asked, pointing to the turban decoration.

Malcolm filled him in with a potted history of the items and how they came to be in his family's possession. John fished out his smartphone and took a number of close-up photos.

'From what you've said, Archie must have told someone else about these jewels, and my guess would be a close family member. You wouldn't trust anyone else with that kind of knowledge. Possibly a son as he was young enough to marry and have kids after the war. Trouble is, we have no idea where Archie lived and that's what's hampered our investigation so far.' He scratched his head and Malcolm could almost hear the cogs in his brain whirring. The inspector had a formidable reputation, or so he'd been told.

'Any other likely family members?

'No, my father was the last of the line.'

John looked thoughtful. 'Which paper carried the latest article on Susan?'

'*The London Evening Standard.*'

'Hmm, covers quite an area, but might help. We're now looking for two men, possibly father and son, with at least one living in the London area. A son could be any age from about sixty-three down, but most likely not less than, say, forty-five—'

Malcolm cut in, 'I've just remembered something Louisa said. She thought the man she saw wasn't young, he moved like an older man.'

'Okay. Well, I'll need to talk to your daughter, see if I can jog her memory some more. You all right with that?'

'Sure, I was expecting you to suggest it. Tell me a good time for you and I'll arrange it.'

A few minutes later, as he showed him out, Malcolm realised that the earlier restlessness had left him, replaced by a surge of adrenalin. He now had a purpose, a mission to accomplish, in honour of both his father and his own lost love, Susan.

'Louisa? Hi, my dear. Can I ask you something, please?'

★

That afternoon Louisa made her way to Malcolm's apartment, only too happy to do anything to help catch her mother's killer. Because that's what he was, in her mind at least. She was buoyed by the idea of using a private investigator; he'd be more willing to keep going with the investigation. She was pretty sure that the police had surreptitiously closed the file, even though the coroner pronounced an open verdict on her mother's death. Terms like aggravated burglary and manslaughter were mentioned, but nothing happened.

'Hi, Malcolm, it's me,' she said into the intercom.

'Good, come on up.'

Once inside the apartment, her father ushered her into the living area where a stocky, middle-aged man stood looking out of the window. He turned round and came towards her, hand outstretched.

'Hello, Louisa. John Ferguson. Please accept my condolences for your loss.' She nodded and they sat down on the sofa while Malcolm disappeared to make coffee.

John continued, 'I know you've already told the police what happened that day, but I'd appreciate it if you could tell me, as I won't have access to your statement. Okay?'

'Sure.' She went on to describe the events of that horrible day, finding it hard to hold back the tears. Every time she had to recount the story it felt as if the wound was being ripped open again, never getting the chance to heal.

The detective wrote it all down and then chewed his pen a moment before looking over at her. 'I know you only had a quick glimpse of this man, but can you try really hard to think of anything, anything at all, that you may have noticed and haven't mentioned.'

Louisa concentrated, but try as she might, other than the impression he was an older man, nothing came into her mind. She said as much to John.

He smiled reassuringly. 'No problem. There might be something we can try. When I was with the London Met, we occasionally used hypnosis to help witnesses remember people or events, and with great results. Would you be willing to give it a try?'

'I…I suppose so. I've never used hypnosis. But if it'll help…' She didn't want to appear a wimp, but visions of swinging watches and staring eyes flashed through her mind.

'Great. Now all we need is a hypnotherapist. Mm, there was a lady who helped in a case a few years ago. Didn't hear her name but–'

'Could it have been Molly Ogier? She's semi-retired but works a few hours a week at the centre. I believe she's good,' Malcolm chimed in, returning with a tray of mugs.

'Might be. I can ring the girl she helped and confirm the name. Excellent!' He rubbed his hands together, adding, 'Even a small piece of information might help us to track this man down and hypnosis can yield things you didn't realise you saw.'

Malcolm handed round the mugs and John asked if he had a phone book. He fetched a copy from his study and passed it over. The detective flicked through the pages and then punched in a number on his phone, moving away to the window to make the call.

'Jeanne? It's John Ferguson. Yes, that's right. How are you? And the family? Good, good, pleased to hear it. Listen, I need to know the name of the lady who helped you with the hypnosis…Right, thanks. Will do, take care. Goodbye, Jeanne.'

He returned to the others smiling. 'Molly Ogier's the right woman. Will you get in touch, Malcolm, and see if she'll help Louisa? Shouldn't take more than a session or two.'

'Will be glad to. What do you plan to do once Louisa's been hypnotised?'

'I'll need to go over to London and chat up some old pals from the Met, do some digging. I'll also focus on finding any trace of Archie Blake in or around London and any male born with that surname since 1946. It's likely to be a slow process, I'm afraid. Could be weeks…'

Malcolm shook his head. 'I don't care how long it takes or how much it costs. Those men must be found!'

Louisa felt relieved. Even though she didn't expect to remember any more about the burglar, she had every confidence that with both Malcolm and John involved, the chances of success were greatly increased.

A little later John left and when Malcolm came back from seeing him out, Louisa stood up, ready to leave. He motioned her to sit down again.

'Don't rush off. I'd like to make a suggestion,' he said. Louisa, wondering what was coming, sat down.

'Your booking in the hotel must be running out soon, right?'

She nodded and replied, 'Yes, in a couple of days. But I can keep the room–'

'There's no need. It's pointless you paying for a room when I've got one available at La Folie. We're not full at the moment so it wouldn't be a problem for you to move in. That's assuming you were planning to stay here a bit longer?' For the first time since they had met he looked unsure of himself.

Louisa hadn't thought beyond each day since her arrival in Guernsey. But she now needed to stay at least until after seeing the hypnotherapist. And if she was honest with herself, returning to London and her empty house didn't hold much appeal. Staying here would give her a chance to get to know her father better and she'd have the company of the staff and guests at the centre. A no-brainer.

'I'd love to stay there, thanks. It's very generous of you.'

'Nonsense! You're my daughter and so far all I've contributed to your well-being is a posh meal. I have a lot of making up to do, young lady.' He smiled. 'I'll inform Paul that you can have as many therapies as you like; enjoy some pampering. I can rely on him to take good care of you.'

Mm, now *that* was a thought!

chapter 12

It was agreed that Louisa would move into the centre on Friday. In the meantime, she decided to explore the island. She had always considered herself to be a true city girl, but the few days she had spent in Guernsey started a shift in her thinking. The ability to walk along unspoilt golden beaches and a seemingly endless variety of cliff paths was definitely preferable to pounding along London's pavements. And although Guernsey was lacking the cultural advantages of London, it wasn't the backwater she had expected. The local paper listed the new releases showing at the multiplex cinema as well as concerts and shows available in the leisure centre's theatre. But she did wonder how Malcolm fared after the buzz of Toronto, although he seemed happy enough on his adopted island. It would have been in his blood, perhaps, she mused; hidden for years until his recent arrival and re-connection with the place of his conception.

The beaches were fairly deserted at this time of year, only the occasional dog walker or jogger keeping her company while she strode along the sand along L'Ancresse Bay in the north. Everyone exchanged a quick greeting or a smile and Louisa felt heartened by the friendliness. But there were still moments when she would be assailed by grief and needed to be alone, taking refuge in the car and weeping until exhaustion kicked in. Just seeing a woman who bore even a slight resemblance to Susan could set her off. And although finding her father had been a bonus, he could in no way compensate for the loss of her mother. She admitted he was doing his best as a born-again father. Or, to be more accurate, a late starter. A *very* late starter. He hadn't tried to smother her, but offered help as needed. Louisa looked forward to moving into La Folie and the promised pampering. But she was still unsure about the hypnosis and the memories it might stir, memories she had tried hard to suppress in the far reaches of her mind. It would be another picking at the scab of the unhealed wound and the unsettling thought followed her back to the car.

Since being on the island, Louisa had made several calls to Margaret to keep her up to speed. Her aunt had been cautious about her trip to meet Malcolm, saying she didn't want Louisa to face more hurt. Meaning rejection. Now, back at the hotel, Louisa phoned her with the latest news.

'Hi, Margaret. How are you? Good, I'm fine. Malcolm's invited me to stay at the centre and I'm moving there tomorrow. And I can have any therapies I want!'

'That sounds lovely, dear. I'm quite jealous! How long will you stay there?'

Louisa chewed her lips. 'I don't know. A week or two, maybe. Malcolm's hired a private detective and he wants me to try hypnosis to see if I can remember more about that…that man. I'm a bit nervous but will give it a go. The session's booked for tomorrow afternoon…' She went on to tell Margaret about the meeting with John Ferguson.

'That's wonderful news, Louisa. What happens if this man is found? Won't you need to identify him?'

'I guess. I couldn't at the moment, but let's hope I remember something under hypnosis.' She sighed. 'One minute I feel quite upbeat about things and the next I feel I'm back to square one. I keep seeing Mum…' Her voice caught on a sob.

'Oh, darling! It does take time, I know. Try to focus on the good times you had with your mother. Remember that wonderful laugh of hers that got everyone else in the room laughing too?'

Louisa forced herself to think back. The memory that flashed into her mind was their last Christmas party at home. People milling about, glasses in hand, while conversations reverberated around the large sitting room. Then her mother, apparently having been told a joke or funny story, suddenly burst out in her deepest, fullest belly-laugh, and a tsunami of laughter spread around the room, leaving no-one immune. Louisa herself had joined in, even though she hadn't a clue what was funny. The memory brought a reluctant smile to her lips.

'Thanks. That helps. I'll remember that next time I'm feeling weepy.'

'There's no shame in shedding a few tears. You *need* to grieve, Louisa. But allow yourself to laugh, too. It's what Susan would have wanted.' Louisa heard the catch in her voice and felt ashamed. Her poor aunt had lost the two most important people in her life in the past year and yet here she was trying to cheer her up.

'Look, when I return to London how about if you come down for a while? We could catch some shows or visit museums. Whatever,' she said.

'I'd like that, but let's wait and see how things pan out for you first. Will you let me know if the hypnosis works?'

'Sure, no problem. Take care and I'll ring soon. Bye.'

By ten o'clock the next morning Louisa was packed and ready to leave the hotel. She had enjoyed one last swim before breakfast, giving her an appetite for the full English on offer. After settling her bill she loaded up the car and drove off towards La Folie. The sun was playing hide and seek behind the clouds, making the day feel cooler than of late and she switched on the heater. Ten minutes later she parked her car and carried her case into the entrance hall.

'Hi, Louisa, it's good to see you again,' called Nadine from behind the desk. 'Leave your case here and I'll get it taken up to your room. Are you looking forward to your stay? Your father's insisted you have one of the best rooms,' she added, with a grin.

'That's nice, I could get used to being spoilt,' she replied, smiling at Nadine whose curls seemed even bouncier today. 'Is...is Paul about? I think I have to arrange any therapies through him.'

Nadine checked the rota. 'He'll be free in half an hour and I'm sure he'll want to have a chat with you. I know you're not here as a regular guest, but if you want any therapies, Paul needs some info to provide the right package. Mind you, you look pretty fit to me,' Nadine said, looking her up and down.

Louisa smiled. 'I *am* pretty fit, thanks, but there's always room for improvement, isn't there? Do you have a brochure with some details?'

'Sure.' Nadine reached into a drawer and brought out a glossy, gold-edged brochure bearing a watercolour picture of La Folie on the cover.

'Mm, nice. The artist has managed to create a very welcoming look. Still, artistic licence and all that...' They both giggled.

'Well, nothing could be done to change the front but it's a lovely house inside now. Mr Roget spent a ton of money on it, you know, and I think he wants it to be one of the top ten centres in the world,' Nadine said, lowering her voice, as a guest clad in the ubiquitous white towelling robe walked past.

Louisa nodded, pleased that her father had set his sights so high. *Pampering, here I come!*

Nadine must have pressed a hidden button as a young man, hardly more than a teenager, and dressed in white T-shirt and trousers, arrived to escort Louisa to her room.

'Hiya, Miss Canning. I'm Doug and I run all the errands around here, so anytime you need anything, you just let me know.' His perfect white teeth dazzled against a non-English tan as he shook her hand. Then he grabbed her case, giving the impression it was as light as a feather. His voice had an accent similar to Malcolm's.

'Morning, Doug. Are you Canadian, by any chance?'

He started to ascend the broad, sweeping staircase, beckoning her to follow him.

'Sure am. My pa's a friend of Mr Roget and suggested I came over here to work for him. Gain some experience from a past master of the hospitality industry.'

As they ascended the stairs, Doug explained that one day he hoped to manage a hotel as his father had for Malcolm, but in the meantime thought he'd try working in a health centre. Arriving at the first floor, he headed off left towards a door at the end. Louisa guessed it was at the back of the house and hoped it would have a sea view. Doug unlocked the door, bearing a nameplate showing the word *Serenity* inscribed in flowing letters. He ushered her inside before following with her case, placing it on a stand. Louisa walked across the expanse of cream carpet to the window, a large bay reaching almost to the ceiling.

'Wow! What a view,' she cried, gazing over the garden towards the cliffs and the sea beyond.

'Sure is,' he replied, coming to stand near her. 'Right, ma'am, the en-suite's through here if I may explain how to work the shower?'

She followed him into a spacious wet room, with soft cream tiling and a teak bath and vanity unit. The walk-in shower boasted an enormous shower head and no visible controls.

'It's remote controlled...' he said, running through the brief instructions. After ensuring she was happy with everything, he left. Louisa moved around the bedroom, letting her fingers slide along the golden maple wood of the four-poster. Looking up she admired the damson and gold silk canopy echoing the silk throw on the bed. She sat down gingerly, always wary of hotel beds, but was delighted with a comforting bounce. After stroking the smooth ivory bed linen, as soft as silk, Louisa walked around, touching the linen covered sofa, the intimate table with two chairs near the window and the dressing table and chest of drawers. A bowl of subtly scented *pot pourri* sat on the chest, a faint waft of frangipani filling her nostrils. The honey-toned maple furniture glowed against smooth, soft-toned walls. She couldn't resist stroking a wall; as smooth as marble, it reminded her of the polished plaster walls found in Moroccan houses. One wall was filled with the mirrored doors of a fitted wardrobe large enough to hold all her clothes from home. But for her the pièce de résistance was the bay window, framed in fine, pale gold silk curtains, and offering the most magical view. Sighing contentedly, she had just started unpacking when the bedside phone rang.

'Oh, hi Nadine. Thanks. Please tell Paul I'll be down in five.'

She quickly hung up the rest of her clothes and threw her undies into a voluminous drawer. Glancing quickly at her reflection in the mirror, she ran her hands over her hair to smooth it before leaving to meet Paul. Her pulse quickened as she ran down the stairs, eager to see him again.

He was waiting at the bottom of the stairs, his face uplifted to follow her descent. The sun chose that moment to peek out from the clouds and his blonde hair took on a golden hue. She stifled a gasp as for a nanosecond, a halo of light framed Paul's head, creating the illusion of an angelic being, clothed in white. Shaking her head, she saw him return to his normal physical self. *God, I'm going doolally.* Taking a deep breath, she joined him in the hall.

Paul's face split into a wide smile. 'Hello again. Welcome to La Folie. Everything okay with your room?'

'It's perfect, thanks. What happens now?' she asked, not feeling entirely calm as yet.

'Let's go to my office and we'll chat about the therapies you're interested in. Won't take long.'

Once in his office, they sat in chairs arranged in front of a desk. Paul asked her to fill in a questionnaire, saying he needed to know if she had any medical problems before she had any treatments. Glancing at her answers, he said, 'You must be one of the healthiest guests we've had so far. You're free to have whatever you want.'

Louisa smiled. 'Great! I'd love to learn how to relax and I've heard good things about meditation. And perhaps some aromatherapy?'

'I teach the yoga and meditation classes so how about joining us? The next class is tomorrow morning at nine. We start with some gentle yoga exercises and finish with a short meditation. Sound okay?'

'Fine.' She shifted in her chair. 'Do you know anything about the hypnotherapist I'm seeing later? I'm a bit nervous…'

'Molly? She's lovely. Not at all scary and I'm sure you'll get along fine.'

'Thanks for that. Oh, are there any restrictions on the use of the pool?'

He explained the opening times and she got up to leave, asking, 'Do the staff live in? Only it doesn't seem big enough for both staff and the guests.'

'Just me, everyone else lives at home. With the island being so small no-one has to travel far. And I need to be here for safety reasons. I live in one of the converted tower attics, enjoying 360° views,' he replied, flashing a big smile.

She cleared her throat. 'Lucky you. Well, I'll see you around.'

She walked up the passage to ask Nadine where she would find Molly later. Opting for a quick walk before lunch, she nipped upstairs for a sweater before heading out to the garden, hoping to see some of her fellow guests. The brochure had stated that the centre catered for up to twenty-four guests in the dozen *"individually styled, luxurious rooms complete with superb, hi-tech bathrooms."* Well, she thought, stepping outside, if my bedroom's anything to go by, I can only agree. The brochure also quoted the aim of La Folie Retreat and Health Centre was to *"provide a full and personal programme of treatments to promote the healing of Mind, Body and Spirit. We offer peace and seclusion away from the stresses of the modern world and advise our guests that we do not provide televisions in their rooms and respectfully suggest that mobile phones and laptops are left at home."* Reading that last bit had made Louisa feel guilty about her own mobile and laptop, but decided that as she wasn't a regular guest then she could ignore the request. Still, she fully approved of the centre's ethos and could see why people in the public eye might want to seek refuge here.

In the garden she spotted a woman about her own age heading in her direction. The other guests she'd seen so far had been much older so, as the woman came closer, Louisa stuck out her hand, saying, 'Hello, I'm Louisa and I've just arrived.'

The other woman, a tall, slightly overweight brunette with a look of sadness about her, stopped and shook hands. 'Charlotte. I've been here a week so you could say I'm an old hand,' she answered in a husky, well-spoken voice.

'How are you getting on? De-stressed yet?' Louisa asked, with a grin.

'I'm feeling tons better than when I arrived, but...' she shrugged.

'Sorry, didn't mean to pry–'

Charlotte waved her hands. 'No problem. We wouldn't be here if we didn't have...issues to address, would we? And it's nice to have someone to chat to; I've been a bit of a hermit since I arrived.'

'How long are you staying? Hope you're not rushing off just as I've arrived.'

'Oh, don't worry. I'm here for a while yet. Were you off on a walk? Fancy some company?'

They fell into step with each other, setting off in the direction of the kitchen garden around the pool. Louisa stole a glance at her companion as they chatted. It was obvious even to her uninformed eyes that Charlotte's clothes were designer label and her hair beautifully, and expensively styled. But she seemed friendly and happy to talk. But only about the usual British safe topics of the weather and what they did for a living. Nothing too personal. She said she was "in publishing" and looked surprised when Louisa mentioned she was a physiotherapist.

'Isn't being here a bit like a busman's holiday for you?' she asked, eyebrows raised.

Louisa laughed. 'Not really. Here, I'll be the one receiving treatment, not giving it. It will be a chance to chill out and recover...' she trailed off, not wanting to say more.

'Of course,' Charlotte nodded her agreement. 'And why not? We all deserve to be spoiled sometimes.'

Louisa noticed she wasn't wearing a wedding ring, but her ring finger bore a white mark where one might have been. Perhaps someone else with something to hide? She had agreed with Malcolm that it was best that other guests did not know she was his daughter. The knowledge might create awkwardness for all concerned. If a guest mentioned seeing her with him, she planned to say he was an old family friend. That much, at least, was true. The staff were to treat her as a normal guest in public.

By the time they had finished their walk it was not only time for lunch, but the women were behaving like old friends, automatically sitting down together at a table in the dining room.

'I can recommend the food here, Louisa. It's superb; I believe Chef was poached from a top hotel. And, thankfully, it's not at all fattening,' Charlotte said, patting her stomach. 'I do need to lose a stone, which is one of the reasons I chose this place. Didn't want to be starved but I do enjoy tasty food that will still help me to lose weight.' She looked across the table at Louisa. 'Not something you have to worry about, is it? You've a lovely figure.'

She mumbled her thanks, saying her work kept her trim. During the meal Charlotte mentioned that she lived in London and Louisa admitted that it was also her home town, leading to an animated discussion about the merits of the city as a place to live.

Charlotte got up to leave at one thirty, saying she had a massage appointment, and they agreed to keep an eye out for each other. Swapping room names, it appeared that Charlotte was in *Peace* and they both said how apposite the names were. And so much nicer than a mere number. Louisa's appointment with Molly Ogier was at two o'clock and she went upstairs to change into joggers and sweatshirt. Even her preferred jeans seemed too formal for the laid-back atmosphere of La Folie.

In spite of Paul's reassurance, Louisa felt apprehensive as she made her way to the room set aside for Molly. Her hands felt moist as she knocked on the door, nervous about what she might remember of that awful day.

chapter 13

The door was opened by a smiling, cuddly woman of about sixty, with grey hair wisping around her broad face.

'Hello, you must be Louisa. I'm Molly. Do come in.'

They shook hands before Molly indicated a reclining chair placed not far from her own seat. Picking up a pad and paper, Molly gave her an appraising look.

'Malcolm has explained what happened to your mother. Please accept my condolences. I do understand that you might well be anxious about meeting me, not wanting to have it all raked up again.' Molly paused and Louisa saw the compassion emanating from her eyes as they held her gaze. She started to relax a little.

'No I don't, but...' she shrugged.

'I understand,' Molly said. 'But we need to try and jog your memory about the man you saw that day, or anything else that might be helpful to the investigation. We can take our time, there's no pressure to come up with anything immediately.'

Louisa felt somewhat reassured. She had visualised the kind of questioning carried out in the interviews in television police dramas. Silly, she knew but...

'Okay.' She managed a small smile.

'Good.' Molly went on to describe the process of hypnosis, or a self-induced deep state of relaxation as she put it. She explained that in today's session she wouldn't be asking Louisa to recall anything, wanting only to take her through the process to see how she responded. A trial run, she called it.

Louisa breathed more easily. She had a reprieve!

Molly asked her to lie back in the recliner and close her eyes. She then began to talk to her in a soothing voice and Louisa felt her body relax first, to the extent that she could no longer feel it. It was as if she existed only in her mind, and even that was being slowly seduced into a state of utter peace.

Twenty minutes later she opened her eyes, gazing unfocused at Molly, as she returned to full awareness. 'That was great, Molly! Not at all like I expected. I heard everything you said. Or I think I did!' she laughed.

Molly's eyes twinkled at her. 'You relaxed very well. We've made a good start and next time I'll guide you into an even deeper state, ready to uncover those missing details.' She reached for her diary. 'Would Monday morning suit you? Say eleven? I don't work at weekends.'

'That's perfect.'

Louisa left feeling so relaxed and refreshed that she fetched her swimsuit and robe before heading for the pool. This was accessed by a corridor on the west of the house, leading to the newly built changing rooms and sauna. Once changed she walked into the Moroccan-style sauna, completely covered in stunning blue and green tiles that created the impression of being under water. The seating area followed the curves of the room and Louisa stretched out, enjoying total seclusion. Faint sounds of soothing, meditative music flowed from hidden speakers and she closed her eyes for a few moments. The intensity of the heat kept her from falling asleep and, when it became too much, she stepped out into a matching tiled shower, letting a powerful jet of water cool her body. It was bliss! She grabbed a white, fluffy towel and walked the few feet to the pool area. Other guests were enjoying a gentle swim, watched by a couple relaxing on loungers, tall glasses of juice by their hands. Powered up, Louisa slipped into the water, speedily completing thirty laps before flopping onto a lounger for a break. She had hardly drawn breath when a young girl came up bearing a tray of freshly prepared juices. Accepting a glass, she took an appreciative sip. Out of the corner of her eye she noticed someone waving from the garden and, recognising Charlotte, she returned the wave. Charlotte smiled and came in through the far door.

'Hi. Had a good swim?'

'Yes, thanks. What have you been up to?' Louisa sipped her juice while Charlotte, after removing her trainers, stretched out on the adjoining lounger.

'Oh, not much. Had an Indian head massage which was so relaxing I fell asleep!' she laughed, throatily. 'I needed to get some fresh air or I'd have been fit for nothing for the rest of the day.'

'Everything seems geared to encourage such a blissful state of relaxation it's a wonder that anyone does anything. I'm just so not used to being pampered like this. What about you?'

Charlotte accepted a glass of juice from the hovering waitress before answering.

'Well, to be honest, I do have some help at home, a lovely woman who does some cooking and cleaning for me. It leaves me free to focus on my work and I never was what you might call the domesticated type.' Charlotte frowned, as if she was recalling something unpleasant.

Louisa, not wanting to pry, changed the subject. 'Are there any particular treatments or therapies you can recommend? I'm happy to be pampered to within an inch of my life,' she said, grinning.

Charlotte seemed to perk up. 'You've come to the right place for that and I'd suggest you try all the various forms of massage, but no more than one a day. The therapist is divine and she seems to know intuitively what I need. Her name's Lin and she's very popular so do book as soon as possible.' She took a sip of her drink before asking, 'How long are you staying? I don't think you said.'

'I'm not sure. It's…a bit open-ended. Luckily they're not full so it's not a problem if I stay more than a week. And from what you've said, two weeks would be heavenly.'

'Sure. I'm here for at least another week and I've met some people who've already been here for three.' She smiled. 'I'm wondering if they put something in the juice to make us not want to leave. Some kind of narcotic so that we lose free will while soaking up subliminal messages from the music they play!'

They laughed. Louisa thought Malcolm would find it an amusing idea and she smiled as she imagined him putting it into practice. Would certainly be good for business! She was having dinner with him that night in his apartment, after he returned from a business trip to Jersey. It would be a chance to catch up.

'Paul has suggested I try the yoga and meditation class tomorrow morning. Do you go?'

'I wouldn't miss it for the world. I'd never tried yoga until coming here but Paul makes it seem so easy. We start with gentle stretches and he never asks us to do any of those weird contortions you associate with yoga.' She lowered her voice, 'Some of the guests here are not exactly young and their joints are stiff so I think Paul makes allowances. Mind you, one of the old dears is obviously a past master and can get herself into some funny positions. Really shows us younger ones up. Naturally, Paul's an expert. I've seen him practising on his own before the start of class and he's incredibly flexible. You will join us, won't you? I'm sure you'll find it fun.'

For a moment Louisa's mind had wandered off, picturing a very "flexible" Paul in some interesting positions. She had to drag herself back to face Charlotte, who was looking at her enquiringly. 'Louisa? Are you with me?'

'Sorry. Drifted off a minute. Think you're right, there must be something in the juice!' she chuckled, before adding, 'Yes, of course I'll join the group. I'm looking forward to it now. And I'll book some sessions with Lin. Anything else you can suggest?'

Charlotte listed other treatments worth trying and after they parted Louisa went off to the reception to book appointments. Nadine worked out a programme for her and included the session with Molly. There was still plenty of free time for more sessions or trips around the island.

'There's a talk on Buddhism tomorrow morning after the yoga class, if you're interested,' Nadine said, pushing over a flyer for her to read. 'We arrange various talks and demonstrations but there's no obligation to attend. But Paul's talks are always popular; he's so knowledgeable about anything Eastern.'

Louisa scanned the flyer, immediately deciding to attend. She liked the idea of learning more about Buddhism, having admired the calmness of her Buddhist colleague from work. And it gave her an excuse to be near Paul. Not that that influenced her in any way. Absolutely not.

'Thanks, Nadine. Put me down for it. Oh, and can you book me a taxi for seven o'clock, please? To go into Town.'

'No problem. Have a nice evening,' she said, with a sly smile.

Louisa returned to her room to shower and change. As she moved around, peeling off her robe, her gaze was caught by a patinated bronze Buddha on the bedside table. She hadn't noticed it before and sat down to look at it more carefully. An aura of peace seemed to emanate from the Buddha's serene face and body. She smiled. *No surprise this room's called Serenity! Wonder if all the rooms have their own Buddha? Must ask my father.* With a jolt she realised she had thought of Malcolm as "her father" rather than by his name. It felt odd, but not unpleasant. She let her fingers trail over the little figure, as one would touch a lucky charm, before jumping up and heading for the shower. For a moment she had felt some peace in her heart but the image of her mother's face soon destroyed it. As she let the hot, soothing water flow over her body, Louisa could only hope that she would find a way to heal. And soon.

'Louisa, my dear, come in, come in.' Malcolm stood framed in the elegant doorway, looking impeccable in cream slacks and a deep blue cotton shirt, opened at the neck.

She hesitated before leaning forward to peck him on the cheek. His answering smile said it all.

Malcolm led the way to the living area before offering her a drink.

'I can shake a mean martini cocktail,' he said, pointing to a collection of spirits and mixers in a cabinet. 'What's your poison?'

'I'll let you choose, thanks,' she replied with a grin, making herself comfortable on the sofa. She watched as he expertly mixed a brightly coloured concoction into a shaker and then gave it a vigorous mix. After pouring it into two cocktail glasses he came over to offer her one.

They clinked glasses and she took a sip. 'Mm, that's delicious! Fruity but with a hit. What's in it?'

'Ah, that's a trade secret. Was the house special in my hotels.' He sipped his own drink before asking, 'So, how was your first day at La Folie? Everything okay?'

'Great, thanks. The rooms are so heavenly it's almost a shame to leave them. Do they all have the same Eastern influence as *Serenity* and with their own Buddha?'

He nodded. 'Yes. That was Paul's idea. We wanted to replicate the sort of ambience you find in Eastern spas, encouraging guests to slow down and rethink their lives. It's not just about getting one's body into shape these days. The mind and spirit are equally important.' He paused, leaning back into the sofa opposite her. 'You remember I said I first met Paul in an Indian ashram?' She nodded. 'Well I hated it!' He laughed at the memory.

'Why were you in the ashram?' Louisa asked, intrigued.

'It's a long story, but basically I'd been talked into it but was about to walk out when I got talking to Paul. I…I wasn't in a good space in those days and I think Paul saw it more than I did. To me it seemed like I didn't know what to do with my life since I'd sold the business, but Paul sussed there was more to it than that. He's very perceptive, you know.'

Louisa remembered the vision she had had of him standing bathed in light, looking like an angel. There *was* something about him that was a bit otherworldly, a bit fey. Those eyes!

'What happened after you met Paul?'

'He helped me get my head straight and I became interested in the spiritual side of life. Not that I've become a Buddhist or anything!' He laughed.

'But there's a strong spiritual influence at the centre, isn't there?'

'Sure is. And it's deliberate. We want to work holistically with our guests or they're likely to go back to their old ways and become sick again.'

She nodded. 'That makes sense, but surely you're reducing the repeat business from satisfied guests? They won't need to come back.'

'Ah, now that's where you're wrong. We've already had guests re-book as they recognise the need to keep in tune with the ideas they learn here.' He took another sip of his cocktail. 'How did the hypnosis go?'

She told him about the session and they chatted a while until the intercom buzzed. While Malcolm went to answer it, Louisa wondered who was going to join them, thinking it was odd he hadn't mentioned anything about another guest. Her question was soon answered when he returned moments later carrying two heavy carrier bags, preceded by the mouth-watering aroma of freshly cooked food. Looking a little sheepish he explained that he'd ordered a complete meal from La Fregate, something they only did as a special favour to him.

'I thought it was brave of you, offering to cook for me,' she said, grinning.

'Decided it would make a change from eating out, even though it's the same food. You go and sit down and I'll bring it out in a minute.' Malcolm pointed to the dining table near the window, set with glasses, cutlery and candles. He was obviously making an effort. She took a seat and gazed into the darkening sky beyond the lights of St Peter Port. Her eye was caught by a ferry coming in slowly to the harbour, its lights seeming to float upon the sea. The sight made her think of Malcolm, a mere babe in arms, being taken by his mother on a ship thousands of miles to Canada, to a new life. And now here they were, in Guernsey where it all began.

'A penny for your thoughts. That's what my mother used to say,' Malcolm said, setting down a tray heaped with plates of mixed fish and seafood, bowls of fresh vegetables and buttered new potatoes. The aroma set her gastric juices flowing in overdrive.

'Oh, I was just watching the ferry arrive,' she said, avoiding his eye. 'Mm, this looks amazing, Malcolm! I'm suddenly very hungry.'

He poured glasses of chilled white wine and they tucked into the most upmarket takeaway that Louisa had ever eaten. In between mouthfuls she asked him about the kind of food that Canadians ate.

'Generally speaking, they eat a lot of fast food. As bad as the Americans. They cover nearly everything with maple syrup and love fried food smothered with cheese. I was putting on too much weight until one day, in my late twenties, a medic told me I was heading for heart problems if I didn't change my diet. From then on, I was a different man. Canada's fortunate to have fantastic game, like venison, duck, grouse and wild salmon, so I made sure I ate plenty of those and vegetables and soon lost the weight.' He picked up his glass. 'Until then we'd been offering all the rubbish food that guests wanted in our hotels; but I insisted we change our chefs and menus and, what was interesting was that we gained more business. So that medic did me a good turn, twice over.'

'Well, the food you're offering at the centre is definitely both healthy and delicious. I met a guest who hopes to lose some weight while she's there and she said the food was one of the reasons she chose La Folie.'

Malcolm looked pleased. 'That's good to know. It's not easy knowing what's the most important attraction for our guests. I can see you'll make a great spy for me,' he teased.

'I don't think you need one. You and the team are doing a great job and I'm looking forward to my treatments. I'm even going to try yoga tomorrow.'

They continued to talk about her plans for the next few days, easing into a more relaxed relationship. Louisa was aware how much effort Malcolm was putting into winning her over, wanting her to trust him. As she enjoyed the dessert, French apple tart served with rich Guernsey cream, she sensed that he wanted to make up to her for what had happened to Susan. Of course, nothing he did would bring her mother back, but she appreciated his trying to be a father to her. And she couldn't, in all honesty, hold him responsible for the attack on her mother. No, she told herself, the responsibility lay fairly and squarely on the shoulders of the man she had seen running away. The man she hoped she would, in a few days, be able to describe.

chapter 14

Louisa groaned as the alarm shrilled into life at eight o'clock the next morning. She had grown accustomed to waking naturally of late, a luxury only possible since giving up her job. Remembering why the alarm was set, she sprang out of bed and made for the shower. Paul's yoga class beckoned and she suddenly felt wide awake. Minutes later, wearing joggers and a T-shirt, Louisa headed downstairs to the dining room.

'Hi, Louisa, over here,' Charlotte called from a table, looking immaculate in a teal blue crossover cardigan and stone-coloured yoga pants. Louisa felt like the poor relation in her baggy joggers and grey top.

'Morning. You're looking perky,' Louisa said, smiling.

'You have to make an effort, don't you? Don't want to look as if one has just crawled out of bed, even if one has. At least I'll be feeling perky, as you call it, after the delicious breakfast that's about to arrive.'

Louisa gazed appreciatively at the selection of sliced fruit, juices, homemade muesli, granola and yogurt being wheeled towards their table. The waitress went off with their order for two green teas while they helped themselves to the food.

'These juices are incredible. The chef told me he mixes in a combination of herbs and spices with the fruit and vegetables to increase the antioxidant and energising properties. I get a real buzz from them,' Charlotte said as she filled her glass. 'I'm taking the recipes home so I can keep up the benefits.'

'They're not secret then?'

'Nooo, not exactly. He's writing a book based on the recipes he uses here and I've, er, persuaded him to let me have a peek.'

'Oh, and why would he do that?' Louisa asked, eyebrows raised.

Charlotte grinned. 'I might be able to help him get his book published, that's why. I'm a publisher.'

'Ahh! Right.'

They concentrated on their breakfast, conscious of the time. Finished, they made their way to the large room set aside for group work, finding Paul setting out a number of yoga mats.

'Morning, ladies. Ready for a good stretch?' Paul greeted them as they made a beeline for the first row, just beating some other guests who had to make do with the second row.

Louisa smiled in return, her eyes travelling over Paul's athletic body, apparent even under his loose-fitting yoga suit. He really is very attractive, she thought, tearing her gaze away to take up her position on the mat.

The session passed quickly. Paul took the ten people present gently, but firmly through stretches and yoga positions that Louisa found comfortable to follow. Throughout, soft music played in the background, encouraging the release of tension. A short guided meditation at the end nearly sent her to sleep, only brought back to full awareness by Paul sounding a tiny bell.

'Well done, everyone. I can see the improvement in those of you who have been coming to the class this past week,' he smiled at Charlotte and a couple of other participants. 'If anyone wants to stay behind for the talk on Buddhism, please grab a chair and form a circle.'

Half a dozen people lined up chairs in front of a projector screen and Charlotte whispered a quick 'See you later' to Louisa before leaving with the others. Paul switched on a laptop for the PowerPoint presentation and as pictures of Buddha filled the screen, he started his talk.

'According to Buddhist tradition, the Buddha, Siddhartha Gautama, lived sometime between the 6th and 4th centuries BC in eastern India, possibly Nepal…'

Louisa was fascinated. Paul delivered a punchy narrative of events, based on the little evidence remaining, even bringing some humour into the talk. When he turned to the issue of karma and reincarnation, laughter erupted when someone asked if it was true that a person could be re-born as an animal if they were "bad" in this life.

Paul nodded. 'According to some traditions, yes. Or as lowly deities or demons. Only humans can achieve the desired state of Nirvana, and only if they have practised the highest forms of meditation. So,' he said, smiling broadly, 'it pays to be safe and not do anything evil or you may come back as a rat!'

Louisa smiled with the rest, but inwardly she wanted to cry as she pictured her mother, frightened to death by the 'evil' man. She fervently hoped that if reincarnation was a possibility, then he'd return as a rat or something equally horrible.

Fortunately for her peace of mind, the talk turned to more pleasant ideas and beliefs and she remained engrossed in what Paul had to say about the different forms of Buddhism. Once he'd answered all the questions, he ended the meeting with a reminder that the next yoga class would be the following morning at nine o'clock sharp.

As she was about to leave with the others, Paul stopped her to ask if she had enjoyed the yoga.

'Yes I did, thanks. It was much more fun than I'd expected and so relaxing. I'll definitely be back tomorrow,' she said, shifting from foot to foot. She didn't know why, but she felt like a schoolgirl in front of a teacher. Very unsettling.

'Great! You looked like a natural and it won't be long before you can manage the Kapotasana or Pigeon pose. I'd guess swimming's made you more flexible than most people I see here.' He smiled warmly and again images of the both of them in 'flexible' positions filled her mind. She felt a warm glow spreading up her neck to her cheeks.

'Right, that's good. I'll...I'll see you tomorrow then,' Louisa said, beating a hasty retreat. The attraction she was beginning to feel for Paul felt wrong, somehow, although she wasn't entirely sure why that was. He didn't seem to be married as he lived alone, but he could have a girlfriend lurking in the background, she mused. Also, as a therapist herself, she was well aware of the client attachment that could develop between therapist and client. As she returned to her room she pondered on her own vulnerability at this time, missing her mother and still smarting from the abrupt end of her last relationship. Any good-looking man who smiled at her would be seen as manna from heaven, poised to sweep her into his arms and comfort her. *I really must get a grip. Fanciful ideas about a gorgeous yoga instructor are not appropriate right now! I'm supposed to be enjoying some R & R not erotic thoughts. Time for a cold shower and a long swim.*

Suitably cooled down from her shower, Louisa made her way to the pool, ready to work on her 'flexible' muscles once more.

The rest of the weekend passed pleasantly enough. Charlotte joined Louisa in a long cliff walk after Louisa had enjoyed her first aromatherapy massage from Lin's soothing hands. Charlotte had received a reflexology treatment and they both floated on air along the cliff.

'I wish I could stay here forever,' Charlotte cried, as they felt the sun's rays on their blissed-out bodies. The days were warming up nicely, kissing goodbye to the winter chill that had tried to hang on longer than was necessary.

'Me too. It's a magical place, isn't it? Seems hard to accept this little haven is only about an hour away from London.' Louisa spun around, taking in the sea glistening beneath her and the green open spaces behind. The towers of La Folie were the only visible sign of civilisation. 'Have you been out exploring the island, yet?

Charlotte shook her head. 'I was completely washed out when I arrived and didn't want to stir further than the grounds. But I'd like to venture out a bit. Shall we go together?'

They agreed to go out for a drive on Sunday afternoon and Louisa said she'd check the best places to visit. She was glad of the chance to have company as it took her out of herself. It was too easy to become maudlin when you spent a lot of time on your own, she thought, as they walked slowly back to La Folie. The place was so big that with only about fifteen guests, you hardly ever bumped into anyone else except at mealtimes. *I've been a hermit far too long, it's time to join the human race again. Or at least the small contingent staying in the retreat!* She would be eating dinner here for the first time that evening and she was looking forward to it. Charlotte had hardly stopped talking about how great the food was and they planned to eat together. She told Louisa that some of the guests were couples and tended to stick together; other singletons tended to form alliances to be spared the horror of eating alone. But she hadn't felt up to pairing until Louisa arrived, she added. Louisa didn't like to pry, but guessed that Charlotte might have been depressed

The island tour was enjoyed by both. Spring remained in situ and jackets were discarded when they explored the delights of the west and north coasts. Stopping the car along the way, they discovered sandy and rocky coves which would make great places to sunbathe come summer. And dotted around the island were various visitors' attractions vying for their custom. Their favourite was Oatlands Village in the north, a rambling collection of buildings clustered around old brick kilns and offering shops and eateries. Guiltily, they enjoyed a lavish cream tea which Chef would have frowned on if he'd known.

'I'll have to join you for a lengthy swim when we get back,' Charlotte sighed. 'And I'd been so good since I came here. Easy when Chef only offers non-fattening menus. But it *was* delicious,' she said, licking her fingers delicately.

'Have you lost any weight?'

'A few pounds. Chef's a trained nutritionist and he's drawing up an eating plan for me to take home. I'll be able to continue the good work as long as I stay away from cream teas!' She laughed.

'Hey, we all need the occasional treat. And you're a very attractive woman, Charlotte, so don't beat yourself up over a cream tea,' Louisa said, envying the other woman's glossy locks and sculptured cheekbones. When Charlotte smiled she looked beautiful; but there was still an air of sadness around her.

Charlotte waved her hand. 'Oh, that's sweet of you to say so, but I'm pushing forty and feeling a bit over the hill.'

'Rubbish! I've heard fifty's the new thirty, so you've nothing to worry about yet.' She looked at her new friend with concern. *Someone's made her feel old and unattractive. Bound to be a man...*

'My...my husband left me for the proverbial bimbo and it rocked me rather.' Charlotte fumbled in her bag for a tissue and patted at the tears slowly running down her cheeks.

Louisa squeezed her arm. 'I'm so very sorry. That must have been awful. Is that why you came here? To help get over it?'

'Partly. He...he left six months ago and initially I was numb with shock. It came completely out of the blue.' Her mouth twisted. 'Shows how naïve I was! Apparently everyone else knew he was having an affair but didn't feel able to tell me. I admit I was pretty well wedded to my work and didn't spot the signs; the late nights, trips away, not much sex...' She blew her nose before fixing a smile on her face.

'Look, I'm sorry to have blubbed like that. I shouldn't burden you with my problems; I'm sure you have enough of your own.'

'Don't be silly. I guessed something like that must have happened; you looked so sad. Has being at La Folie helped?'

Charlotte nodded. 'Definitely. I've been receiving counselling from a lovely woman called Molly, as well as the physical treatments which have been a godsend.'

'I'm seeing Molly too. Not for counselling but for hypnosis...' Louisa saw Charlotte's eyebrows rise in surprise and decided to share the story of her mother's death, but not that of her new-found father. Not yet, it was too soon.

When she had finished Charlotte reached across to give her a hug.

'You poor girl! Losing an errant husband is nothing compared to the loss of a mother. Husbands can be replaced, but not one's mother. But I'm sure you'll receive the very best help here, the staff are particularly dedicated. I've tried a few health spas in my time, but this one is in a league of its own.' She pulled back and added, briskly, 'Right, perhaps it's time we made our way back. And I think a bottle of the best bubbly La Folie can provide will be in order at dinner tonight. My treat,' she added as Louisa tried to protest. 'We can take it up to one of our rooms afterwards and have a good piss-up. Do us both good and to hell with the diet!'

The next morning Louisa woke with a throbbing head and a throat like sandpaper. Reaching for the glass of water she'd left on the bedside table, she swallowed deeply and propped herself up on the pillows. With a wry grin she mentally replayed the previous evening's drinking session which had finished up in her room. As the champagne flowed serenity had flown out of the window, with both women veering between hysterical giggles and morose re-telling of their stories. Swallowing a couple of paracetamol, Louisa had to concede that, in spite of the sore head, the evening had been cathartic for them both. It was if they had each given the other permission to let go without fear of judgment. She could only hope that Charlotte wouldn't feel uncomfortable with her after baring her soul the night before. It was clear that she was used to being in control, not letting go easily. In that they were alike, she thought, padding into the shower for a quick burst of cold water before turning the temperature back to normal. She just had time to pull on her joggers and top before heading downstairs to the yoga class. Breakfast would have to wait.

She arrived with moments to spare, surprised to see an immaculate Charlotte smiling serenely at Paul as she took her place on a mat.

'Good morning, Louisa. Glad you could make it,' Paul greeted her, grinning. *He knows! Surely it's not common knowledge that we got blasted last night?* She shot a quick look at Charlotte who winked as she indicated the vacant mat next to her own.

'It's okay, I only said we enjoyed a bottle of champers last night. And he said he'd have been happy to join us,' Charlotte whispered to her as Paul moved away to welcome a newcomer. 'How are you feeling? I noticed you missed breakfast.'

'I've felt better. I'll grab something after class. But you look great! How...'

'Oh, I have the constitution of an ox when it comes to booze. Not even a headache. And I slept better than I have for months, so thank you. It did me good.'

Charlotte patted Louisa's hand as they prepared for the first stretch.

By the time the class had finished, Louisa felt back to normal and ravenous. After a brief chat with Paul, who asked how she was, she shot off to the dining room. Fortunately for her, breakfast was available until the civilised time of ten thirty, and she placed her order for a double-strength café latte as she helped herself from the trolley. She finished in good time for her appointment with Molly, quickly popping upstairs to clean her teeth and slap on some make-up to cover the dark shadows.

'Hello, Louisa, do come in,' Molly said, as she opened the door.

Settling into the recliner, Louisa experienced some qualms. Until then she had been too busy to think about what it would be like to recall that awful day. She shivered.

'Are you cold?' Molly's face creased in concern.

'No. It's the thought of having to dredge it all up again...'

Molly nodded. 'Of course. But remember we're only looking for a description of the man you saw. It probably won't be necessary to probe deeper than that.' Molly smiled reassuringly and Louisa took a deep breath. *Come on, girl! Don't be a wuss!* She told herself firmly, not wanting to let everyone down. Especially her mother.

Molly went on to explain that once Louisa was deeply relaxed, she would direct her to return to the day concerned, asking her to describe what happened as she arrived home. Louisa nodded her understanding and, on Molly's instructions, closed her eyes.

Some minutes later Louisa felt herself sinking down into a blissful state of relaxation, soothed by Molly's gentle voice.

'Now, Louisa, I want your subconscious mind to take you back to Friday 16th January 2009. It's around half past six in the evening and you're on the way home. I want you to tell me what's happening.'

'I've just left Angel station and I bought Mum some roses. Her favourite. I'm running a bit late and Mum's cooking dinner so I start to hurry.' Her voice was clear, enabling Molly to make notes.

'Good. Have you far to go?'

'No, only another five minutes and I'll be there.' A pause. 'I'm just opening the front door and calling out to Mum when...when this man rushes towards me...down the hall...barges into me.' Louisa shifted in her chair as images fill her mind.

'Can you tell me anything about this man, Louisa? What he looks like, what he's wearing.'

'Um, he's very thin...scruffy...about sixty. He's wearing a dark mac...over a navy fleece...has something on it...a logo of some sort.' She frowned in concentration. There's something familiar about that logo. 'I've got it! It's the London Undergound logo! He must work there.' She felt herself falling as he pushed into her. 'I...I fall when he collides with me. He's running off as I'm picking myself up.'

'Okay. Do you catch another look at him before he disappears?'

Again Louisa saw a picture form in her mind. 'Yes. Not tall...grey...lanky hair. Oh! He's got a limp! He can't run properly...sort of shuffle...but I'm worried about

Mum…turn back into the house.' Louisa could feel herself becoming anxious. Mum! Is she all right?

'That's very good, Louisa. Now, I want you to leave that time and return to the present. So I'm asking your subconscious…' Molly continued to guide her back from that January evening, eventually asking her to open her eyes, telling her she would feel calm and relaxed.

Louisa blinked, her gaze falling on Molly's friendly face. Her heart rate was still a bit high, but she was no longer filled with anxiety. It was over. And she had remembered things she hadn't realised she'd seen. Perhaps now they would catch him the man who killed her mother.

chapter 15

Malcolm was lost in thought as he stared out of his apartment window. Louisa had only said that her hypnosis session had produced results, but from the excitement in her voice he guessed it was significant. He really hoped whatever she recalled could help to nail the bastard who'd robbed a lovely lady of her life. He clenched his hands so tightly that the knuckles glowed white through the skin. The memory of the night that had, ultimately and tragically, brought about Susan's death flashed into his mind.

'Can I really? You're not kidding me are you?' Susan asked, her soft grey eyes round with excitement.

'Hey, 'course I'm not. That would be cruel. I'd love you to wear the jewels; the rubies will positively glow against that creamy skin of yours. You'll be the belle of the ball!' he said, giving her a kiss. Susan looked radiant in a deep blue satin sheath, encasing her svelte figure to perfection. As he fastened the necklace around her neck his fingers trembled as he felt the familiar onslaught of passion. There was no time now, but later…

Forcing himself to stand back, he admired the effect of the huge rubies and diamonds filling Susan's décolletage. Stunning, absolutely stunning. She swung round to see her reflection in the mirror and gasped.

'It's beautiful! You are absolutely sure–'

He pulled her into his arms. 'Yes. I'll be the envy of all the men with the most beautiful woman on my arm tonight.' At that moment he realised how much he loved her and he was scared. Scared of what that meant.

Commitment. Marriage and children. He wasn't sure if he was ready. Not yet…

And then, days later he got the call that his mother was seriously ill and he left. Never to see Susan again. And not knowing she was carrying his child.

★

Louisa rang the intercom and Malcolm buzzed her in. Adrenaline coursed through her bloodstream as she rode up in the lift to the penthouse. The thought that they now had something concrete to go on in the search for That Man, went some way to assuaging the pain of her loss. Until then she had felt guilty for being so useless.

Malcolm led her into the living area, offering her a cup of coffee as she sank onto a sofa. He returned a moment later with two cups.

'Okay. I can tell from your face that whatever you've remembered is important, so shoot,' he said.

She told him everything.

Malcolm's face, initially sombre, now lightened. 'That's terrific, Louisa. Well done! I'm sorry you had to go through the ordeal again but…'

She shook her head. 'It was okay, really. We didn't go further than my encounter with That Man so it wasn't as if I had to recall what happened after…' She bit her lip then continued, 'I'm glad I did it and John Ferguson was right to suggest it. Will you tell him what I've remembered?'

'Sure will. You drink your coffee while I give him a ring.' He picked up his phone and wandered off to the window, giving Louisa's shoulder a quick squeeze on the way.

'Hi, John, it's Malcolm…Yes, she did, this morning…Yep, quite a good description…sure, that sounds a great idea…let me know when…right, talk later. Bye.'

Returning to the sofa, he explained that John would chat to a photo-fit expert who could help them build a life-like picture of the suspect.

'Sounds good. Once we have a picture what happens next?'

'John will go over to the UK and start digging around amongst his contacts in the Met. Of course, if the guy doesn't have a record, then we'll be no further forward. In that case, John will search the birth records to see if Archie had a son and, if he did, track him down and see if it's him. Either way, John feels confident it will lead us to the killer. Just may take some time,' he said, sighing. 'We need to be patient, my dear. Meanwhile, we'll be able to get to know each other better while you relax at La Folie. Is that a deal?'

Louisa, worried exactly how long was "some time", managed a smile. After all, although she desperately wanted justice for her mother, she also wanted to build a relationship with her father. Once she returned to London that might be more difficult to maintain.

'Great. Now, how about I take you out to lunch? Assuming you haven't gotten any other plans.'

'Thanks, I'd like that. I've nothing booked until four o'clock when I'm due for a full body massage.'

'You love those too? I've got one tomorrow. Helps to keep this ol' body of mine moving around,' he chuckled. 'Right, I'll phone for a table and then we can be off.'

Minutes later they were settled at a table in La Fregate studying the lunch menu. Glasses of low-alcohol lager were testament to their desire for sobriety. Although they had walked from the apartment, she had to drive out to La Folie for her massage. It didn't take long to choose their food, leaving them free to chat. Malcolm appeared keen to know more about her childhood and Louisa was happy to answer his questions. Time drifted by as they became immersed in their conversation and the good food.

'I guess I'd better be heading back, Malcolm. I planned to get in a swim before my massage. Thanks for a lovely lunch.'

'You're welcome, my dear. I enjoy your company, you remind me of your mother. Both of you lovely to look at and listen to.' He squeezed her hand, looking wistful.

Louisa swallowed a lump in her throat. 'Thanks.'

She drove back to Torteval pondering on her father's words. She had never really considered how much she took after Susan; like most women she wanted to be her own person and not a carbon copy of her mother. Much as she loved and admired her. Thinking about it, they were both quite independent, although her mother had been much more so. More of a risk-taker than Louisa would ever be. She couldn't help wondering if the lack of a father had impacted on her self-confidence. Susan, on the other hand, had been the apple of her father's eye and a bit spoiled by him. Louisa had completed a course in psychology at university and it had taught her about the intricacies of family dynamics, and the effect of fractured or incomplete families on the children. As a child without a father, she had lost out on the opportunity to test out her female wiles on her father, as daughters so often do. She had witnessed it amongst her school friends on sleepovers, slightly shocked by the kind of flirtation that took place between daughter and father. She bit her lip as she now recalled how girls often looked for father-replacements when choosing boyfriends, wondering if she had been guilty of that. Mentally reviewing her relationships, she had to concede that she'd probably been too willing to let the man control her, letting them be always right. An uncomfortable thought. *Right, girl, from now on, you'll make better choices and stick up for yourself. Be more like Mum!*

The swim helped to clear her head and she felt more at ease as she headed up to her room, meeting Charlotte on the stairs.

'Hi! Haven't seen you all day. How did the hypnosis go?' Charlotte asked, giving her a quick hug.

'Well, thanks. I'll tell you later as I'm due for a massage in a minute. Shall I see you at dinner?'

'Sure. I'm off for a *very* long walk as that cream tea still haunts me.' She patted her stomach in disgust.

Louisa grinned and dashed up to her room to change into her joggers and T-shirt, ready for the massage.

An hour later she floated out of Lin's therapy room, trailing the heady mix of rose geranium and frankincense, feeling on top of the world. Rounding a corner, she bumped into Paul. He grinned. 'No guesses needed as to where you've just been! Enjoy it?'

'Mm, it was delicious, thanks. The smell of the oils alone sends me off even before Lin lays a finger on me. I feel as if I could sleep for a week!'

'Then why not lie down for a while? Although a week's probably pushing it! An hour or two should be enough to give those oils time to work. A massage always zonks me out, too, so I have to be careful when I have them. That's assuming I can fit one in amongst my work sessions,' he said, his eyes crinkling up as he smiled.

'Glad to hear I'm not the only one who succumbs to drowsiness. I always thought that a massage energised you not wiped you out.'

'Ah! Depends on the massage. Lin's aromatherapy is renowned for its relaxing effect, but you'll have the extra energy tomorrow. Promise.'

'Good. Well, I'll toddle up to my room and chill out for a bit. If I'm not down for dinner will someone give me a shout? Don't want to miss one of Chef's masterpieces, do I?' she said, pushing her hand through her hair.

'Don't worry, I'm on the case. See you later.' He shot her a smile as he walked away and Louisa's legs felt even more wobbly than before. Definitely time for a lie-down!

She didn't miss dinner, thanks mainly to a phone call from Malcolm about an hour later. John Ferguson had phoned to say that the island policeman experienced in e-fits could see Louisa at the station the next morning. John had told his old boss that the suspect could lead them to the killer of Malcolm's father, so he'd approved his request. It was only a slight fudge of the truth, John had assured Malcolm. Louisa was happy to agree, and Malcolm said John would pick her up.

The phone call brought her wide awake but it was a little early for dinner, so she called her aunt to bring her up to date. She usually phoned every few days, knowing Margaret worried about her. As Louisa thought, her aunt was pleased about the outcome of the hypnosis.

'If this man is tracked down, then I presume you'll come home to identify him?'

'Yes, but I've been warned it could take a while so don't expect me back just yet. And, to be honest, I'm quite enjoying being pampered. And I've made a friend...' Louisa told her about Charlotte and how they had spent Sunday together. Omitting its drunken end.

'That's nice, Louisa. You needed to come out of yourself a bit and have some fun. And are you seeing much of your father?'

They continued to chat for a few minutes, leaving it that Louisa would call again in a few days. As she put down the phone, it struck her that Margaret had sounded a little brighter than she had on their last call. Perhaps she, too, was slowly coming to terms with her loss. She hoped so. As she got off the bed, she stroked the Buddha. *Perhaps I'll be as calm as you one day soon.* With that thought in her head, she slapped on some make-up and brushed her hair in preparation for supper. Her stomach rumbling, she ran downstairs. In her book, any meal she hadn't had to cook would make it enjoyable, but one cooked by La Folie's talented chef would be extra pleasurable.

Neither Charlotte nor Louisa were up for another drinking session and both declared themselves ready for an early night by ten. Louisa took a while to settle, anxiety about the upcoming e-fit session pushing away the desire for sleep. She was afraid she wouldn't recognise the picture as that of the man she saw. Or rather, didn't see. Had her mind played tricks on her? Made up the description of That Man? Molly had tried to assure her it was unlikely but…At last she let go, not waking until seven thirty, in good time for breakfast and yoga.

As she rolled up her yoga mat, Paul asked how she was getting on and if she wanted to try more therapies.

'I'm enjoying everything so far, thanks. Perhaps in a few days…I really want to spend time outside too. Go for long walks.' She kept her eyes down, ostensibly fastening the ties on the mat, but really to avoid catching Paul's eyes. They had such a strange effect on her and she wasn't sure how to handle the feeling, like being swallowed up in his gaze. She was finding him too damned attractive and it wouldn't work. Her father was his boss and she was a guest at the retreat. And anyway, her head and heart were all over the place. Too soon…

'Okay. Let me know if there's anything you need; I want you to enjoy your stay here.'

She nodded, muttered a quick goodbye and followed a grinning Charlotte out of the room.

'You fancy him, don't you?' Charlotte said as soon as they were on their own.

'I…I. No, of course not! He's good looking, I grant you but…'

'But nothing! I can see it in your face.' Charlotte must have noticed the warmth in her cheeks as she added quickly, 'Hey, don't worry. Only a woman would know. Men can't see further than the end of their noses. But what's wrong with you finding him hot? Neither of you are spoken for.'

Louisa stared at her friend. 'How do you know that?'

'Oh, it's no secret he's single.' She waved her hand airily. 'Most of the girls who work here are a bit in love with Paul.' She smiled at Louisa. 'And perhaps one or two of the guests…'

'Hmm, I *like* him but I'm not in love with him. I hardly know him!' She protested. Inside she wasn't so sure. She certainly felt *something* for Paul…

John Ferguson collected Louisa and drove to the police station in St Peter Port. As he was parking the car, she felt pangs of anxiety bite at her stomach and, not for the first time, wished she was made of sterner stuff. Like her mother. She chewed on her thumb, a habit from childhood.

'You okay, Louisa? There's nothing to worry about. Sergeant Davis will be doing all the work, you only need to describe what you remember.' John's calm voice broke into her thoughts as they climbed out of the car.

'I'm fine, thanks. A slight attack of nerves, that's all.'

John smiled encouragingly and, placing his hand under her elbow, guided her to the reception desk. The duty sergeant grinned at them.

'You can't keep away, John, can you? Retirement proving not as it's cracked up to be?'

John laughed. 'Retirement's great, Pete. Just tying up loose ends on that last case of mine. Sergeant Davis is expecting us.'

'He is, is he? Righto, I'll let him know you're here.' Pete made a quick call and buzzed them through to the inner offices. A young man was hovering in a doorway and, after nodding at John, beckoned them through to a small room dominated by a desk burdened with files and a large computer screen. John made the introductions and the sergeant asked Louisa to make herself comfortable in one of the two chairs facing the screen. He took the other one while John perched on a stool nearby. The sergeant explained how he would select images of parts of a face based on Louisa's description, eventually building up to a whole picture, like a jigsaw. The computer software would then harmonise the result, producing a lifelike image.

It was a slow process. Sections of the face were built up until Louisa was satisfied that the resulting image was accurate. Or at least as accurate as her memory allowed. It resembled a photograph and she was startled by its uncanny likeness to the man she'd recalled under hypnosis. He looked like a weasel, she thought, shuddering. A sharp nose and thin mouth sat under small eyes on a thin, stubbled face. Greying, lank hair hung down below the jawline.

John leaned in and patted her shoulder. 'Well done. Is there anything you'd like to change?'

She shook her head. That Man's face was now engraved on her mind. The sergeant printed off several copies of the picture and they left the station. John was in buoyant mood.

'This is going to be a big help, Louisa. And the fact that this guy probably works on the Underground. I'll check in with Malcolm before setting off to London tomorrow for some digging around.' His eyes gleamed and she sensed the excitement emanating from him.

'You miss being a detective, don't you?'

He cleared his throat. 'I do like solving mysteries, I admit. Like to keep the "little grey cells" working, to quote that famous detective, Hercule Poirot. To be honest, Pete was right, and retirement doesn't suit me. And I'm glad of a chance to do some proper detecting after the petty stuff I've been doing of late.' He opened the car door, adding, 'And I promise you, Louisa, I'll not stop until we've got this guy banged up. And I never break a promise.'

Louisa joined Charlotte for lunch, telling her about the outcome of the e-fit session. Charlotte was suitably impressed.

'Great news! So your detective's going on the manhunt? Let's hope that it won't be long before the case is closed and you can get on with your life. Any plans for the future?' she asked, tilting her head on one side.

Louisa frowned. 'Nooo. I haven't given it much thought. Suppose I'd better look for a job in London as at least I have a home there. But I'm not sure it's what I really want…' She sighed.

'Hey, there's no need to make a decision yet. All in good time. Is the, er, island seducing you?' Charlotte asked, straight-faced.

'I know what you're thinking!' Louisa laughed. 'It's not like that. But I admit Guernsey is proving quite seductive. I love the slower pace of life and the gorgeous scenery and the sea.'

'Mm, I'm with you there. But my work is based in London and I do love the social scene in the city. But I'm planning to take more holidays once I've learnt to delegate. Then I can pop over here and chill out,' she said, putting down her knife and fork. 'Speaking of which, are you free to join me in a walk this afternoon? I haven't any treatments until five.'

'Yes, I am. Any particular place in mind?

'Nadine mentioned that the bluebell woods are now in bloom and worth a visit. Fancy going there? Just south of St Peter Port so we need to take the car.'

After parking in a lane off Fort Road they made their way towards the cliff path and the woods. A dazzling carpet of sapphire lay spread before them, covering every inch of the ground around the trees, while dappled spring sunshine filtered through the leaves.

'This is heavenly! Haven't seen a bluebell wood since I was a child,' exclaimed Charlotte, eyes wide as she stopped and stared.

'It's gorgeous. And, like you, it's years since I saw such a display. Oh, I'd like to be a kid again and run barefoot through the flowers,' said Louisa, laughing as she whirled around on the path.

Charlotte began to recite:

> *'The Bluebell is the sweetest flower*
> *That waves in summer air;*
> *Its blossoms have the mightiest power*
> *To soothe my spirit's care.'*

'How lovely! I haven't heard that before,' Louisa said, entranced.

'My mother used to quote it when I was a child and exploring the bluebell woods. It's called *The Bluebell* by Emily Brontë. Happy times,' she said, gazing across at the slightly waving flowers, giving off their distinctive perfume. 'And she also told me legend has it that their perfume is so intoxicating that anyone walking into a field of them would fall asleep. Something passed down from ancient Greek mythology, apparently.' She grinned at Louisa, 'Feeling sleepy?'

'Not yet! But perhaps we'd better keep walking just in case.'

They strolled down the paths, stopping occasionally to admire the views as they reached the cliff path. A couple of hours later they decided it was time to return to La Folie and much needed refreshment.

Laughing at a shared joke, they were just entering the hall when Paul dashed up, his face creased with worry.

'Louisa, thank goodness! I've been trying your mobile, but it kept going to voice mail.'

She checked her bag. 'Oh, I must have left it in my room. Why, what's the matter?'

Paul took her elbow, moving her away from Charlotte, who took the hint and headed towards the dining room. 'It's Malcolm. He had a fall and hit his head soon after arriving for a massage. I called his doctor and an ambulance and they should both be here any minute.'

She felt the blood drain from her face and she grabbed Paul's arm. 'Can I see him, please?'

'Of course, come on.'

She held on as he guided her down the hall. *Please God, let him be all right. I can't lose my father now; I've only just found him!*

chapter 16

Louisa's legs trembled as she saw her father. He was lying on the floor near the massage couch, deathly pale and with his eyes closed. For a terrible moment she thought he was dead, but then his eyelids fluttered open, and she let out a sigh of relief. His eyes were unfocused and didn't seem to see her; then they closed again.

Paul whispered, 'I think he's had a TIA, causing him to fall and hit his head on the edge of the couch. He knocked himself out for a few moments and there's a nasty dent in his skull, near his left eye. Probably concussed. We'll know more when the doctor arrives.'

She nodded, too numb to speak. She knew how serious it was. A TIA was commonly known as a mini stroke and it sounded as if Malcolm also had a fractured skull. Falling to her knees, she picked up Malcolm's right hand; it was heavy and floppy. Giving it a squeeze, she leant over his prone body to kiss his cheek. A livid mark surrounded the dent; fingering it gently she was relieved to find the skin unbroken, minimising the risk of infection. But she knew that Malcolm needed an operation. And soon. Looking up she saw her own fear reflected in Paul's anxious face.

'The hospital knows my father will need surgery?' she said, forcing out the words.

'Yes, I explained about the fracture. Louisa, I'm sure he'll be–'

'Paul, the ambulance's here,' Lin said, opening the door.

Following on her heels were two paramedics wheeling a stretcher, accompanied by a tall, slim man carrying medical equipment.

'Hello, Ben. This is Louisa, Malcolm's daughter,' Paul said, moving aside for the medical team.

Ben shook her hand, looking serious. 'I'm sorry, I didn't know Malcolm had a daughter. Ben Tostevin, his doctor. I'd better have a quick look.'

'Of course.' She found herself guided by Paul to a chair in the corner while Ben knelt by his patient, checking the vital signs and the head injury.

'Right, it looks as you said, Paul. We'll get him off to the Princess Elizabeth and I'll confirm with the surgeon that we want to go straight into theatre.' He nodded to the paramedics who slipped on a neck brace before carefully manoeuvring Malcolm onto the stretcher and lifting it onto the trolley. Ben made his call before turning back to Louisa. She was living a nightmare. The sight of a deathly pale, unconscious Malcolm being stretchered out mirrored the image of her mother being carried out of the house. Suddenly she felt overwhelmed and loud sobs bubbled up from deep within. Held-back tears coursed down her cheeks as she struggled to breathe. Oblivious of everything other than the pain of her loss and the fear of losing again, it was a while before she realised arms were wrapped around her, offering comfort.

'It's okay, Louisa, let it out. It needs to happen,' A distant man's voice, as if from the end of a tunnel.

Slowly the wrenching sobs subsided and she regained some control of her breathing. She opened her swollen eyes to find Paul's face inches away, concern etched in his features. Struck by how awful her face must look, streaked with tears and snot, she pulled away enough to grab a tissue from her pocket and blew her nose. 'Sorry, I…I don't know what came over me…'

'There's nothing to apologise for. It's a perfectly natural reaction under the circumstances. Here, drink some water,' he said, handing her a glass.

She took a grateful sip and the throbbing in her head began to ease. She looked around and saw Ben hovering by the door.

'Where's Malcolm?'

'On the way to hospital. I'll take you there soon, don't worry. He's going into theatre once a CT scan has checked the extent of his head injury. There's nothing you can do at the moment as you won't be able to see him until after the surgery, but I don't think there's any imminent danger.' Ben patted her hand in reassurance.

Paul chipped in. 'Ben's right, Louisa, we're sure Malcolm will be okay. I'll come up to the hospital later, after I've made arrangements here with the staff. We don't want anyone to panic, do we?'

She shook her head. 'Of course not. But surely people must know…'

'We've just said that Malcolm's had a fall and has gone to hospital as a precautionary measure. Lin's the only one who knows the truth and she's too loyal to say anything. And I'm sure he wouldn't want a fuss.'

'No, he…he wouldn't.' She looked at Ben. 'Can we go now, please? I know I'll have to wait but–'

'Of course. As long as you're all right?'

'I'll just go and wash my face. Be right back.' She ran along to the nearest cloakroom and repaired the damage as best she could before dragging a comb through her hair.

She returned to find Paul and Ben waiting outside the door. Paul leaned down and gave her a quick kiss on the cheek. 'Take care and I'll be as quick as I can,' he murmured. She mumbled a quick thanks before following Ben. Her worry about Malcolm vied for space with the feelings aroused by Paul's kiss. The concern for her father won out and she could only pray that Ben was right and that he was indeed in no danger.

Time crawled by, only leavened by regular cups of tea served by the cheerful nurses. Ben had left her in a waiting room while he went off to discover the latest news. On his return he announced that Malcolm was already undergoing various tests and a CT scan prior to going into theatre.

'It's likely that the surgeon will only need to remove the bone and return it to the original position. At the moment I don't know if there's been any bleeding in the brain,' Ben said, frowning.

Louisa felt her stomach muscles tense. 'Will the scan show what caused the TIA?'

'Yes, but–' Ben was interrupted by the beep of his mobile. Glancing at the screen, he stood up, saying, 'I'm sorry, but I need to dash. My wife's gone into labour and I...'

She forced a smile. 'Go. I'll be fine. Thanks for your help and...and good luck. Is it your first?'

'Yes, it is. I'll check on your father later. Bye.' He hurried off and Louisa sat back, thinking what a caring doctor Malcolm had. Left on her own the time continued to drag as her anxiety increased. It was nearly two hours later before Paul dashed in, apologising for taking so long.

'I had to sort out a mix-up over a booking and pour a large dollop of oil on troubled waters before I could make my escape,' he said, his forehead creased with worry. 'How's Malcolm? Any news?'

She told him what Ben had told her and that it was now expected that Malcolm would be out of the theatre shortly. 'Oh, and by the way, Ben's baby's on the way so he shot off to join his wife.'

Paul smiled. 'Great. He's been like a cat on a hot tin roof the past week or so and the baby's not due for another four days. I think his wife Nicole's been more laid-back.'

'You two know each other, I take it?'

'Yes, I met him when we were both surfing one day. We got chatting and became good mates. Since then he's introduced me to a number of his friends and we've had some good times together.'

She nodded, aware of how lonely she felt without the support of friends around her. Not that she had many in London. Over time, girlfriends had moved to other areas and she had lost touch with some of them. There were a couple from work, but since she'd left the hospital she hadn't been in touch. They were not close enough friends for her to reveal how badly she was coping with her mother's death. Perhaps Charlotte could be her confidante... *Oh, Malcolm please get well!*

'You okay? Can I get you a cup of tea or something?' Paul asked, touching her shoulder.

She jumped. 'Sorry, I was miles away. No tea, thanks. I've had more than enough and I don't particularly like the stuff they serve here!' She smiled at him. *Hmm, now he would make a nice friend. But could I settle for that?*

'Malcolm's a tough nut, Louisa. He'll pull through and be back to normal before you know it. He looks after himself and that makes a huge difference in cases like this,' Paul said, gripping her hands.

She was about to reply when a doctor came up and introduced himself as the surgeon. Her heart thumped as she waited.

'I'm pleased to say that your father is doing very well. I managed to repair the fracture to the skull and, luckily, the bone hadn't pierced the brain; there was no internal bleeding or swelling.' He coughed. 'The scan showed the presence of a recent Transient Ischaemic Attack, or TIA, but it appears to have been a brief and isolated event. So, it's good news,' he beamed.

She felt almost dizzy with relief. 'Oh, thank you, doctor. Can I see him?'

'Shortly. He's being moved to a private room in Victoria Wing and we'll keep a close eye on him for the next forty-eight hours. Mr Roget's recovered consciousness, but he's still drowsy so please don't stay long.'

'All right. What happens next?'

'Assuming we have no concerns, your father will be able to return home in two or three days but it's best if he's not alone. Would that be a problem?' He looked from one to the other.

'I think it would be best if Malcolm stayed at La Folie, don't you, Louisa? He can be well taken care of with the therapists on hand.'

She nodded. 'Good idea. Will my father need any further treatment?'

'Yes, we'll be starting him on medication and he'll be monitored regularly. But there's no reason to doubt that Mr Roget won't make a complete recovery and lead a normal life. In the meantime he'll have to take it easy, which he might find frustrating. But he's very fit for his age,' he added.

Louisa thanked him and, after saying that a nurse would fetch her soon, the doctor left.

She slumped down into the chair, drained after the sustained surge of the now depleting adrenaline. Paul put his arm around her, and she found herself relaxing into his embrace, her head resting on his shoulder.

'I told you the old devil would be all right, didn't I?'

'Hey, less of the "old devil"! That's my father you're talking about,' she replied, giving him a playful punch. 'You should show more respect,' she added, trying to sound severe.

Paul just grinned. 'It's a term of endearment, as well you know. But I tell you one thing about your father; he won't make a very good patient! I can't see him taking it easy, can you?'

'No, I can't. But he'll have to do as he's told if he wants to avoid it happening again.' For a moment the image of a caged, angry lion came into her mind and she smiled. Just then a nurse arrived to take her to see Malcolm and she left Paul waiting for her.

The spacious room looked as comfortable as any hospital room was likely to be. But her heart sank at the sight of her father lying stiff on the bed, encased in white sheets closely matching his complexion. Tubes and wires sprouted obscenely from different parts of his body and his head was encased in a thick bandage. His eyes were shut and he bore little resemblance to the man she had grown to care for.

'Malcolm, can you hear me? It's Louisa.' She sat down in the armchair next to the bed, reaching to touch his hands, clasped together on the sheet. Machines on stilts beeped, numbers glowing red or green.

His eyelids fluttered. He turned his head towards her, pale blue eyes blinking as he focused on her face. He grimaced.

'Hi. It seems I...took a tumble and hit...my head. But I don't remember...' he said in a croaky voice, twisting his fingers on the bed sheet.

'It's okay. I'm sure you'll remember later and the surgeon assured me you'll make a full recovery. But you have to rest and I've been warned not to tire you. Paul's here and sends his love.' She gripped his hands, feeling them tremble in hers. Doing her best to sound cheerful, she added, 'I'll be back tomorrow, and can bring you stuff from the apartment if you like.'

'Keys in...my jacket. Ask the...nurse. Like clean...clothes and...toiletries.'

'I'll sort it. You'd best sleep now and I'll see you in the morning.'

She kissed his cheek and Malcolm managed a small smile. 'Thanks.'

Outside the room she checked with the duty nurse who fetched the keys, locked in a drawer in his room with Malcolm's wallet, loose change and phone. Louisa joined an anxious Paul in the waiting area, telling him how it had gone with Malcolm.

'He's disorientated and weak, which is to be expected, but it's still upsetting...' she brushed away a tear, and Paul hugged her. 'Course it is. Why don't we head on back to La Folie and get something to eat? We'll get Chef to rustle up something and send it to my rooms so we don't have to face everyone just yet. And perhaps a glass of wine wouldn't be amiss,' he said, stroking her hair back from her face.

'Sounds good, thanks. Let's go.'

Later that evening Louisa finished the last of the seared pork medallions and fresh steamed vegetables, breathing out a contented sigh. 'That was delicious! Just what I needed – good food and wine,' she said, raising her glass of rosé towards Paul, sitting opposite.

'There's baked figs with Greek yogurt to follow so I hope you're not full,' he teased, clearing away the plates.

'Yummy, sounds perfect. And I'm so glad you suggested avoiding the other guests tonight. I'm sure I'd have found it hard to pretend nothing's happened.' She focused on her glass as Paul collected the desserts from his mini-kitchen. 'But I don't see how I can avoid admitting I'm Malcolm's daughter. What do you think?'

He placed the dishes on the table and sat down. 'I think you should tell Charlotte first, as you two seem pretty

139

close.' Louisa nodded. 'The staff already know, and if other guests find out, I don't see it's a big deal. Some are leaving in a few days, anyway. Malcolm's well liked so I'm sure everyone will be pleased he has family here while he recovers. The room next to yours will be vacant tomorrow so he can stay there,' he said, adding with a grin, 'You've probably noticed it's called *Balance*. Appropriate don't you think?'

'You'd better hope Malcolm hasn't lost his sense of humour!' she laughed. Sitting here in Paul's tower eyrie, she was able to let go the tensions and anxiety of the day. The room was light and airy and decorated in inimitable Asian style; colourful Indian rugs covered the floor and silk wall hangings vied with watercolours on the pale walls. Book shelves encircled the room and an array of Indian artefacts formed a feature on a side table; pride of place being given to a bronze Buddha. She imagined that Paul found it the perfect retreat after a busy day downstairs; wealthy guests could be pretty demanding, he'd told her. As she glanced around now, her eyes were drawn to the man himself. Concentrating on his dessert, he didn't see her looking at him. Which was just as well, as she felt herself flushing at the potential of his bedroom only feet away. *How can I be so turned on by the thought of going to bed with Paul when my father is in hospital? I should be ashamed of myself!* But the desire didn't leave and she began eating her figs, thinking they were an unfortunate, albeit delicious choice, given her state of arousal.

'Good, aren't they?' Paul asked, looking up.

'Mm, yes.' She lifted her eyes to a spot on his shirt. 'Paul, I–'

His mobile beeped and he picked it up, glancing at the screen. 'Hey, what do you know, Nicole and Ben have a baby girl!' He grinned delightedly.

'That's great news. She didn't mess around, did she? Does he say anything else – name, weight, how they both are?'

'They're calling her Eve, after Nicole's grandmother, who used to own this house. Did you know that?'

'No, I didn't. That makes it a bit more personal doesn't it? So, did Nicole live here too?'

He shook his head. 'Not exactly, but it's a long story. Anyway, they're both fine and little Eve weighs in at over 3.4 kilos, which I presume is a good weight. Don't know much about babies.'

'It's fine. I must tell Malcolm tomorrow, it will cheer him up. Ben's been a good doctor, I gather.'

'Yes, and Malc met Nicole a few months ago when the centre opened. Perhaps we should send flowers or a card,' he mused.

'Good idea. Mm, it's getting late and it's been a long day…' She stood up, desperate for the solitude of her room. The upsets and excitement of the day were taking their toll.

Paul shot to his feet. 'Of course. Will I see you at yoga in the morning?'

'Hopefully. I'll ring the hospital first thing to make sure Malcolm's all right.' Picking up her bag, she shifted from foot to foot, wondering how to say goodnight. Paul took the initiative by giving her a hug, followed by a kiss on the cheek.

'Goodnight, Louisa. Sweet dreams. And don't worry, Malc's a toughie. He'll be his usual buoyant self before you know it.'

She nodded, muttered good night, and left. As she walked downstairs to her room, her body felt as if it would barely make it back; complete and utter exhaustion claimed her. Her emotions were a mix of worry over Malcolm and the realisation that she was falling for Paul. In a big way. Arriving back in her room, she threw off her clothes, and with a heartfelt groan, crawled under the duvet, seeking oblivion.

chapter 17

The Ward Sister reassured Louisa that her father had spent a comfortable night, enjoying tea and toast for breakfast. Louisa was free to visit whenever she wished. Saying she would be in later that morning, Louisa rang off before going along to Charlotte's room. She needed to come clean, but in private.

'Hi, can I come in? I wanted to have a quick chat before breakfast.'

'Sure. How's Mr Roget? You had said he was a family friend so I assume that's why Paul needed to speak to you,' Charlotte said, waving her to a small sofa.

'He's…better, thanks. But he's more than a friend, he's my…my father.'

Charlotte's eyes opened wide and she sat down abruptly. 'My, that is a surprise! You never mentioned a father and I didn't like to pry.' She cocked her head, looking expectantly at Louisa.

She explained about having just met Malcolm and why she hadn't said anything, but realised that it could no longer be kept quiet.

Charlotte looked thoughtful. 'I understand your need to be wary. Must have been a bit odd for you ending up staying here in his centre.' She touched Louisa's arm, adding, 'But I'm so glad you did, otherwise we wouldn't have met! And I'm sure your father's glad too. Now, tell me what really happened; there seems to be some mystery around his fall.'

Louisa, after swearing her to secrecy, told her about the TIA and the head injury. Her friend was shocked.

'Oh, I am sorry. We were told it wasn't serious but it would have been so frightening for you both. You poor girl!' Glancing at her watch, Charlotte added that they needed to get downstairs for breakfast if they were to make the yoga class and they agreed to talk later.

They made it to yoga in good time and Paul came across to ask Louisa about Malcolm. She felt the now familiar flutter in her solar plexus as he gave her a hug. Did she imagine it or did his eyes light up when he saw her? And if he did feel something for her, could it work? She gave herself a mental shake and relayed what the Sister had said. His smile broadened and he asked if he could accompany her to the hospital.

'Sure. I have to collect some things from his apartment first and plan to visit about twelve if you're free then?' Her heart skipped a beat at the thought of the two of them spending more time together.

'Great. See you later.' He turned to face his class, 'Right, ladies and gentlemen, are we ready to start?'

Charlotte was grinning as they left after the class. 'You and Paul seem to be getting, shall we say, friendly? Anything happening between you?'

Louisa felt herself redden. 'Not exactly, but we did spend a lot of time together yesterday as he's very fond of Malcolm.'

'Mm. Me thinks it might not just be Malcolm he's fond of! There's definitely an extra twinkle in his eye when he looks at you,' Charlotte said, seeming determined not to let the matter drop.

She caved in. 'Well, if you must know, Paul was very…supportive yesterday at the hospital and…and when we came back last night.'

Charlotte's eyebrows arched. 'Supportive, eh? I wondered where you were at dinner, so where did you eat?'

'It was late and Paul suggested it would be better to ask Chef to send us some supper to…to his rooms. To avoid having to face lots of questions about Malcolm.'

'Well, that's a new way of getting a woman to visit one's room,' she chuckled as they were nearing their own. Charlotte stopped and gave Louisa a hug. 'Look, I'm pleased for you. It would be lovely if you two became an item; you deserve some happiness. Guess I'm just jealous,' she said, ruefully.

Louisa hugged her back. 'I'm sure you'll meet someone soon. You're far too attractive not to catch some dishy man's eye. And anyway, there's no guarantee that Paul and I will get together and in the meantime there's my father…' she sighed.

'Yes, he's the priority now. Please send him my best when you visit, won't you? I'll catch you this afternoon sometime, okay?'

Louisa wanted to change into her favourite jeans and top for her visit to Malcolm. She also needed to phone her aunt with the news of his fall. Once they had said their goodbyes, it was time to leave for the apartment.

It felt odd for her to enter Malcolm's home without him being there, and she quickly made for the bedroom; a room she had not previously seen. As with the rest of the apartment, there was a pre-dominance of maple furniture; from the floor to ceiling built-in wardrobes to the king-size bed covered in a pale grey duvet. Everything was immaculate and she wondered if his cleaner had been in that morning. Tentatively, she pulled out drawers to find the required pyjamas and clean underwear. The wardrobes housed shelves of neatly folded shirts and she chose one at random. She reached up for a small overnight bag from a shelf and packed the clothes, together with slippers and a dressing gown. The en-suite, a shiny marbled wet-room, held an array of toiletries and she grabbed what she felt would be necessary. As Louisa returned to the hall the phone rang.

'Mr Roget's residence,' she answered.

'Is that Louisa? John Ferguson. Is Malcolm there?'

She explained about Malcolm's accident and that she was only there to collect his things. John sounded shocked, saying he had only spoken to him yesterday afternoon, before booking a ticket on today's ferry. He was due to leave shortly and was ringing to advise Malcolm of that fact. When he ventured that perhaps he should postpone his trip, Louisa assured him that there was no need, that her father would want him to continue his investigations as arranged. Malcolm was out of danger and would be leaving hospital in the next day or two. The detective, seemingly mollified, asked her to ring him if there was any change and she agreed, noting his number. As she replaced the receiver, Louisa hoped she had said the right thing.

Malcolm looked better. The colour had returned to his face and his eyes were more focused. He smiled weakly as they entered his room.

'Hey, good to see you. Come to check on the ol' codger, have you?' He spoke slowly, as if it was an effort. Normal after what he had gone through, Louisa thought.

She kissed him, pleased to see he hadn't lost his sense of humour. 'How are you? I was told you'd slept well.'

'Better, thanks. And I slept like a baby. Probably thanks to the…anaesthetic and pain killers. The surgeon told me about the TIA,' he said, frowning. 'That was…scary, but he seems to think it might not…happen again, as long as I take the meds.' He took a deep breath.

'Talking of babies, Ben and Nicole's baby daughter was born here last night. So all in all, an interesting day,' Paul said, settling on the other side of the bed.

'That is good news. Lovely couple.' Malcolm turned towards Louisa. 'Thanks for bringing my stuff,' he nodded towards the overnight bag.

'No problem. Oh, and John Ferguson phoned while I was there.' She gave him the gist of what had been said and he nodded slowly.

'Good.' He shifted uncomfortably, prompting Paul to help him to sit up straighter. 'Thanks. Everything…all right at La Folie?'

Paul assured him all was well and that his fall had been played down to the staff and guests. Malcolm looked relieved.

'What has the doctor said about your coming out?' Louisa asked.

'Should be out day after tomorrow. They want me…to get up this afternoon and start walking. Said something about moving into La Folie. That right?' He glared at Paul.

'They think it's best if you're not on your own and you'll be well looked after there. Added to which, Louisa can spend more time with you. So, don't be pig-headed, Malc, and follow doctor's orders for once,' Paul replied, calmly.

'Humph, I'm not…an invalid and won't be treated as such. Okay?'

'Sure thing, Malc. You're the boss,' Paul said, straight-faced.

Louisa suppressed a smile. Talk about male ego! But she was glad that her father had given in; it was the best solution.

Paul was explaining that there was a room free next to Louisa's when he was interrupted by a knock on the door.

A nurse stuck her head in to say that Malcolm had more visitors if he was up to it, and he nodded his agreement. Ben came in first, beaming from ear to ear, closely followed by a young woman Louisa assumed was Nicole, carrying a bundle in her arms.

Paul stood up and threw his arms around Ben. 'Congratulations, mate. Great news. And you, Nicole, how are you?' He kissed her cheek and she smiled, looking tired but happy.

'I'm fine, thanks, Paul. I didn't expect to find you here, hope we're not interrupting?'

'No, 'course not. Can I...see your daughter?' Malcolm said, beckoning her to his bedside.

Nicole smiled at Louisa, who stood up to give her space. 'Hi, I'm Louisa, Malcolm's daughter. Nice to meet you.'

'And you. And this is *our* daughter, Eve,' she said proudly, pushing back the blanket. A tiny head, topped by a mop of dark hair, emerged, together with a small curled up fist. Bright dark eyes stared up at them. She was passed around and admired by all. Ben, looking the epitome of the proud father, sat on Malcolm's other side, asking how he was.

'Oh, I'm fine,' he said, not really looking it. 'Thanks for your...help yesterday, Ben. Good of you considering...' He nodded towards Nicole and the baby.

Ben grinned. 'Luckily I didn't know Eve was on the way when Paul phoned or I might have delegated to another doctor. Glad I was able to help and that you're on the mend.' He bent down and whispered in his ear, 'You've a lovely daughter there, Malcolm. I'm pleased for you, as one father to another.'

Malcolm murmured, 'Thanks, I...happen to agree with you.'

Louisa saw them whispering to each other, but was distracted by the beautiful baby she had been allowed to hold. Babies hadn't figured large in her life and, if asked, she would have said they didn't interest her. But Eve's bright-eyed stare and soft downy skin tugged at her heart. Surprised by her reaction, she wondered if she did have a maternal instinct after all.

Back at La Folie Louisa caught up with Charlotte in the dining room; she was finishing her lunch but stayed to chat while Louisa ordered her food.

After being filled in with the details of the visit to Malcolm, Charlotte remarked that the story of the real relationship between Louisa and Malcolm was circulating among the guests. 'But don't worry, no-one is being unkind or anything. In fact, those I've spoken to are only relieved that he will be all right.' She poured herself a glass of water before continuing, 'It's just occurred to me that the reason you didn't say how long you were staying was because of Malcolm. And how things developed between you.'

'Yes, it was a bit surreal. Within days of arriving on the island, in pursuit of a father I'd never met and who didn't know I existed, I was living under his roof! Or rather, one he owned,' she said, pushing her hair back. 'Although, after the initial shock and the...checking me out, he did seem genuinely pleased to discover he had a daughter. Then I wasn't sure if he'd go off the idea or I might decide I didn't like him.' Pausing to thank the waitress for her food, she then went on, 'Now I realise that I've become very fond of him. It was scary thinking he might die, like Mum. It...it brought it all back.' She took a deep breath to calm herself.

Charlotte gripped her hand. 'Hey, I understand. Déjà vu. I...I lost my father a couple of years ago and I was devastated. We'd been extremely close and everyone said how like him I was. Physically and personality-wise. And then my mother became ill about the time my husband walked out and...and it all became too much.' Tears glistened in her eyes and she pulled a tissue from her bag, dabbing at them and blowing her nose.

Louisa's heart went out to her friend. 'I'm so sorry, Charlotte. How awful for you, no wonder you needed to get away. And...and your mother?'

Charlotte sipped her water. 'She made a full recovery, thanks. And although it would be fair to describe our relationship as not close, I do love her and was relieved when she was out of danger.' She grinned at Louisa, adding, 'She's now back to being her usual critical self and I can do nothing right, but I can cope with that.'

They continued to chat as Louisa ate, sharing memories of their formative years. It became clear that Charlotte had enjoyed a privileged upbringing, but it had been lonely and she compensated by immersing herself in books. It was her pleasure in reading that led to her to the world of publishing after leaving Oxford. Louisa sensed the air of sadness exuded by her friend, and wished she could help. It seemed money did *not* buy happiness; what Charlotte wanted, like most people, was to be loved. The thought prompted Louisa to think about her feelings for Paul. Was it love or lust? Only time would tell.

Lost in her reverie, she didn't hear Charlotte at first.

'Louisa, are you there? I said how about we visit St Peter Port for some retail therapy. Might do you good, after the drama of yesterday.'

'Mm, yes, great idea. I can buy a card for Ben and Nicole, and arrange for some flowers. I'll get their address from Nadine. I wouldn't mind some new clothes, too; getting a bit fed up of the ones I brought with me. And now it's warmer...'

Charlotte laughed. 'You don't need to justify buying new clothes to me! Come on, let's go. I can hear those tills ringing already!'

Louisa was impressed with the small capital of the island. Even in April the streets buzzed with life. And what a setting! The town rose up majestically from the harbour; glimpses of the sea peeped through the gaps between buildings. And the whiff of sea air always apparent in the mainly pedestrianized streets.

'It's a Lilliputian London,' Charlotte declared, after they had sauntered up and down the High Street and Pollet, the central shopping area. 'Not quite in the same league as Bond Street or Oxford Street, but some decent shops,' she said, putting her arm through Louisa's. 'How about that boutique over there? I love those colours…'

A couple of hours later, happy with the results of their shopping, they headed to a café-bar for a drink.

'I think the sun must be over the yardarm, by now, don't you?' Charlotte asked, grinning. 'Let's have a glass of something naughty. To hell with my diet!' Beckoning the waiter, she ordered two glasses of champagne.

'I had thought tea,' Louisa murmured, half-heartedly. It did sound more fun…

'We'll be good tonight to make up for it. Cheers!' They clinked glasses and took a sip.

'I enjoyed myself, thank you for joining me, Louisa. It's much more fun to shop with a friend isn't it? And you have a good eye. I love that trouser suit you chose; trés chic! But there, you have the figure for it, whereas I…' Charlotte pulled a face.

'Hey, don't be so hard on yourself. That dress you bought really flatters your curves and is *so* sexy,' Louisa said, giving her friend a playful tap on the arm.

'Thanks. You're too kind. But it is rather glam, isn't it? I plan to wear it for the next black tie event. That's the thing about publishing, I'm inundated with invites to social events. And it's tricky without a partner,' Charlotte said, looking pensive.

'Well, in that dress, you might find that's about to change. You'll knock 'em dead!'

Charlotte flushed and took a sip of her champagne. 'We'll see. But thanks for the vote of confidence.'

Once they had downed their bubbly, they headed back to the car. Flowers had been ordered for the new parents and the florist had agreed to enclose Louisa's card. Mission accomplished.

Louisa visited Malcolm again before dinner, and was pleased to see him up and sitting in an armchair. She did not stay long as he looked tired, and offered to call back in the morning.

The next morning Louisa skipped downstairs, in buoyant mood. She had enjoyed the afternoon's shopping with Charlotte; it had helped her to loosen up after the drama of the previous days. Her friend was good company and Louisa had been cheered when told she was now staying till the end of the following week. Her grief for her mother was still liable to surface unawares, but it did not feel quite as raw or overwhelming. She recognised that the healing process had been assisted by both the new environment and becoming involved in the lives of others. Moping on her own in London had done her no favours, she acknowledged.

Stepping into the dining room with a smile on her lips, she faltered at the sight of Paul sitting with Charlotte. She had never seen him at breakfast before, and wondered if they were having a private conversation. Should she sit elsewhere? But Paul spotted her and waved her to the table.

'You don't mind if I join you, do you? I'd run out of milk upstairs so thought I might as well eat here,' he said, his eyes twinkling at her.

'Course not. You're in charge, after all.'

Paul grinned.

'Right, I'd better order breakfast or I'll be late for yoga,' she said, pretending to read the menu when she knew the choice off by heart. It was disconcerting sitting so close to Paul after the intimacy of their dinner in his room. She wished she could be at ease with him, but her insides insisted on looping the loop every time he was close.

Charlotte, giving her a wink, turned to Paul and engaged him in a conversation about the weather. Louisa wasn't fooled and left them to it, concentrating instead on her breakfast. He left shortly after, saying he would see them soon and Louisa burst out, 'The weather! Couldn't you think of something a bit less…less boring?'

'It was all that came into my head. At least it proved a diversion and a chance for you to recover your composure. Your face was quite pink, you know,' she replied, smiling.

Louisa's hands flew to her face. 'Oh no! It's so embarrassing. Do you think he noticed?'

'Probably not, as he was facing me most of the time, remember. I'll be relieved when you two finally get around to telling each other how you feel. And I hope it happens while I'm still here to see it.'

'But I don't even know if he likes me–'

'Of course he does! And I suspect it's more than *like*. There's a way he looks at you that speaks volumes.' Charlotte patted her hand.

Before Louisa could comment on what her friend had said, she saw from the clock that it was time to leave. They pushed back their chairs and made their way to yoga, Louisa wondering if Charlotte was right and Paul did fancy her. But if he did, why didn't he say something?

chapter 18

The next day Malcolm was safely settled in his room at La Folie, having been given the all clear by his doctor. Not that he showed any inclination to spend much time there; as soon as he had unpacked his belongings, he expressed the desire to go and sit in the garden.

'Are you sure you're up to it?' Louisa asked.

'Wouldn't do it if I wasn't. I need to breathe in that sea air after that stuffy hospital room. You can accompany me, if it will make you feel better.'

Malcolm was right. The invigorating air brought a healthy colour to his cheeks as they sat on a bench. The walk downstairs had been slow as he insisted he could do it unaided. Louisa stayed by his side at all times, as she would have done with her physio patients. Guests and staff kept coming up and asking how he was. Louisa quietly observed her father making light of his fall. The occasional curious glance was cast in her direction, but she simply smiled in return. When Malcolm decided he had sat enough they walked the few yards inside for lunch. Fortunately, they were allowed to eat undisturbed before Malcolm was collected for his physio appointment. He made it clear he hated being escorted everywhere, but Paul had made it obligatory if he did not want to spend all the time in his room. Louisa headed off for a massage. She had missed Lin's soothing touch the last few days and it was not long before she drifted off, lulled by softly playing music and the heavenly scent of the oils. Bliss!

The following afternoon, coming back from a swim, Louisa bumped into Paul.

'Ah, Louisa, was hoping to see you. I've invited Malc to join me for dinner tonight in my rooms and would love you to join us. And you needn't worry about my cooking as Chef's preparing the food again,' he said, smiling broadly.

'Right, that would...be great, thanks. What, um, time?' she replied, taken aback. At least it wouldn't be as intimate as last time, Malcolm providing a substantial chaperone.

'Say seven-thirty? I look forward to seeing you later. Bye.' He gave her a quick hug and left.

As she continued her way upstairs, Louisa remembered what Charlotte had said about the way Paul looked at her. His smile had been warm, lighting up his eyes. But didn't he smile like that at everyone? She couldn't remember, but would take more notice in future.

★

Malcolm did not want to admit it, but he had been shaken to the core by his TIA and the resulting skull fracture. For the past few years he had made a determined effort to become as fit and healthy as possible, not wanting to die of the invidious disease that claimed his mother. His embracement of healthy living informed the ethos behind La Folie. So it came as a shock to be told he had suffered a minor stroke. But he concealed his reaction well, his pride did not allow for any public display of weakness. Although apparently critical of the suggestion he move into the centre for a few days, he was actually quite relieved. The fear of suffering another TIA while on his own sucked at the core of his being. He wanted – needed – time for the meds to kick in before he returned to his apartment. And physically, he was nowhere near up to par. As he sat at his bedroom window, watching the ever-present gulls swooping up over the cliff, then down again to the sea, he felt as vulnerable as he had when a small boy. Then, he had yearned for the support and protection of a father, not understanding why he was absent.

His mother had tried to explain.

'When you were still a baby in my tummy, darling, a bad man got angry with your daddy and hit him very hard. Daddy...was hurt badly and...and he died and went up to heaven, with the angels. But he...didn't want to leave, he loved me very much and...and was so happy that you were growing inside me. He'd put his hand on my tummy to feel you kicking and...laugh,' she said, wiping away tears from her eyes. It had made him sad too, to think of his father in heaven with the angels; whenever he had to recite the prayer, beginning, 'Our Father, who art in Heaven...' he thought it referred to *his* father and it pleased him that everyone was praying to him. Until one day he learnt the truth. And he had lost even that comfort.

Malcolm was the odd one out at school; everyone else had a father and he got picked on by the class bully. He learnt quickly that he needed to stand up for himself or he would be lost. As soon as he was old enough, he learnt karate from an old Japanese guy who had settled in Canada before the war. From then on, he was left alone. But he still missed the father he could never know.

He continued to stare, unseeing, out of the window, knowing his fear was of death; his own mortality. He had not given it much thought till now, somehow feeling he was invincible. Or at least that death was a mere speck on the horizon. But now that speck had morphed into the ubiquitous grim reaper and he could almost feel the sound of the scythe slicing through the air. He shuddered, telling himself to stop being so fanciful. Yeh, he'd had a scare, but so what? Didn't mean he was about to "shuffle off this mortal coil" or whatever it was Hamlet had harped on about. *Get a grip, man! If you go on like this, you'll have another stroke and it'll be goodnight, Malcolm!* He stood up and stretched. Glancing at his watch, he saw he had an hour before dinner with Paul and decided to catch up on his emails. It would be ironic if people thought he had died because they had not heard from him for a few days. Waiting for his laptop to boot up, his mind wandered to his daughter. A pleasurable glow warmed his heart. Now, there was someone to keep him going for a few more years! Louisa had shown real concern for him when he was taken ill and it had been a long time since anyone had done that. Except Paul, of course. He was the son he never had, but now there was a flesh and blood daughter too and Malcolm considered himself very fortunate to have two such caring and bright young people by his side. Dinner promised to be fun. If a little tiring.

That evening Chef sent up a mini-banquet, albeit an extremely healthy one. As Malcolm had to forgo alcohol for the moment, fresh juices accompanied the food. But the mood was still buoyant as Paul entertained them with stories from his trips around the world, geared to make them laugh. Malcolm was touched; the two people he was fondest of seemed determined to make him forget the drama of the past few days and simply chill out.

'Do you have any amusing tales from your trips abroad, Louisa?' Paul asked as they were finishing their fresh fruit and yogurt.

Her face screwed up in concentration for a moment and then she laughed. 'Well, there was this time when I was in Madrid with a girlfriend and we wandered into the red light district by mistake. This Spanish guy came up and asked how much for a threesome...' As she described what happened next Malcolm joined in with the laughter. Facing them, he noticed Paul lean towards Louisa, touching her arm in a particularly friendly way; his smile lighting up his eyes. Louisa's answering flush spoke volumes. *Ahah! These two fancy one another. Wonder if they've said anything? Would be great if they got together. I'll have to encourage Paul, let him know I approve. Might be awkward for him, me being her father.*

★

The next few days passed quickly for Louisa. Alternating her time between Malcolm and Charlotte, enjoying long chats and walks with her friend and more sedentary time with her father. Even after Malcolm declared himself fit enough to return home, he popped back to La Folie each day for physio and a swim. It became a regular occurrence to see him pacing Louisa up and down the length of the pool before flopping onto adjoining loungers for a juice. She was happy to see her father slowly recovering the vitality he had shown before his fall and her worry about him eased. One day, after seeing Malcolm drive off to his apartment, she turned to find Paul watching her.

'Hi, were you looking for me?'

'Yes, do you fancy a quick turn around the garden? I've got a free half-hour and thought we could have a chat.'

'Sure.'

They walked around to the side garden adjoining open fields. Grazing cows lifted up their heads; liquid eyes cast a quick glance in their direction and, not seeming to find them interesting, returned to the serious business of eating.

Louisa, wondering what was on Paul's mind, broke the silence.

'Was there something in particular you wanted to chat about?' Surely it wasn't bad news about her father? Her heart lurched. But he seemed so well…

'I wondered if you'd like to go out for a drink one evening. You remember I said Ben and I were friends?'

Letting out a tiny sigh of relief, she nodded.

'Well, I sometimes join him and a few others for a drink. He hasn't been out since the baby was born and we're all meeting up tomorrow evening. Thought perhaps you'd like to join us; there'll be a couple of other girls as well so you won't feel outnumbered.'

She wasn't sure whether to be pleased or relieved that there would be others around. Not exactly a date then. But he had asked her out, which was a sign he liked her, for sure.

'Love to. Where do you meet?'

'At The Rockmount, a pub in Cobo, on the west coast,' he replied, grinning. 'Glad you can come. I plan to leave at eight, if that's okay?'

'Yes, I'll have an early dinner. So, tell me more about these friends of yours.'

Paul chatted about the group as they circled the garden. As he left for his appointment he gave her a peck on the cheek, saying he looked forward to seeing her later. Louisa headed off in search of Charlotte. She needed a girl chat.

Thinking the best person to ask would be Nadine, Louisa stopped at her desk in the hall.

'Hiya. What can I do for you?' Nadine asked, glancing up from the computer screen, her curls bouncing around her head.

'I'm looking for Charlotte. Any idea where she is?'

Nadine returned to the screen and scrolled through the appointments.

'She's due to finish a session with Molly in ten minutes. Do you want to wait or shall I give her a message?'

Louisa checked her watch; nearly three. 'Could you ask her to meet me in the sun lounge for a drink, please?'

'Sure thing.' Nadine smiled before focusing once more on the screen.

Entering the sun room, Louisa was struck by the scent of freshly mown grass. The door to the garden stood open, letting in one of her favourite smells from childhood. For her it epitomised summer and the long school holidays. Although only spring now, the scent from the garden was equally as powerful. The days were becoming warmer, gearing up for the following Easter weekend and the official start of the holiday season. Louisa stepped out onto the terrace to take a deep breath and decided it was warm enough to sit at a table while waiting for her friend. Lulled by the scent and utter peace of the garden, she closed her eyes, letting her mind drift. Images of herself as a child, running around her grandparents' garden, chased by their elderly and arthritic dog, made her lips curl into a smile. Although not very hands-on grandparents, they had been happy to have her stay for two weeks in the summer holidays while her mother worked. Their rambling house in Surrey had appeared palatial after Susan's tiny two-bed terrace with a sunless back yard. It felt good to be able to run free before collapsing, spread-eagled on the lawn, to be thoroughly licked by old Benji. Mr and Mrs Canning were old school and believed in setting ground rules for her stay, but tended to let her have the run of the garden, it being completely enclosed and safe. Her grandmother was a keen gardener, encouraging Louisa to learn the names of plants and trees and to help with weeding as she grew older.

Susan had inherited her mother's love of gardens, but it was not until after her parents' deaths that she was able to afford the house in Islington, complete with a thirty foot long walled garden. Tiny compared to the Surrey house, but enough for her to enjoy pottering for hours after a stressful week at work. Louisa felt her eyes begin to water as she pictured her mother, on her knees, planting in the latest purchase from the gardening centre. *Oh, Mum! You'd have loved it here! Not just because of Malcolm, but because it's beautiful and so, so peaceful.*

'Drifting off in the sun? Gorgeous, isn't it?' Charlotte said, sinking into a chair.

Louisa opened her eyes and smiled. 'Yes, it is. Thought we could have our tea out here. The usual?' she asked, getting up to place their order. Charlotte nodded and she went inside to ask for a pot of the mixed berry tea to which they were both addicted. When they were not drinking wine.

'Right. What's on your mind? Something happen since this morning?' Charlotte frowned.

'It's nothing bad. I…bumped into Paul and he's asked me to go for a drink–'

Charlotte cut in. 'Hey, that's great news. I told you he was interested–'

'Yes and no. It's not just the two of us…' She explained about the group of friends and her continued doubts about what Paul really felt about her.

Her friend rolled her eyes. 'In my book it counts as an invitation to spend time with him and his friends. Nothing wrong with that, he wants to take it easy, which is fine. The word is Paul hasn't been in a relationship for a long time; he's been too busy with his work. So, he's cautious. As are you. He knows you're grieving and that you've just found your long-lost father; who, by the way, happens to be his boss, which might complicate things a tad. You know, the over-protective father bit.' Charlotte sipped her tea before continuing, 'Personally, I don't see Malcolm playing the Victorian father role. He seems pretty fond of Paul and might see it as a match made in heaven,' she grinned mischievously, as Louisa tried to interject.

'You've already got us walking down the aisle and we haven't even been on a date!' she exclaimed, aiming a mock punch at Charlotte's arm.

'Forgot to tell you I was psychic, didn't I?' Charlotte teased.

Louisa's jaw dropped. 'You're not, are you?'

She shook her head. 'No, only kidding. But it's not that bad a scenario, is it? Handsome, caring and intelligent man ready to whisk you off your feet and up to his ivory, or should I say, granite, tower. A lot of women would be very jealous!'

Louisa shifted in her chair, made uncomfortable by the image Charlotte had presented so vividly. A very attractive, but unsettling image of Paul carrying her to his rooms. Not that even he would be physically capable of that; the stairs were far too steep...She pulled herself together and glared at Charlotte.

'Can we stop daydreaming please and re-enter the real world. I do concede that Paul is...interested in me – and I in him. So let's see what happens. I may be leaving Guernsey soon, anyway, if the detective finds That Man. I came here on the assumption it would be for a week max, and it's been three so far. Once I leave, there wouldn't be a reason to return.' As she said this, Louisa felt a heaviness fill her being. A feeling of loss. Could she really face returning to London and never coming back to this magical place? Or Paul?

chapter 19

The following evening Louisa shrugged on her beloved jeans and a pale blue long-sleeved T-shirt; ubiquitous uniform for a pub get-together. As she checked in the mirror, she noticed that the sun had brought her freckles to life, albeit still faintly. By the time summer was in full flow her nose and cheeks would display a light sprinkling that she did not find at all attractive, hiding them as best she could under make-up. The trick was to shade her face as much as possible and use high-level sunblock. Being fair-skinned she did not tan easily and tended to cheat with the fake stuff when it was time for the beach. For now, she dabbed on an extra layer of foundation before grabbing her biker jacket and heading down to an early supper with Charlotte.

An hour later she stood in the hall waiting for Paul. He dashed down the stairs, apologising for keeping her waiting. They walked out to his car and set off towards the west coast. The light was beginning to fade, creating speckled shadows as they drove under the trees. As the sun was setting, the moon appeared above them as a pale translucent disc. Through the open window Louisa heard the twittering of birds as they settled in the trees for the night.

'Did you have a good day?' Paul asked.

'Yes, thanks. I'm really enjoying the cliff walks with Charlotte. We went westwards today and ended up at a charming little bay with a pub. We had to walk through some woods to get there.'

'That would be Portelet Harbour. A nice walk. Did you stop at the Fairy Ring?' he asked with a grin.

She laughed. 'The map said something about that but we didn't notice anything specific. It was a pretty area, though. A bit off the beaten track.'

'Sounds like you're getting to know the island. Not finding it too quiet after London?'

'Nope. I love the quiet. Until I came here I hadn't realised how enervating London was. All that noise and people pushing and shoving on the underground, crammed like sardines into the Tube. No wonder I sometimes felt tired even before I got to work!' She shook her head. 'I was thinking yesterday about when I used to stay with my grandparents in the country; how much freer I felt. And that's how I feel now.'

'Good. Pleased to hear it. I hope that La Folie is playing its part in your rejuvenation?'

'Sure is. I've...I've really enjoyed staying there. But all good things come to an end, don't they? Then it's back to reality,' she said, with a sigh.

'Malc never said how long you were staying.'

She heard the hesitation in his voice and turned to look at him. Could she discern a slight sadness? Would he be sorry to see her leave? Her heart skipped a beat.

'It might not be for much longer; once the detective finds the...man we're looking for, I'll go back to London. I guess, once everything's settled, I'll pick up the pieces of my old life. Or a new version of it. I don't plan to work in a hospital again, for sure.'

'I see.' He looked pensive for a moment, concentrating on the numerous bends on the narrow roads. Louisa had been this way before; she and Charlotte had taken this route to the north of the island a few days previously. She gazed out of the window at the calm sea, now a dark blue as the light faded and the horizon became tinged with gold. Oh, how she would miss these gorgeous sunsets!

'Beautiful, isn't it?' Paul said, seeming to catch her thoughts.

'Yes. We sure don't get sunsets like this in London!'

'Mm. Louisa, have you thought about working here, at La Folie? Our physio is already saying he's a bit stretched, and with the bookings coming in, we'll soon need more therapists.' He flashed her a smile before turning back to the road.

She sat still, barely daring to breathe. Had she heard right? Paul was offering her a job at La Folie?

'I...I don't know. It had never occurred to me. I'd just assumed I'd return to London...' She chewed her thumb, trying to envisage what it might mean. Could she give up her home in London? Possibly. It had been her mother's and held a lot of memories; not all were good. Especially one... But could she live in Guernsey? Another possible. She had grown to love the island in the past few weeks and, after all, it wasn't a million miles away from England. She could fly over regularly, work permitting. Work. Ah! That was the rub. Could she work at La Folie, with Paul not only as her boss but in such close proximity? It would depend...And then there was her father...

'Sorry, looks like I've taken you by surprise. To be honest, I surprised myself!' He laughed. 'I hadn't planned to suggest you worked with us, it kind of popped into my head. As you seem to like Guernsey, I thought...' Paul said, pulling into the car park behind The Rockmount. Switching off the engine, he turned towards her, saying, 'Look, I'm not asking for an answer now, think about it. Okay?' He squeezed her arm.

'Will do. Now, hadn't we better go and meet your gang?' Louisa replied, smiling as she swung herself out of the car, glad of the reprieve.

As they entered the crowded bar, a voice called out from a group in the window.

'Paul, we're over here!'

Louisa recognised the voice as belonging to Ben; the only known face among the sea of strangers. As she and Paul walked across to join them, she recalled something her mother used to say. "Remember, a stranger is just a friend you haven't yet met." Right, time to make more friends!

'Hi Louisa! Glad you could make it. Paul said he was hoping to bring you. How's Malcom?' Ben said, standing up to give her a hug.

'He's a lot better, thanks. I think the rest at La Folie did him the world of good. Naturally, he was spoiled rotten by everyone! I wouldn't have been surprised if he'd stayed longer, but he wanted to get back home.' She smiled up at him. 'Thanks again for all your help last week. And how's your wife and daughter? Both well?'

'Blooming, thanks. Though Eve hasn't yet learned that night time is for sleeping, but it is early days,' Ben said, the shadows under his eyes confirming his words.

Paul went to the bar to get them both a drink and Ben introduced Louisa to the others.

'First, this is Jeanne and her husband Nick. They had their first about eighteen months ago and the second's due in what, four months, isn't it Jeanne?' He asked a dark-haired girl entwined with a man whose deep-blue eyes shone out of a deeply tanned face. Jeanne's stomach was nicely rounded and she gave it a gentle pat.

'Hi Louisa, good to meet you. Yep, the next little Mauger is due in August. Hope it's not too hot!' She moved up to let Louisa sit down and Nick reached across to shake her hand, murmuring 'Hi.'

Ben continued the introductions. 'Next to Nick is his little sis, Colette and her brand new fiancé, Jonathan. Got engaged last weekend.'

Louisa offered her congratulations as they shook hands. Paul returned with the drinks, squeezing in next to Louisa. Within minutes they were all chatting happily; the main topic being what plans they had for the Easter break. The newly-engaged couple rather sheepishly admitted that they had booked a night away in Jersey; they couldn't go away for longer as Colette owned a restaurant and it was a busy weekend. Nick said he was taking his family to Sark for the long-weekend and Ben admitted that he and Nicole would probably aim to catch up on their sleep.

'Tell me about Sark. It's the larger island beyond Herm, right?' Louisa asked.

'Yes it is and it has a totally different atmosphere to Herm, but still laid back. There's no traffic; only cycles, horse and cart or tractors are allowed. It boasts several hotels which have been smartened up recently, although personally I have a soft spot for the old Dixcart.' Nick shrugged. The others nodded their agreement. 'But times change, so…We usually stay onboard our boat but this time we've booked a B&B, to give Jeanne a break,' he said, grinning at his wife, 'and we'll hire cycles to get around. This will be the first time we've taken young Harry and he can sit on the back; much easier than pushing a buggy on the dirt roads. You do get some great views cycling thanks to the steep cliffs, but it can be hard work getting down to the beaches.' He took a sip of his lager. 'You and Paul should come over and we could show you around.'

'Oh, that's kind of you but–' Louisa wondered if Nick thought they were a couple. What had Paul told him?

'Thanks, Nick, but I'm working over Easter. We have a lot of new guests arriving. Pity, would love to see Sark. Perhaps when I can get some time off.' Paul chipped in quickly.

'Sure thing. You can get there in a day trip on the ferry if you're short of time.' Nick turned back to Louisa.

'Have you visited Herm yet? Now, that's my favourite getaway place, isn't it, Jeanne?'

'And mine. We've enjoyed some magical times there, Louisa. The beaches are stunning; you can almost imagine you're in the Bahamas on a good summer's day.'

Jonathan and Colette added their endorsement, saying they were planning to get married in Herm, as had Nick and Jeanne. For a moment Louisa wondered if Paul had put his friends up to extolling the virtues of the islands as an incentive for her to stay.

'I haven't been off Guernsey since I arrived, but that was only three weeks ago. If…if I do stay a while, I'll certainly visit the other islands. They sound irresistible!' She noticed Paul give her a quizzical look, but only smiled. She still needed time to think about his offer and it involved a major life change. And if she continued to feel the way she did for him, it would be impossible for her to stay if the feelings were not reciprocated.

The evening was full of chat and laughter and Louisa felt herself drawn into the camaraderie of the little group. It seemed that Paul had been accepted into their number without question, and now they were pulling her in as well. From what she heard, it was clear that the others had, for the most part, known each other from schooldays, creating a strong bond. It was not until she thought of herself and Paul as the "outsiders", the only non-Guerns, that Louisa reminded herself she had Guernsey-born grandparents. So she was part-Guern too! *Maybe that's why I love it here so much. Perhaps I'm carrying a genetic memory from my ancestors. And why Malcolm was drawn to come here.* As she listened to the conversations going back and forth, it seemed that fate might be playing a part in bringing her here now, at a time when she stood at a crossroads in her life. Showing her that, if she did decide to stay, there was a ready-made group of friends waiting. Definitely a plus, she thought, as they said their goodbyes.

'Enjoy yourself?' Paul asked as they strolled back to his car.

'Yes, I did. They're a great bunch. I can see why you like getting together with them. It was nice of Nick to invite us over at Easter, although–'

'Look, I'm sorry about that. I can see that you might wonder what I've said to him about us.' He stopped and turned to face her. 'I didn't say we were an item or anything,' he said, looking embarrassed. 'Nick must have presumed we were, as you're the first girl I've taken along to meet them. Please don't let it affect your decision on whether or not to work at the centre. If we *were* a couple then working together might not be a good idea.'

Louisa felt her heart lurch. So he wasn't interested in her as a girlfriend. Only as a physio. So why introduce her to his friends? To say she was confused was putting it mildly.

'It's okay. I can see how Nick might have got the wrong idea,' she said, suddenly wanting the evening to end. Not wanting to say anything now, she knew she would refuse the offer of a job. Her hopes for the future had been lifted and dashed in one evening. Once in the car, she closed her eyes, hoping Paul would take the hint and leave her in peace. He did. As soon as they arrived back at La Folie, Louisa muttered a quick good night and escaped to her room to nurse her wounded feelings. Reluctantly deciding it was too late to talk it over with Charlotte, she went to bed and spent a restless night wondering how soon she could leave. Without upsetting her father.

The next morning, having finally drifted off about five, Louisa woke to the sound of knocking on her door.

'Louisa! Are you all right? It's Charlotte.'

Glancing at the clock she saw it was eight thirty. Groaning at the memory of the previous evening, Louisa dragged herself out of bed and padded to the door.

'Hi. I...I overslept. Come in.'

'You look dreadful! Are you ill?' Charlotte said, giving her a hug.

'Not exactly. But I didn't sleep well and I...' she felt herself crumple.

Charlotte guided her to the sofa and sat them both down.

'I smell man trouble. Tell me all,' she said, patting her arm. Louisa obliged. 'Mm, it sounds like Paul isn't being honest with himself. On the one hand, he wants you to meet his friends, which is fine and dandy. And usually indicates the start of a relationship. But then he offers you a job, which would keep you here all right; the downside being it would be difficult to be more than friends. Or at least, in his opinion,' Charlotte said, looking thoughtful. 'It is generally considered to be bad form to mix business with pleasure, so he might be right there. And with the added complication of your being the boss's daughter.' She crossed her legs and leant back.

Louisa digested her words and sighed heavily.

'So what you're saying is that, although he might have some feelings for me, he doesn't expect us to become a couple, just friends. I would find it too difficult to stay here if that's the case. Which means I'll turn the job offer down and go back to London.' Her heart felt leaden at the thought.

'Hey! That's not quite how I put it. What I said was that he *does* have strong feelings for you but hasn't fully acknowledged them. You know what men are like! Always the last to admit to how they feel. As if it would un-man them, or something,' Charlotte said, waving her arms. 'From what you've said, it was a spur of the moment suggestion that you work here. He wants you to stay so you can get to know each other better. Makes sense. But I'd guess he hadn't thought it through until later; feeling obliged to say that a couple couldn't work together. He's trying to be professional but has made a right hash of it. In my not so humble opinion,' she added, with a grin.

Louisa was about to answer when the phone rang. She got up to answer it, mouthing 'sorry' to her friend. It was her father and he sounded excited.

'Louisa, I've just had a call from John Ferguson. He's found out that the old rascal Archie had a son in '48. To a woman called Isabel. And he was named Edward. Isn't that good news?'

'Yes. That would make him about the age of the man I saw. So it could have been him!' Her earlier feelings of woe were replaced by an excitement that they were on track to finding That Man. 'What happens now?'

'John is liaising with some old colleagues from the Met. He needs their co-operation in tracking down this Edward's address, starting with the staff listed with the Underground. Only the police would have the authority to request that information. He did say it could take a few days, however. So we won't need to go over yet.' He went on to ask how she was and what she was up to and Louisa skirted around the truth by saying she was fine. She did not mention Paul.

Replacing the phone she turned to Charlotte and told her what Malcolm had said.

'That's great. Look, I'll have to shoot or I'll be late for yoga. Shall we catch up afterwards? We could take a walk along the cliff, well away from everyone,' Charlotte said, heading for the door.

'Sure. See you later.'

As Louisa padded into the bathroom she thought about what Charlotte had said about Paul and his perceived feelings for her. The bottom line was that it was all conjecture. Neither of them knew with any certainty what Paul actually felt. So, what should she do? Go or stay?

chapter 20

Spring was showing off its technicoloured coat of many colours as Charlotte joined Louisa in the garden. Tulips, massed in rows of red and yellow, stood proudly with their heads opening up to the sun. Daffodils were still in evidence amongst their younger bed-mates of grape hyacinths and irises. Shrubs of viburnum and lilac scented the air. Small pockets of wisteria buds peeped from behind the shelter of green leaves criss-crossing the rear wall of the house. As the women strolled towards the gateway to the cliff path, they stopped to drink in the smells and vibrant colours assailing their senses.

'It's as if the garden has suddenly woken up and put on its best clothes to beguile us,' Charlotte said, admiring the pink and white flowers of a japonica.

'I've always thought spring's the best time for gardens. And whoever planted this one knew what they were doing. My grandmother would have approved,' Louisa said, feeling uplifted in spite of herself.

'I don't possess even a fraction of a green finger, but I do like gardens. Other people's, that is.' After walking through the gate, they linked arms and headed eastwards. For a moment they were quiet, thinking their own thoughts. Then Charlotte asked quietly, 'Have you come to any decision? About the job?'

'I'll turn it down. Nicely, of course. Make up some excuse about needing to be in England, I guess. And if the man is found, I will need to go back–'

'Yes, but not for long. It's your decision, naturally, but if you *were* to stay then Paul might finally wake up to the fact that he fancies you like mad and wants you as a girlfriend. Not a work colleague.'

'Then I'd be out of a job!'

Charlotte raised her eyebrows. 'So? That's not the end of the world, is it? I'm sure you could work somewhere else on the island if necessary. And who's to say you couldn't carry on working together? If you were happy, it wouldn't be a problem.'

Louisa kicked at a stone on the path. 'I know there's some sense in what you say, but in the meantime I'd have to work with Paul while…while hiding my feelings. And if he didn't "wake up" as you put it, I'd be worse off than I am now. It's the thought of rejection…' she felt tears well up and brushed them away, angry with her own weakness.

'Hey, I understand! Don't beat yourself up about it, Louisa. You've been hurt. We both have. You must do what feels right and I promise not to say any more.' Charlotte gave her a hug and Louisa smiled. They continued on their walk, and by tacit agreement, the subject of Paul was left behind.

Louisa knew it was cowardly, but she managed to stay away from Paul that day. She planned to tell him her decision after yoga the next morning, hoping to find a suitable excuse in the meantime. That evening Malcolm was taking her to dinner at La Fregate and she was looking forward to getting away for a few hours. A soothing aromatherapy massage with Lin had helped her to feel calmer and more certain of her decision. As she changed into the smart trouser suit bought the previous week, it occurred to her that Charlotte might be able to recommend other centres, like La Folie, where she could apply for a job. The thought cheered her. Much as she would hate leaving La Folie and Paul, it would be easier if a new life beckoned.

Malcolm hummed to himself. He was pleased with the progress Ferguson had made and had every confidence that, before too long, Edward Blake would be traced and would prove to be the man who had attacked Susan. At this point he was not sure how that could be proved, but in his view that was a minor concern. On top of this, he had received good news from the surgeon. The fracture was healing up nicely and his blood pressure was down. He had been reminded to watch his diet and take gentle exercise, but that was something he was happy to do. As he changed his shirt for dinner, he found himself smiling at the third piece of good news of the day. Paul had phoned to say that the bookings were up, with very few spaces left over the coming months. Glowing reports had been appearing in the media; a couple of their guests had been undercover journalists, returning home to write articles praising La Folie for its "unique ambience, faultless attention to detail and the high standard of the staff", to quote one of them. Malcolm could not be more proud. Although his hotel empire had been much bigger and sold for many millions of dollars, he felt more in tune with La Folie. He liked the thought that the guests were experiencing much more than a mere holiday. They were, according to their feedback, finding a way back to health, on all levels. Letting go outmoded and unhealthy lifestyles and becoming enriched by an inner peace. Just like himself. He never stopped feeling grateful for that chance meeting with Paul, who had opened his eyes to a whole new world. And a chance to show everyone that there was still life in the old dog yet. He grinned at his reflection in the mirror as he adjusted his tie. Paul had also mentioned that he had offered Louisa a job and hoped that Malcolm was okay with that. Of course he was okay with it! It would mean his daughter would be living nearby and they could spend as much time together as they liked. Apparently she had not yet given her answer, but Malcolm shrugged that aside. Why on earth would she say no?

'No? You're going to say no? But why? It's perfect! I thought you'd be happy to stay here, so we could be closer,' Malcolm said, staring at Louisa in disbelief. They were sitting at a table in La Fregate, waiting for their starters, and he had just told her he knew about Paul's offer. She had gone quite pale and stammered that she was planning to say no.

Malcolm was hurt. Did she not want to be near him? Had he overestimated her affection for him?

'It's…it's not that I wouldn't like to be near you. Of course I would. But it's…complicated. It would be so easy to stay and work at the centre, but…I need to find my own way. My working there smacks of nepotism and the other therapists might resent me–'

'Nonsense! It's quite normal in the hospitality business for family to work together. And you're *my* family. If I say it's okay, then to hell with anyone who thinks otherwise.' He could feel his blood pressure rising and took a few deep breaths. Louisa lowered her head, biting her lip. She looked very unhappy, intent on pulling her bread roll to pieces. Malcolm realised he was not helping by pressurising her and softened his tone.

'Look, my dear, I'm not trying to bully you into staying. I'm sorry if I came on too strong. I was so pleased when Paul told me about the job offer and only saw the benefit from my point of view. You, quite rightly, have to satisfy your own needs and desires. Have…have you made other plans?'

She lifted her head, her eyes suspiciously over-bright. 'I'm looking at other centres in the UK, perhaps nearer to my aunt. But I can't make any definite plans while this business with That Man is still unsolved. But if you need my room–'

He grabbed her hand, forcing her to stop murdering the bread roll. 'There's no problem with the room. You can stay as long as it takes. Although, after the call from John, I'm hopeful that it might be quite soon.' He cleared his throat. 'I understand that you want to get on with your life, Louisa, and I respect you for that. But I will miss you when you leave and would hope that you'll keep in touch. Perhaps come over sometime.'

'Of course I'll stay in touch! And I'd be happy to see you whenever I could. My not wanting to…to take a job at La Folie is absolutely not a reflection on my feelings for you. I've grown quite fond of you and enjoy our time together,' she said, managing a smile.

He was reassured. Pleased that it wasn't because of him that she was turning down the job, he began to wonder what *really* lay behind her decision. Something didn't quite add up and he wanted to know what it was. But now wasn't the time to probe; he had to be patient. Not easy but…

★

Louisa, for the first time, was glad when the meal was over and she could scuttle back to La Folie. It had been such a shock when Malcolm announced that he was looking forward to seeing her become a new member of staff. Damn Paul! She thought, driving home. He had no right to say anything to her father before she had given him her answer. *Men! Who do they think they are, making decisions for us?* Her initial shock had given way to anger, seething slowly inside through what had seemed an endless meal. And Malcolm's initial response hadn't helped. Another man who liked to take charge – as he had with her mother all those years ago. But he had, at least, backtracked from that first reaction and they had agreed not to discuss it further. Thinking about that, she allowed her breathing to slow, letting the anger ease. It hadn't been Malcolm's fault; it was Paul's. He was guilty of making her feel he was interested in having a relationship with her, and then promptly sabotaging the chance by offering her a job instead! As she pulled into the drive she remembered what her father had said about family working together. That was all well and good, she conceded, but didn't apply to working with someone who apparently didn't reciprocate your feelings for them. Switching off the engine, Louisa got out of the car and headed inside, hoping she could return to her room unnoticed. She was in no mood to talk to anyone. She was in luck and shut the door behind her with relief. Next stop: Paul.

At breakfast the following morning, Louisa described to Charlotte what had happened.

'Oh dear, that's made things a tad awkward, hasn't it? I assume you haven't spoken to Paul yet?'

She shook her head. 'No, I'm planning to corner him after yoga. Malcolm agreed not to speak to him before I had the chance. I'll have to make light of it, I suppose, as I don't want him knowing what my true feelings are.' She let out a groan. 'Everything would have been fine if he hadn't offered me the blooming job!'

Charlotte sipped her tea. 'That's not strictly true, is it? With your departure growing more imminent, you two would have had hardly any time to explore your feelings for each other – meaning you could have left without anything being said. I do agree Paul has messed up, but there's no easy answer is there? If you two are meant to be together, then...' she waved her arms like a magician pulling a rabbit out of a hat.

Louisa could not help but smile. 'So we leave it up to fate, do we?'

'I didn't say that exactly. One can always give fate a helping hand,' Charlotte grinned. 'Now, come on or we'll be late. And that would not do, would it?'

Paul raised his eyebrows when they walked in and asked why she had missed the previous day's session. Louisa had mumbled something about over-sleeping and moved off quickly. He looked puzzled but before he could say anything, was cornered by another guest asking him a question. Charlotte chose a spot further back than normal, for which Louisa was grateful.

Once the session was over, Louisa waited until the others had left before approaching Paul.

'Um, Paul, about that offer of a job. I…I'm afraid the answer's no. Tempting as it is, I really do need to…to be nearer my aunt. But thank you, anyway.' She turned to go but he held onto her wrist.

'Hey, what's wrong? You seemed quite keen on the idea the other evening. You said how much you liked it here. Loved it, in fact.' His eyes bored into hers and she felt a painful lump in her throat. God, it was hard to lie to him!

'I do love it here. But that doesn't mean it's the right place for me to live. I…I have another life…family in England. But I'll be coming over to see Malcolm when I can. I…I appreciate your offer, Paul. Now, I must dash as I have a session booked.'

She almost ran out of the room before he could reply. But she had time to notice the look of hurt on his face. Biting her lips, she rushed off to find Nadine to ask if any therapist was free. She was in luck, the reflexologist could slot in a half-hour if she hurried. Louisa smiled her thanks and set off. Reflexology, like massage, usually calmed her so it was a fortuitous choice. She didn't think it would help with a breaking heart, though.

The next few days leading up to Easter were filled with a mixture of therapy sessions, swimming and walks or drives with Charlotte. Louisa wanted to spend as much time with her friend as possible, dreading her leaving on Easter Monday. It also meant that she was out a great deal, and less likely to bump into Paul. Somehow she managed to get through the yoga sessions, the benefit outweighing the heaviness in her heart. Just. On Thursday morning she and Charlotte set off on another trip to St Peter Port. The sky was a dull slate and the sun was hiding like a sulky child. They had decided a spot of browsing around the shops, followed by a visit to Victor Hugo's house would be the perfect way to avoid any threatening rain.

'I can hardly spend a few weeks here and not visit Hugo's house, can I? I'm a publisher, for heaven's sake! And I've heard it's quite something: it's been left exactly as he left it. You don't mind going, do you?' Charlotte asked as Louisa switched on the engine.

'Not at all. I'd love to see it. Although I haven't read his books, I loved Les Miserables on the stage. I am not adverse to a spot of culture, you know,' she said, putting on a plummy accent.

Charlotte grinned. 'Touché!'

The plan was shopping first as Hauteville House, Hugo's old home, was not open until midday. Nadine had suggested they park near the marina while shopping and then drive up Cornet Street towards Hauteville. It proved good advice, as by the time they had explored previously missed shops and relaxed over a cappuccino, their parking clock had expired. They both agreed that free parking on Guernsey was a welcome change after London. Even if it did mean moving the car.

They found a spot a reasonable walk from Hauteville House and joined the queue gathered on the front steps of the white stuccoed house. It stood out as being foreign as the French flag flew proudly above the front door. Once inside and having obtained a tour guide, the reason for the flag became clear. The property was preserved by the City of Paris in honour of one of their most famous sons. Even the guide was French, however her English was impeccable.

Louisa and Charlotte spent most of the tour open-mouthed at the décor and furnishings. The guide informed them that both the house and garden had been designed by Hugo, who had apparently wanted a medieval, slightly Gothic look. Heavy dark oak furniture fought with painted ceilings and damask lined rooms to be noticed.

'Wow! I hadn't expected anything like this,' Charlotte whispered to Louisa as they stood in a room lined with red damask and topped with a carved, decorated ceiling. 'One tends to think of writers living in rather humble abodes, even when they were as successful as Hugo. But he obviously revelled in opulence.' She threw her arms wide.

Louisa nodded. 'Not only that, but according to this guide book, he kept a mistress for fifty years, and she followed him here when he was exiled from France. Even though his wife and children lived here. He sounds quite a character! I might consider reading one of his books. In English, naturally,' she said, chuckling.

They continued upstairs, admiring the Crystal Room where Hugo wrote his books, and the glazed conservatory perched up high and offering wonderful views across from Castle Cornet and out to the islands.

'He would have been looking out towards France whenever he was up here. It's not that far away,' Charlotte said, gazing out of the window. 'Must have been strange for Hugo. He was here for fifteen years before he returned to Paris. By all accounts he fell in love with Guernsey and the people and was sad to leave.'

'Mm. I can relate to that and I've only been here a few weeks!' Louisa said, wistfully.

Charlotte grabbed her arm. 'Come on, let's go down to the garden before it rains. It looks nearly as lovely as La Folie's. And don't get maudlin! You might not have to leave. Or perhaps only for a little while.'

Louisa was not convinced but gave in to her friend. She might as well enjoy what the island had to offer while she could. And the garden did look beautiful.

They were both in reflective mood as they drove back to La Folie. Whenever Louisa glanced across at Charlotte she seemed deep in thought, as if she were miles away.

'Penny for them,' she said as they neared the airport.

'Mm? Oh, my thoughts! Well, if you must know I was thinking that I'm going to make some changes when I return home. Seeing Victor Hugo's house, with his wonderful writing room and the views, has reminded me of my old desire to write. And really, there's no reason why I can't do it. I could cut back my hours in the office and work more from home, freeing up time to write my own book, not just publish other people's.'

'That's a great idea! What would you write? Fiction or non-fiction?'

'Definitely fiction. I've been toying with an idea based on real historical characters. My degree was in history so I'm au fait with historical research. I used to love it at uni and considered staying on for my post-graduate degree. But…life got in the way,' Charlotte said, shrugging.

'Well, at least you could be your own publisher.'

'Actually, I couldn't. We only publish non-fiction. It's a small independent publisher, founded by my grandfather. I inherited it from my father and have been fulfilling the role of editor ever since. Interesting work, but not as fulfilling as writing something myself.' Charlotte turned to

Louisa who glanced across to her. 'Coming here has given me the chance to re-assess my options. I no longer want to be that woman who inherited a publishing company. I want to achieve something for myself. Something I can be proud of.'

Louisa smiled. 'You show 'em, girl! Now, tell me a bit more about your idea for a novel...'

Easter Friday heralded the arrival of several new guests, bringing the centre up to full capacity. Whenever Louisa passed Nadine in reception she seemed to be either signing in new people or arranging therapy appointments. She still had time to give her a smile and a cheeky wink. Louisa smiled in return before making her way to wherever she was meant to be. In spite of the new arrivals, no part of the house was crowded and she was able to keep up her swimming. It looked as if the age range was reducing: no longer were the majority of guests in their autumn years as thirty-and forty-somethings, sporting the latest fashions and carrying designer-label bags, formed the new intake. Louisa was glad; if she were to be here for a while it would be nice to be around people more her own age. As she ploughed up and down the pool the thought of Charlotte disappearing on Monday left her feeling low. They had so much enjoyed their day together that they planned to take a trip to Sark on Sunday. Charlotte had therapies booked for Saturday and Monday and Louisa planned to spend time with Malcolm. Just as she thought about this, she spotted Charlotte talking to Malcolm outside the pool enclosure. He looked as if he was coming in for a swim when Charlotte must have spotted him. Louisa idly wondered what they were talking about before she pulled herself out of the pool. She wanted a few minutes in the steam room before continuing with her swim.

Returning, she saw Malcolm was in the pool and Charlotte had disappeared. She slipped in to join him and they paced each other for a few lengths before she left for a hot stone massage. They arranged to see each other for lunch on Saturday, Malcolm offering to pick her up and drive to a restaurant he wanted to try.

As she was about to turn into the corridor leading to the massage room, Paul appeared by her side.

'Hi, stranger. Have you been avoiding me? Haven't seen you around much this week.' He gave her a searching look.

'No, of course not. I've…been busy. Charlotte and I have been out and about, making the most of our time together. You know she's leaving on Monday?'

He nodded. 'Yes. You've become good friends then. I'm pleased. But I hoped that you and I could go out for a drink sometime. After the weekend, perhaps?'

'Oh, right. Thanks. I'll let you know. Look, I'll be late for my massage, can we talk later? Bye.' She sped off, glad of the excuse to get away. Why on earth did Paul want to go out for a drink? He knew she wasn't staying on the island, so what was the point? And, more importantly, how was she going to say no?

chapter 21

Fortunately for Louisa, Paul was tied up with new guests after yoga and she was able to slip away, accompanied by a grinning Charlotte, without having to talk to him.

'That was lucky! But you're going to have to speak to him sometime. The man's asked you out and it's rude to keep him waiting,' Charlotte said, trying to sound severe.

'I know, I know. But he did say not until after the weekend so…' she said, trying to make excuses for herself.

'Okay. I'm off, catch you later, right? Have a nice lunch with your father.'

Charlotte walked away and Louisa returned to her room to change. She planned to swim then take a cliff walk before lunch. The concentrated exercise was paying off. She was no longer as depressed as when she arrived, although the thought of Paul threatened her peace of mind. Charlotte had agreed to give her a list of health centres to approach once she was back in London. It was time to move on.

Malcolm took them along winding roads into the hinterland of the west coast. 'I've heard about a quaint old place in St Saviours with a good restaurant that grows a lot of herbs and vegetables. Thought it might be fun to check out. The gardens are lovely, I'm told, and surrounded by woods.'

'Sounds good. Are you working your way around all the island eateries? In the name of research?'

Malcolm chuckled. 'It's a nice idea but might not be approved of by my doctor. But it's good to see what's on offer locally, while exploring the island. And it's a lot more fun with company,' he said, patting her hand.

He steered the car around a steep bend and pulled into the car park. Louisa saw that the sign over the front door, *Auberge du Val,* was nearly obliterated by the foliage covering the facade. Malcolm took the last parking place, commenting that it was lucky he had booked.

Although tables were set out in the garden, Malcolm admitted that he preferred to eat inside and they were shown to a table in the beamed restaurant. After choosing their food they slipped into an easy conversation and the time passed pleasantly. They both commented on how good the food was and, once they finished, went out to the garden to admire the herbs.

'This is how I see it developing at La Folie,' Malcolm said as they walked around the garden. 'As I told you, I want to grow our own herbs as well as vegetables and I'm planning to build a small greenhouse for less hardy specimens. It'll take time to be as established as this one is, but worth it, don't you think?'

'Yes. The more home-grown produce the better. Particularly as it's organic. Chef seems pretty dedicated to providing the best ingredients; he told us he won't use anything that isn't organic. Probably why the food tastes so fantastic. Charlotte was particularly impressed and plans to spread the word when she's back home,' she replied, sneakily rubbing lavender stalks through her hands.

Malcolm nodded, looking pleased, before continuing his walk.

After being dropped off at La Folie, Louisa went in search of Paul. She could put it off no longer. She found him in his office and it was hard meeting those smiling blue eyes with her own.

'Louisa! Did you have a good lunch with Malc?' Paul looked so pleased to see her that her heart sank.

'Yes, thanks. It…was great. Paul, about that offer of a drink. I…I think it's better if I say no. I'll be leaving any day now and we might not meet again for ages. If at all, so…' she trailed off, not sure what more to say.

He frowned. 'I see. Are you saying we can't be friends? I got the impression we hit it off, but if I was wrong–'

'It's not that I don't like you, Paul. But it's clear there can't be anything between us so…' she shrugged, knowing she was digging herself into a bigger hole with every word.

Paul looked as if he was about to reply when the phone rang and his attention shifted. Cowardly, she took the opportunity to mouth 'sorry', and left. *Right, you've burnt your bridges now, girl. He'll be glad to see the back of you.* The thoughts whirled around her head as she sought the safety of her room. Needing a diversion, she rang her aunt for a lengthy chat.

As the ferry to Sark was at ten on Sunday morning, Louisa and Charlotte were obliged to skip yoga, enabling time for a leisurely breakfast. Louisa was happy not having to face Paul.

The weather was perfect. Hot for April and it looked set to stay sunny all day. They joined a happy throng of day-trippers queuing for the ferry at White Rock and waited patiently until they were allowed to embark. While most of the passengers went inside, Louisa and Charlotte stayed on deck, keen not to miss anything.

'This is fun! It's been ages since I took a boat trip and felt the sea breeze on my face. We should finish the day with glowing cheeks,' Charlotte said, lifting her face towards the sun, eyes closed.

'Good thing we packed the sun-cream then! I'll have to watch it or my dratted freckles will come out in their thousands,' Louisa replied, sighing. She reached into her bag for the high-factor sun block.

'There's nothing wrong with freckles. Some of my friends have them and their menfolk think they're cute, so there.' Charlotte opened her eyes as the boat moved out of the harbour and past Castle Cornet. 'Isn't this view to die for? I do think one gets a different perspective looking back on a place, don't you? We've been up and down those little streets of St Peter Port a few times and thought we knew it. But now we can see the whole picture and it looks so…so much more than streets full of shops. And so steep!' They both gazed back towards the harbour and the buildings now facing them. A mixture of white, cream and granite, they rose up from the seafront; a mass of windows glinting in the sun.

'It's as if we're the ones being observed. All those windows are like eyes!' exclaimed Charlotte.

'Mm. It's quite something, seeing the town rising up in tiers towards those towers on the skyline. I wonder what they are? Look, now we're pulling away, you can see the cliff walk leading to the bluebell woods. And over there…' Louisa continued pointing out places they had visited, Charlotte vying to compete with her own choices.

Within moments the town was left behind and, with one accord, they turned to face their destination.

'It looks so far away! No wonder it will take about an hour to reach it. That tiny island of Herm is just a skip and a jump away by comparison. Looks pretty, too. Still, I'm told Sark is also lovely and we'll be able to cycle around it. Something I wouldn't consider trying in London, for sure! Mind you, I don't want to cycle for five hours. We'll need to find other ways to amuse ourselves that aren't as energetic,' Louisa said, taking in the island her Guernsey friends seemed to think was magical. Thinking of them made her wonder if she would bump into Jeanne and Nick in Sark.

'No problem. If all else fails we'll retreat to one of the pubs and sink a bottle or two. It's my last full day and I intend to make the most of it,' Charlotte said, throwing out her arms, as if to embrace all and everyone around.

Louisa grinned. 'A bottle or two will play havoc with your avowed intent to keep to Chef's diet plan. And you're looking so fab, Charlotte. You must have lost a few more pounds this past week.'

'Why, thank you, kind lady! I lost five pounds and my clothes fit much better now. Chef didn't say I had to avoid alcohol, just drink in moderation. I'll drink plenty of water and the cycling will help. Um, it's becoming a little chilly now. Shall we go below decks?'

They settled themselves on window seats for the remainder of the journey. Small motor cruisers and speed boats rode the waves around the ferry, all heading towards Sark. Louisa and Charlotte chatted quietly amidst the hub of their fellow passengers. Small children ran around excitedly, until their parents finally called a halt, settling them on their laps with picture books. The ferry's engine slowed as they approached the harbour, distinguished by a high granite and concrete wall, offering protection and shelter to the few boats at anchor. The boat moored alongside granite steps and the crew gave a hand to the disembarking passengers. Parents, collecting their respective children and bags, strode off, talking excitedly about their plans for the day. Louisa and Charlotte followed, keeping clear of the crab and lobster pots piled on the wall's edge. The way out was through a short tunnel cut into the granite cliff. Louisa clutched a copy of a short guide to Sark, which informed her that the steep hill ahead was the only route up to the village centre and the rest of the island. Awaiting them was a tractor bus, known locally as the "toast rack", according to the guide.

The choice being either to walk or take the bus, the two of them decided the bus might be quicker. Possibly. It was simply comprised of a tractor pulling an open-sided cart lined with rows of basic seats.

Charlotte grinned. 'This will be a new experience! We can walk down on the way back. That's if our legs are still functioning after cycling around the island.'

Once the bus was full, the tractor began its slow progress up the kilometre of hill. They passed a number of fellow travellers making their way towards the adjoining woodland path. Colour abounded: primroses, thrift, bluebells and wild garlic jostled for space on the grassy banks and the trees showed off their new leaves. Although the ride was bumpy, there was plenty to admire, breathing in the heady scents wafting on the slight breeze.

Once at the top, they found themselves at the start of the island village. Dirt roads, lined with painted buildings reminiscent of a bygone age, led off in different directions. After collecting their cycles they set off along what was grandly named The Avenue. Their destination was Little Sark, an even smaller island at the opposite end of big Sark, connected by a narrow isthmus, known as La Coupee. They had booked a table for lunch at La Sablonnerie Hotel, suggested to them by Malcolm. Apparently no hotel or restaurant was off his radar.

'This is heavenly. I can't believe how peaceful it is after the arrival of so many people. And it makes Guernsey seem positively hectic in comparison,' Louisa remarked, as they cycled along quiet country lanes bordered by open fields. Blackthorn and hawthorn blossom added colour to the hedgerows.

'You're right. I haven't cycled in England since I was a child, the roads became so clogged. And London…! Well. But I'm enjoying this. Thanks for suggesting we came here.'

They passed a few walkers and a horse-drawn carriage full of excited tourists on the way, but by way of "traffic" it was minimal. Charlotte remarked on the absence of noise. All that could be heard was the cawing of seabirds wheeling overhead.

'It looks as if we're heading for the ends of the Earth,' said Louisa, giggling. They were approaching La Coupee, freewheeling down a slight hill. 'Let's stop for a proper look before we go over.'

Leaning their cycles against the railings, they looked down from their eighty metre high vantage point.

'Wow! What a view!' exclaimed Louisa, taking in not only the small bay beneath her, but various rocky outcrops and, in the distance, Guernsey.

'It's very pretty, isn't it? And there's an aroma of coconut coming from somewhere,' said Charlotte, sniffing the air.

'I think it must be from the yellow gorse flowers. See? There's loads round here. Oh, and look! I think those are puffins.' She pointed to some black and white birds clinging to the cliff face beneath them.

After spending a few minutes absorbing the sights and smells surrounding them, they pushed their bikes across La Coupee, sharing greetings with a family coming the other way. The hotel was roughly in the centre of Little Sark, and it was not long before they wheeled their bikes into the courtyard.

The restaurant buzzed. Families were out in force for their Easter Sunday lunch and it had been a good idea to book. They were shown to their table by a smiling waitress and left to peruse the menus. The white painted granite walls helped the room to feel cool after the heat of the sun.

Louisa looked around at the deep red furnishings against the dark wood of the furniture.

'Very olde worlde! But cosy. I feel as if I've stepped into another age, don't you?'

Charlotte looked up from her menu and smiled. 'A bit. But the whole island seems as if it's stuck in a time warp. Which is no bad thing, in my book. There's too much rushing around these days. I'm really looking forward to working from home more when I start my writing. But research comes first, which means visits to the British Library. Once I've restructured my work in the office, I'll be raring to go.' She rubbed her hands together, looking like a child anticipating Christmas.

They ordered a bottle of chilled Pinot Grigio to accompany their roasted sea scallops and fresh local vegetables. And a jug of water to keep them hydrated. They finished the meal with a light crème brûlée topped with assorted fruit.

'That was delicious! Your father knows a good restaurant when he sees one. Please do thank him for me if I don't happen to see him before I leave.'

'Of course,' Louisa said, sipping her wine. So far it had been a perfect day and she was falling in love with Sark the way she had with Guernsey. Paradoxically, it wasn't entirely a good feeling. In days she was likely to be heading back to England and a new, unknown life, leaving these islands behind for the foreseeable future. Possibly only returning briefly to see her father. She felt a sense of loss; whether for the place or a particular person, she didn't allow herself to dwell.

'You all right, Louisa? For a moment there you looked so sad...' Charlotte said, touching her hand.

'Oh, it's me being silly. I'm going to miss Guernsey, and Sark is lovely and...and there's Paul.' She took a deep breath, swallowing the lump in her throat.

'Hey, there's still a chance it will work out with Paul. It's not as if you have no connections here. You'll be back to see Malcolm, and Paul will be around too. Think of it as a slight delay in getting together. If you don't have to start a new job straight away, why not return once you've identified the burglar? Assuming there is enough evidence to charge him, of course.'

Louisa frowned. 'I don't need to get a job immediately as I have an income from the business, but I feel uncomfortable doing nothing. Mum worked hard all her life and she expected me to do the same. Which is fine by me; I love my work.' She bit her thumb. 'There might be a problem with evidence against That Man. No prints or DNA were found at Mum's, so even if I can identify him, that wouldn't be enough. Not according to the detective. We have to find something else that puts him at the scene.' Louisa sighed, wishing once again that it was all a horrible nightmare: she would wake up to find everything was as it used to be, her mother still alive.

'Oh, Louisa, that's tough. But I'm sure Malcolm and the detective won't stop until the guilty man is brought to justice. The bottom line is you might need to be in London for a while. Is that what bothers you?'

'Yes, I guess. You know, "out of sight, out of mind" and all that. Paul could well have forgotten me if I'm away for weeks. Or worse, months.'

'If he did, then he wasn't right for you. Have faith! Now,' she added briskly, 'come on and let's stop being maudlin and enjoy ourselves. We're on a heavenly island, the sun's shining and I want to make the most of it. Back to the grindstone for me on Tuesday,' Charlotte said, pulling a face.

After they paid the bill, they were on the way outside when a voice called out 'Louisa! Over here!'

She turned round to see a couple in the corner behind where she had been sitting.

'Hi Jeanne, Nick. How nice to see you,' Louisa said, walking back, Charlotte by her side.

Next to Jeanne was a high chair holding a dark-haired, grinning little boy with food smeared over his face. 'This must be Harry. Isn't he like you, Nick?' Louisa smiled, before introducing Charlotte to the couple.

'I didn't recognise you from the back,' explained Jeanne. 'It's good to see you. I didn't think you were coming over. Is Paul working?'

'Yes, I…I think so. Charlotte is going home tomorrow and I will be leaving soon, so we thought it would be a good opportunity to see Sark. Are you having a good weekend?'

Nick's broad smile said it all. 'Great, thanks. It's been fun introducing this little guy to cycling. He's taken to it like a duck to water, hasn't he, darling?'

Jeanne laughed. 'Yes. He keeps shouting out more, more, when we go downhill. A bit of a speed fiend, is Harry.' She popped a kiss on his head before cleaning his face with a wet wipe. 'Look, we were about to go outside for our coffee so that Harry can run around a bit. How about joining us?'

Louisa checked with Charlotte who was happy to agree and they found a table in the garden. Not having had coffee, they ordered theirs with the others. Nick took Harry off to the lawn to play.

The girls chatted while waiting for their drinks and when it came out that Jeanne was an author, she and Charlotte fell into an animated discussion about books and publishing. Nick returned with Harry and sat next to Louisa.

'Will he let me hold him?' she asked Nick, looking at Harry.

'Sure. Come on, Harry, say hello to the nice lady.'

Harry gazed solemnly at her, his dark blue eyes taking her in. Then a smile lit up his face and he reached out his arms. Louisa lifted him onto her lap and said hello.

Harry mumbled ''ello' before using his fingers to explore her face. 'He's lovely, Nick. Do you want another boy or a girl next time?'

'Don't mind. But a girl would be nice for Jeanne. Every woman wants a daughter, don't they?'

'I guess. I haven't thought that far ahead. Need to find a partner first!'

Nick frowned. 'I thought that you and Paul…'

She shook her head. 'No, we…we're just friends. We haven't been out together, apart from that night we met you and the others. I have to return to England soon so…' she shrugged.

'Odd. I could have sworn Paul told me the evening we met that you were staying on. And he hoped to be seeing a lot more of you. As in, he fancied you.' Nick's forehead was creased in thought. 'Sorry, must have got my wires crossed. No harm done, I hope?'

Louisa felt light-headed. 'No, no of course not.'

chapter 22

Somehow Louisa managed to keep up a conversation with her new friends. It helped that Charlotte and Jeanne had so much to talk about that they did not appear to notice that Louisa said little. Nick, after finishing his coffee, took his son off to run around the garden. Eventually Louisa announced that if she and Charlotte wanted to see more of Sark, they needed to leave.

Goodbyes were shared and Louisa and Charlotte retrieved their bikes to head back over La Coupee. The others were remaining to explore Little Sark. Once back at the point where they needed to dismount, Louisa told her friend what Nick had said.

Charlotte's eyes opened wide. 'Now that *is* interesting! I told you Paul was keen on you. But then he realised that by offering you a job it might complicate a relationship. Soooo, what are you going to do, now?'

'What can I do? It's up to Paul to say something. I'm not supposed to know how he feels. That's assuming Nick got it right. You know what men are like for not listening properly.'

'Ah, that's only when a woman is talking to them. When it's a man, they're all ears. No, I think we can safely assume Nick is telling you the truth. But, as to what *you* can do, I'm not sure. Remember what I said earlier. It might be that you two don't get together just yet, but it now looks even more likely that you will. One day.'

Louisa hoped her friend was right and she smiled, determined to enjoy the rest of their trip.

They managed to take a brief look at a few of the sights, including La Seigneurie, the manor house belonging to the Seigneur, the 'feudal owner' of Sark. Until a few months previously, the island had been the last feudal state in Europe. Now it possessed a more democratic government.

With a total area of two square miles, it did not take long to cycle from one point to another and they just had time to explore the quaint shops in The Avenue before returning the bikes to the hire shop. Then it was time to walk down to Maseline Harbour to catch the ferry. The woodland walk proved a fitting end to their stay, scented flowers accompanying their downward steps. The both agreed it was an improvement on the bus.

Sitting on the harbour wall, Charlotte stretched her arms. 'What a day! A brilliant end to my time here. Can't wait for my next trip, hopefully in September. You've enjoyed yourself, haven't you? And not too many new freckles,' she said with a smile.

Louisa's hands went automatically up to her face. 'I did pile on the sun-cream, but I think I still caught the sun. It's been a wonderful day, yes. Thanks for everything, Charlotte. I'm going to miss having you around.'

'I'll miss you as well. You made it much more fun for me, I was becoming too much of a hermit before you arrived. When you get back to London, give me a ring and we can meet up. And I will want to know the latest news from your detective. And any other, er, interesting developments,' she said, raising an eyebrow.

'Hmm, I doubt there'll be anything else to report, but I'd love to see you.'

They watched as the ferry manoeuvred its way to the harbour steps. There only looked to be a few passengers arriving, while there was a long queue to depart.

'It's odd, but for the first time ever, I'm not mad about returning home. Usually, whenever I've been away on holiday, I can't wait to get back and stuck into work. But this time, it's going to be a wrench. The islands have seduced me. Or perhaps it's that stuff they put in our juice at La Folie!' Charlotte said, smiling.

Louisa grinned at her friend. 'Maybe. But remember you've got a book to write and I'll be rooting for you. It's the beginning of an exciting new chapter in your life. If you'll excuse the pun!' Laughing, they dropped down from their perch to join the queue.

As Louisa drove her friend to the airport the following afternoon they were both quiet. Charlotte insisted that Louisa not wait around so, after a hug, they parted and Louisa returned to La Folie, feeling empty inside. She had always hated goodbyes, particularly if she was the one left behind. Giving herself a talking-to, Louisa reminded herself she would be seeing Charlotte again soon and, in the meantime, could spend time with Malcolm. In fact she was spending that evening with him. He had invited her to a jazz concert at St James Hall in St Peter Port, preceded by dinner in town. She was looking forward to it, aware that she had not spent much time with him the past week. Not that Malcolm had complained. He wore his independence on his sleeve, always reiterating that he was used to going it alone. Driving back now, Louisa felt how sad that was and determined to play a bigger role in his life. It would not be a hardship, he was good company with plenty of stories to tell.

With a couple of hours to kill before Malcolm collected her, Louisa headed for the pool. As she counted the lengths, her mind flitted to the problem of Paul. What to do? She and Charlotte had attended the yoga class that morning and it was the first time she had seen Paul since turning him down for a drink. And finding out that he did fancy her after all. She had not known how to react to him, but Charlotte had taken over, gushing to him how much she had enjoyed the yoga and how much she would look forward to returning. Paul had tried to catch Louisa's eye when there was a brief break in Charlotte's flow, but she had pretended not to notice. *Oh, God, I'm such a coward! And I won't have Charlotte here to help me now, so I'll have to speak to him. Although what is there to say? "Oh, hi Paul, I hear you really fancy me. So, shall we go out on a date?"* The thought caused her to choke on a mouthful of water, and she had to lean onto the side of the pool until the coughing stopped. Waving away an assistant who had come to see if she was all right, Louisa carried on with her swim. She would think about Paul later.

'Right, where are we going on our magical mystery restaurant tour?' Louisa asked, grinning. Malcolm had just started the engine and turned to face her, laughing.

'Somewhere you'll like, I promise. It's a hotel around the corner from St James and I stayed there when I first came to Guernsey, checking out La Folie. We'll only have time for a main course so it's ideal.'

The car purred down the drive and Louisa relaxed into the leather seat, looking forward to good food and jazz. She had been to a few jazz sessions in pubs with friends, but never to a concert with top notch artists. Malcolm assured her she was in for a treat, having heard this quartet play at a major festival. As they made their way into St Peter Port she told him how much she and Charlotte had enjoyed Sark.

'And you were spot on with that restaurant. We had a lovely meal and even met a couple Paul had introduced me to the other evening. They were there for the weekend and looked pretty chilled. But that's what seems to happen in the islands. Not exactly like the Mediterranean countries, but there does seem to be a sense of *mañana* here. Guess there might be a downside to it.'

Malcolm chuckled. 'There sure is, when you're trying to get a property renovated and opened on time! It was lucky a lot of the work went on in the winter or the builders might have been tempted to hop in their boats and go sailing. The guys worked incredibly hard when on site, but they didn't quite agree with my sense of urgency.' He glanced towards her. 'Sounds like you're enjoying the lifestyle. Could do a lot worse.'

She gave a non-committal grunt, not wanting to get drawn into an argument about her taking the job. It seemed that her father felt the same, as he promptly changed the subject to the less controversial one of her taste in music.

The next morning found the island covered in a light mist. As Louisa threw back the bedroom curtains she could see little beyond the garden. She shivered, although not from cold. There was an eeriness about the mist that she found unsettling. After the bright sunshine of the past few days it felt as if she had woken up in another world. One not as friendly. She knew it was silly, but she could not shake off an air of foreboding. The only thing she really dreaded at this point was confronting Paul at yoga without Charlotte at her side. It was lucky for her friend that she had left yesterday; the mist would prevent flights until it lifted.

Feeling low, Louisa stood under the shower, hoping the hot water would wash away her negative thoughts. It was partly successful: by the time she pulled on her leggings and T-shirt her mood had lifted enough to view the prospect of coming face to face with Paul with less dread.

'Morning, Louisa. Did you enjoy the jazz last night?'

She cleared her throat. 'Mm, yes thanks. How did you…?'

Paul, looking his usual breezy self, grinned. 'Malc told me he was taking you. I hadn't realised you were a fan.'

'I've been to a few gigs, that's all. But this was in a different league and we...both thought it was very good.' She went to move to a place near the back but Paul took her arm, saying he wanted her to sit by a new guest who had not done any yoga before. She could not very well refuse, and ended up being introduced to a woman in her fifties who did look as if she was regretting coming along. Louisa smiled and introduced herself, assuring the other woman that it had been a new experience for her only a few weeks ago. The woman, giving her name as Wendy, seemed to relax and they settled on their mats together ready for Paul to make a start.

After the session Wendy went to chat to Paul. It looked as if he had made another convert, Louisa thought, flashing him a quick smile as she left. At least they could be friends, even though nothing had been resolved. As she passed through the hall, Nadine called to her.

'Louisa! Your father's been trying to phone you. Could you ring him back, please? He said it's important.'

'Sure, will do. Thanks.' Louisa bit her lip as she ran up the stairs. *Surely he's not ill? No, he would ring the doctor not me.* Not entirely convinced all was well, once in her room she dialled Malcolm's number.

He answered on the first ring. 'Louisa! Glad you got the message,' he said, sounding in good spirits, much to her relief. 'I've had a call from John Ferguson to say he's traced an Edward Blake who works for the London Underground.'

'Brilliant! That was quick. Has...has he seen him yet?' Louisa's heart was pounding.

Her father coughed. 'Yes, he went to the address given to him by his police colleagues and saw him leaving the house. He was able to take a photo and he's compared it to the e-fit and he thinks it's a good match. But to make sure, he's emailing it to me so you can see for yourself. If you let me have your email address I'll forward it as soon as I receive it. Should only be a few minutes. You did say you have your laptop with you?'

'Yes, yes I have.' She gave her father the address before hanging up and then switched on her laptop. Nadine had given her the Wi-Fi access code previously so that she could check her emails, something prohibited for the other guests. Louisa's palms began to sweat as she waited impatiently for the computer to connect to the internet and her email account. The screen filled with emails not yet checked, but none were more recent than the previous day. Taking calming breaths to slow the ever-faster heart rate, she spotted it – an email from Malcolm Roget with an attachment. Ignoring the brief message from John, she opened the file and in a moment found herself staring at the full-length photo of the man known as Edward Blake.

chapter 23

The insistent ring of the phone finally grabbed her attention.

'Is it him?' Malcolm barked.

'Yes, it is. Or at least as much as I can be sure given…Did John say if he has a limp?'

She heard a release of breath. 'He does. The word is he's had it since birth; something went wrong when he was born. John got the info from his Met colleagues who were granted access to the personnel files. He's shared our leads with them and they're aware there's another outstanding crime, linked to this man's father, my cousin.'

Louisa had been so wrapped up in the search for her mother's killer that she had forgotten Malcolm also wanted to find the man who killed *his* father. She felt a pang of remorse. They were linked by a painful history.

'What happens now?' she asked, pulling herself together.

'We must fly over tomorrow. The mist should clear later today and hopefully the flights will be back to normal by then. After we meet with John he can take you to see this guy in the flesh. Unseen of course!' he added hastily as she gasped. 'It's the only way to be sure; you understand that, don't you, Louisa?' His voice sounded more gentle.

'Yes, yes of course. I've always realised I'd have to see him again at some point. Are you sure you're okay to travel and follow this through? I can always go alone–'

'I'm fine. Never better. The doctor's said I'm making a faster recovery than expected, so there's nothing more to be said. I certainly wouldn't want you to face this alone, my dear. It's the least I can do: for you and your mother.'

She wiped away the tear threatening to slide down her cheek. *Yes, this was all for Mum. And he's right, he should be there. Just hope he's as fit as he says he is.*

'All right. You can stay at my house, there's plenty of room. I have my own little apartment in what were the attics, so we won't be on top of each other and it will save time travelling.' *And I'll be able to keep an eye on you.*

'That's kind of you, Louisa but I don't want to intrude...'

'Nonsense! You're my father. Of course you're not intruding. And we can use the house as a place to confer with John. That way there's no risk of being overheard,' she said, pleased with her argument.

'Okay. Thank you, it does make sense.'

'There's one thing that puzzles me. Without any forensic evidence, how are we going to prove it was Blake who wanted to steal the jewels?'

Malcolm was silent for a moment. 'John has an idea or two, but we'll need the support of the Met. Don't worry, if Blake is the man, we'll prove it.'

She had to be satisfied with his answer and Malcolm rang off to book their flights. Louisa remembered, belatedly, that she had invited her aunt to join her in London. And she had now asked Malcolm! Could be tricky, she thought, dialling Margaret's number.

'Hi, Margaret, it's me. I've got some news...' She went on to describe the outcome of John's investigation so far, finishing by saying she would be in London the next day.

'That's wonderful, Louisa. I'm so glad things are finally moving forward,' Margaret said, before a fit of coughing stopped her from continuing.

'Margaret, are you okay? I'm so sorry, I didn't realise…'

She heard her aunt take a sip of something before she spoke again.

'It's a bad cough, that's all. Started as a cold, before going onto my chest. The doctor's told me I have to rest and I'll be right as rain.' She stopped to draw breath. Louisa was worried. Her aunt lived on her own, how would she manage? Margaret's voice cut into her thoughts.

'You don't have to worry about me, my neighbour pops in every day to check on me. And gets my shopping. So I'm fine. But I won't be able to come down to London just yet. As soon as I'm better I'll come, as we arranged.' She stopped as a coughing fit claimed her. Louisa, though still concerned about Margaret, was relieved to avoid the problem of her coming while Malcolm was staying. After a brief chat, Margaret rang off, still coughing.

Louisa stared out of the window. The mist still swirled outside, giving the impression that nothing existed beyond the garden hedge. She felt paralysed. There was much to do but…Did she pack up everything, expecting to stay in London for good? Or would she be there only a few days? Thinking about it, it had to be for longer. Even if she wasn't needed in London, there was Margaret. If she remained ill, Louisa would go and see her. If she recovered then Margaret would come to London to stay with her. Either way, it looked as if her time on the island had come to an end. For the present, at least. And that meant saying goodbye to Paul. A piece of lead settled heavily in her stomach as she reached out again for the phone.

'Hi, Nadine. Could you tell me when Paul's free for a chat, please? Okay, thanks. I'll catch him then.'

She had an hour to kill and rousing herself, grabbed her swimsuit and towelling robe before heading down to the pool. She needed exercise.

The swim helped. By the time Louisa had showered and changed she felt clearer-headed. Coincidentally, the mist had thinned, allowing glimpses of a watery sun to be seen. Once dressed in jeans and T-shirt, she made her way to Paul's office. The lead was still in place, but she decided to ignore it, fixing a smile on her face as she knocked on the door.

'Come in.'

'Louisa! This is a surprise. Please, sit down. What can I do for you?' Paul's eyes crinkled up as he smiled. *If you only knew!* She found herself dropping her own eyes, focusing on a plant on the desk.

'I...I'm going back to London tomorrow. With Malcolm,' she said, and then filled him in with the latest development. She risked an upward glance and saw his smile had died.

'I see. Well, that's good news then, isn't it? What you hoped for. And Malc. How...long will you stay?'

'For good, I guess.'

He looked shocked. 'But you will come back? To see Malc?'

'Sure. But for the moment he will stay with me in London. Does he need to be here? For the centre?'

Paul pushed a hand through his hair. 'No, no he doesn't. He's given me full control as he never wanted to be tied down again.' He seemed to make a big effort and smiled at her. 'I'll miss you, Louisa. I had hoped we'd have time to get to know each other better, but...' His eyes locked onto hers.

Louisa wanted to cry. She had hoped so, as well. But it couldn't work. She needed to be in England. Standing up, she took a deep breath before saying, 'I'll miss you too, Paul. I...I have to go. Things to arrange...' She turned towards the door but Paul got there before her.

'Hey, not so fast. You can't go without a goodbye kiss. Okay?' he said, encircling her with his arms and pulling her close. Not having the will to fight, she gave in and let his lips find hers. The piece of lead melted and she found herself not wanting the kiss to end. Every part of her body tingled, as if properly alive for the first time. She sagged against him, any remaining stiffness in her body dissolved. An annoying voice in her head shouted, "Stop! This can't happen. Leave *now!*" As Paul's tongue began to gently probe her mouth, Louisa knew she had to be strong and walk away. She pulled back, muttering, 'Goodbye, Paul,' and fled out of the door and up to her room, passing a bemused looking Nadine. It was not until she was safely back that she allowed the tears to flow. Tears for a love that was not meant to be.

The plane taxied on the tarmac, pulling into the space designated by the man with what, to Louisa, always looked like table tennis bats. Brightly coloured ones, too. Shortly after the passengers began to disembark, their flight was called and she and Malcolm headed to their gate.

The mid-morning flight to Gatwick was busy: cancelled flights on the previous day had created a backlog of passengers. The mist had cleared by lunchtime, and the rest of the day had seen brilliant sunshine. Today promised to be a mix of sun and clouds, but Louisa hardly cared. She was leaving part of her heart behind and it was not a good feeling.

'You're looking very serious, my dear. Something wrong?' Malcolm's voice seemed to come from a distance and she forced herself to smile at him.

'Just thinking about…you know. It's feeling very real now after weeks of waiting.'

He gripped her hand. 'I understand. But I'll be by your side so you're not facing this alone.'

She nodded and before either of them could say anymore, they were at the front of the queue and handing over their boarding cards. A short walk along the glazed corridor and they were outside following the marked-out path to the plane. Once ensconced in her business class seat, Louisa stared out of the window as men bustled about, preparing for departure. Within minutes the pilot was building up speed down the runway and then they were airborne. Hoping to see La Folie, she looked down as the plane banked over the coast, but was disappointed. She continued to watch as the patchwork of fields dotted with cows the size of ants, and clusters of houses looking like pieces of Lego, peeled away out of sight. Then they were over the sea, heading north to England and whatever lay ahead.

She closed her eyes, wanting to relive the moment when Paul kissed her. She had taken ages to get off to sleep that night; part of her wanted to run up to Paul's room and tell him what she felt. That she loved him. But another part, the cautious, led by the head part, held her back. It was too soon, and she only had Nick's word that Paul had feelings for her. Okay, that kiss seemed to support that, but he hadn't *said* anything, she told herself. Now, as the plane took her ever further away from Paul and La Folie, she fell into a doze. Images filled her head: Paul, smiling and golden in the light through the stairwell, and That Man Edward, with his grey, lanky hair, thin face and stubbled chin. One minute she was in Paul's arms and the next in That Man's. He was pulling her towards him, shouting at her, she could feel his spit on her face…she cried out.

'Louisa, are you okay? You shouted something.'

She opened her eyes to see her father's concerned face and flushed when she realised what had happened. But apart from Malcolm, no-one else seemed to have noticed.

'Sorry, bad dream. I...I didn't sleep well last night. Guess I'm a bit stressed.'

Malcolm squeezed her arm. 'Understandable. I'll ask the stewardess to bring you a drink.' He ordered a small brandy for Louisa and a coffee for himself.

Not normally keen on alcohol in the middle of the morning, nevertheless, the brandy hit the spot, and she relaxed.

'Better? We'll be preparing for landing any time soon so we'll need to drink up shortly.'

The disembarkation proceeded smoothly and, after the usual long wait for their luggage, they finally cleared the arrivals area. Amongst those waiting was a chauffeur holding a card with the name "Mr Roget". Louisa flashed a grin at her father, who admitted that he did not like hanging about for taxis and usually hired a car and driver. Fine by her, she was quite happy to be driven home in comfort. The chauffeur explained that it would take about an hour and a half to drive to Islington so she sat back in the sumptuous seat to take a leisurely look at the passing countryside. Initially, it was slow going on the M23, but the driver picked up speed once they were clear of the airport traffic. The contrast with driving around tiny Guernsey really hit her. Louisa, like a lot of Londoners, did not drive much. Used to a good public transport system and the evils of driving in the city, there was no point. She had shared the use of a car with her mother and more often than not, it remained parked for weeks at a time.

As they neared the outskirts of London the traffic again built up. Once they had cleared Vauxhall Bridge it was virtually nose to tail for the remainder of the journey, but it did give plenty of time to take in the sights.

'Do you spend much time in London, these days?' she asked Malcolm, who had appeared lost in thought for most of the journey, staring out of the window.

'Not much. I think in some ways it hasn't changed a great deal since I lived here, which I like. But I'm not so keen on all these high–rise buildings that seem to proliferate everywhere you look. To me London's lost some of its character. What do you think?' He turned towards her, with a smile.

'I understand that we need to build upwards, and I'm sure the views are fantastic. But I wouldn't want to live or work so high up. To me it's a way of shouting "money" rather than a real answer to the lack of housing. No average person could afford to live in those towering edifices. And I always think about what happens if there's a power cut and the lifts stop working!' she said, grinning.

'Fair point. My hotels were never more than five or six storeys high, which was manageable.' He waved his hand and added, 'But this is more like the real London. A mix of really old buildings next to some great modern architecture.'

Louisa followed his line of sight, taking in the area of the Strand and Aldwych. 'I agree. I love this part of the city. Where did you live when you were here?'

'I had a pokey little flat in Greek Street, handy for the hotel where I worked. So I got to know this part of London pretty well.'

'What about Mum? Where was she based when…when you saw each other?' Louisa found it uncomfortable visualising them as a couple. A lifetime ago. Literally. Hers.

Malcolm shifted in his seat. 'Susan shared a flat with another girl in Holborn. A friend from school, if I remember rightly.'

'Mm, I think she did mention something about sharing with a friend.'

They fell into a companionable silence. Louisa did not want to dwell any more on her mother's past and she guessed that it was equally awkward for her father. After all, he had not behaved very well at that time, had he? As they drew closer to Islington, she began to regret asking Malcolm to stay with her. It would be as if he was invading her mother's personal space, even though she was no longer around. Her stomach clenched at the unwanted memory. It was too late to change her mind so she would have to make the best of it. As she was trying to tell herself it would be fine, the car turned off City Road into the small terrace of Georgian houses tucked away behind Angel station.

The car stopped outside a house with shuttered windows and Louisa found herself saying, with a brightness she did not feel, 'Here we are. Home.'

chapter 24

Malcolm stood by the car, staring at the house, while the chauffeur unloaded their luggage. He liked what he saw – part of a row of classical Georgian houses, three storeys high and with the traditional stuccoed fronts and original sash windows. It was reached by a short path bordered by a small area of shrubs and hedges now displaying their bright spring colours. A pair of twisted bay trees guarded the deep blue painted front door. The closed shutters of the windows of the lower two floors created the impression of a house asleep. Would his presence disturb the house's equilibrium? *Please forgive me, Susan. I should have been there for you. But I'll do my utmost to bring you justice and to protect our daughter. You did a great job bringing her up alone. She's a girl to be proud of...*

'Malcolm? Shall we go?' Louisa's voice cut into his thoughts and he took a deep breath. Time to face his memories of Susan.

Louisa led the way, unlocking the front door while he carried the cases. Light filtered through from a room at the end of the passage, but the hall was still dim. Louisa went off to open the shutters in the front room, which appeared to be a study. Returning, she led him to the kitchen at the back and suggested he sat while she made them both a cup of coffee.

'Glenn from the office has stocked me up with a few basic essentials. I left him a key so that he could keep an eye on the place.'

Malcolm admired the light oak free-standing units topped with bronze coloured granite worktops. The wall cupboards, of various shapes and sizes, were painted in the pale shades of green and cream reminiscent of the Georgian era. In the middle of the room stood a battered refectory table and old mismatched chairs. The overall effect was an effortless mix of old and new befitting the age of the house.

'This is lovely, Louisa. Did your mother design this?'

Louisa looked up from the cafetière. 'Yes, Mum chose everything in the house. She loved pottering around old second-hand shops and antique markets and would bring back something most weeks. Some of the furniture is from my grandparents' house as they collected antiques. I guess that's where Mum got the bug from. I'll show you around once you've had your coffee. The only drawback of these houses is that there's a lot of stairs.'

Malcolm nodded, before walking over to the window to gaze outside.

'That's some garden you have here. Large for this type of house isn't it? And beautifully cared for, too,' he said, taking in the manicured lawn, herbaceous borders and the old walls covered in climbers. There was a miniature patio outside the back door with room for a small table and chairs.

'Mum loved her garden. It's what sold her the house. 'Course, it didn't look as good as it does now. It was a real labour of love, a way of de-stressing after a week in the office.' Louisa fiddled with cups and saucers, looking strained. He guessed she was finding it difficult talking about her mother and he felt the familiar twinge of guilt.

'Sorry, my dear. My being here is dragging it all up for you, isn't it? Perhaps I should find an hotel–'

She shook her head. 'No, you mustn't do that. I have to learn to live with what happened and you have every right to be here.' As he raised his eyebrows, she continued, looking flustered, 'You're my father. And Mum would want you to be here.'

He moved towards her and hugged her close. 'Thank you. You have no idea how much that means to me.'

'Oh, I think I do,' she said softly. 'I think I do.'

★

Once they had finished their coffee, Louisa showed Malcolm around the house as promised. He was right: it *was* difficult having him there, and talking about her mother. But she had to get over it. Nothing either of them could say or do would change the past and, if it wasn't for Malcolm, she would not be in a position to bring her mother's killer to justice. And he was proving to be a caring, loving father even if it was more than thirty years too late.

She hesitated before entering the sitting room and Malcolm seemed to sense her unease.

'This is where it…happened?' he asked, squeezing her hand.

She nodded, hanging onto his hand as they went in. Gazing around at the familiar room, full of the clutter her mother had acquired over the years, she realised that the old feelings of panic were no longer there. Perhaps it was the reassuring grip of her father's hand, but whatever it was, she felt safe. Or at least, safer.

'What a cosy room. Susan had very good taste. She could have been an interior designer,' he said, still gripping her hand.

'Funny you should say that, but Mum used to tell me she wished she'd become a professional designer instead of a travel agent. But I think she had the best of both worlds; the business was – still is – a great success, and she got to be creative at home.'

'I always knew Susan would do well at whatever she turned her hand to. She was managing a small travel agency when I met her.' He appeared to drift away for a moment.

Louisa waited. Then he turned to her, adding, 'It's where we met. I went in to book a vacation somewhere, can't recall where, and fell for this beautiful blonde, English lady with smiling grey eyes.' He smiled at Louisa. 'I didn't bother with the trip but stayed in London to see more of her.'

'Oh, Mum never told me! That's sooo romantic. If only…' she bit her lip, knowing she couldn't go there.

'I know. But at least we made a beautiful daughter, of whom we can both be proud. So let's focus on the positive, shall we? As Paul would say.'

Her heart quickened at the mention of Paul. But that was another subject out of bounds. Instead she went over to the bookcase and picked up the photo of her mother and Malcolm at the charity ball.

'This is the only photo I had of you and it was years before Mum let me see it. Then I insisted that she leave it out instead of buried in a drawer. I wanted to *see* that I had a father even if he wasn't around.' Louisa felt the long-buried hurt bubble up inside her; tears welled in her eyes and when her father threw his arms around her, she allowed herself to let go. He steered her to the sofa and stroked her hair while the tears fell unchecked, soaking his shirt. Her body shook as the pent-up emotion took control. It was if she had regressed to childhood, being comforted by her grandfather after some upset or accident. It was a while before the tears eased and she regained some control. Wordlessly, Malcolm handed her a large linen handkerchief, and she blew her nose and wiped her face before lifting her head away from his damp chest.

'I'm so sorry, I–'

'Don't be silly, darling. You have nothing to apologise for. I'm the one who caused you all that pain. I can only hope that one day you will forgive me and be free of the hurt.'

She gazed with blurred vision at Malcolm's face; saw the sorrow etched in lines around his eyes and mouth as he continued to stroke the hair away from her wet face. She registered the endearment, spoken for the first time. It felt good.

Pulling away, she managed a faint smile.

'I think I've already forgiven you. It was a combination of your being here…and talking about Mum that set me off.' She stood up, her legs wobbly. 'Sorry about your shirt. I'll show you to your room so you can change.'

'You'd better have a wee brandy first. You're looking pale. I'll get it.' Malcolm walked over to the drinks cabinet and poured a small brandy into a glass. 'Here, drink this. Then you can point me in the direction of my bedroom.'

While Malcolm was changing, Louisa took the opportunity to disappear up to her own rooms. After splashing cold water on her face she re-applied her make-up. Her eyes were still puffy but a touch of eye shadow and mascara hid most of the damage. She dragged a comb through her hair before changing. Streaks of mascara had managed to creep onto her top as well as Malcolm's shirt. Although the outburst had been exhausting, she now felt cleansed. The life-long hurt of not having a father, followed by the loss of her mother, had lessened. She knew her grief for her mother would continue to ambush her for some time to come, but at least she had turned a corner. Her father's love was proving to be the best healer.

Once they were both downstairs, Malcolm suggested they went out for lunch. Louisa, suddenly ravenous, was happy to agree and led him to a nearby pub offering all-day food. Not as healthy as that served at La Folie, nevertheless, they both tucked into a steak sandwich partnered with salad.

'I needed that,' Malcolm said, finishing his meal. 'Right, now I must phone John and arrange for him to show us where this Edward fella lives. We'll keep out of sight, naturally. Do you think you can handle that or–'

'I'm fine. This is what we came back for, so let's do it.' Louisa sipped her juice while Malcolm went outside to make the call. Not as confident as she sounded, she wanted it over and done with.

Malcolm appeared back at the table. 'John suggests we meet tomorrow morning just after ten. The guy leaves the house at half-past to get to work; he's on an afternoon shift. John's been watching him for a couple of days now and his routine doesn't vary.' He looked around at the tables filling up around them before adding, 'Let's go home. We can't talk here.'

As they made their way back, Malcolm told Louisa what John had learned.

'Edward lives with his father, Archie, who's frail and never leaves home.' Louisa noted the gleam in his eye when Malcolm mentioned that Archie was alive. 'They rent a run-down flat in a less than salubrious part of the East End. So I guess that's why they wanted the jewels.' He stopped talking while they crossed a road with a young woman pushing a buggy. Once at the other side, he continued, 'Archie lost his wife ten years ago and Edward's been divorced for the past fifteen. He moved in with his dad when his mother died. His wife re-married and their two kids, now grown-up, never speak to their father. Some big row between them all, John said. Edward is the carer for Archie, although a nurse comes in a couple of times a day to check on him.'

'Not what you'd call a happy family, then,' Louisa remarked, glad that she wouldn't have to feel sorry for them.

'No. Edward's divorce was bitter and his wife took him for every penny. Not that he had a lot, by all accounts. He lost his home and family and took to drink, costing him his job. He only got back to work a few years ago, as a ticket collector on the Underground. His health isn't great and he's permanently broke, according to John's sources. Both Archie and Edward are considered to be bitter old men, with chips on their shoulders,' Malcolm said, grim-faced.

'So you think Archie put Edward up to stealing the jewels?'

'For sure. My guess is he held a grudge for years about my father not making him his heir. And then, adding insult to injury, my mother spirited away the money and jewels he had stolen from my father's safe.'

They arrived at the house and Louisa let them in before heading to the kitchen to put the kettle on.

Looking at Malcolm's sombre face, she said softly, 'Do you have any way of proving that Archie killed your father? That would stand up in court?'

'I've thought about that a lot. It's possible. There were traces of DNA found on my father's ring that were not an exact match with his. We figured that Archie had tried to pull it off, so it could be his.' He let out a long breath and Louisa handed him a mug of coffee. 'Thanks. But even if we could prove it was Archie, I doubt it would go to court. He's got to be ninety-two and in poor health. What would be the point in locking him up now? After seventy years?' He shook his head. 'What I really want is to meet him face to face and hear him admit to what he did. From what John's learnt his life hasn't been a happy one, so he's had the karma he so richly deserved.'

'I think you're right. He's been punished. But Edward hasn't…' She took a sip of coffee, forcing herself not to re-live what occurred that awful day in January.

Malcolm patted her arm in silent agreement.

The next morning Louisa offered to drive them to meet John, pointing out that they would need to take cover in a car while they watched. Malcolm agreed and they set off after advising John to watch out for a dark blue VW Golf. It took a while to negotiate the busy streets snarled up with traffic and, as Louisa did not know the area, she had to pay attention to the instructions passed on by John. The street they were headed for was a mix of social housing flats, maisonettes and shops that had seen better days. As Louisa turned into the end of the road her heart sank. Most of the shop fronts were either boarded up or protected with thick metal grills: lounging against them were groups of surly looking young men who cast suspicious looks towards the car.

'Keep driving. John said to go right to the end and he'll be outside the pub.'

Relieved, she continued as fast as allowed before spotting a pub that looked as run down as the rest of the street. A figure detached itself from the doorway and pointed to the opposite side of the road. Louisa pulled over to park and switched off the engine.

John came over and slid into the back of the car.

'Good to see you both again.'

Louisa and Malcolm turned round to exchange greetings. She was grateful for the comforting presence of two strong men in the car. This would not be an area she would want to venture in alone.

'Grim, isn't it?' John said, as if reading her thoughts. 'Don't worry, we won't have to hang around long.' He glanced at his watch. 'Ten minutes, I'd say. It's that building over there,' he said, pointing to a two-storey block of flats. 'It's the one with the red door and when he comes out he'll be walking right past us so you can get a good look at him. I'll get out and ask him for directions, saying we're lost. It'll give you plenty of time to study him without him noticing you. Okay?' he asked, pulling out a map.

They nodded and Louisa counted down the minutes. She wanted to get it over and go.

Right on time, the red door opened and a man appeared, pulling it shut behind him. Louisa couldn't see his face clearly but the figure looked familiar; lank grey hair and walking with a slight limp. As he drew closer she saw his face: it *was* him. Her breath caught in her chest and Malcolm gripped her hand as John got out, waving the map. The man – Edward Blake – stopped and scowled at John but appeared to listen and, turning, pointed left at the end of the road and then right. A moment later John thanked him and returned to the car. Blake limped past, showing no interest in the car or the occupants.

'It was the man I saw. For sure. Can we go now, please?' She felt sick, seeing him like that again…

John offered to drive and Louisa, after making sure Blake was out of sight, swapped seats.

Safely back at home, Louisa made a pot of coffee. John mentioned that he always used the Underground while in London, and was bunking down with an old mate from the Met.

'Lovely house, you have. And in such a great area! Very nice,' said John, gazing around the kitchen.

Louisa placed the coffee pot and mugs on the table and fetched the milk from the fridge.

'It is. But Mum wasn't able to buy anything decent for years. When her business took off she bought a small flat not far from here; it was only after she inherited money from my grandparents that she was able to buy this place,' she said, pouring the coffee. 'But now…I don't feel at ease here since Mum died. I may sell it and buy something smaller.' She bit her lip, not happy about the inevitable upheaval if she did.

'I'm sure you don't need to make that decision yet, darling. You know you'll always be welcome at La Folie or at my apartment, if you need to get away.'

'Mm, thanks.' She smiled at Malcolm before taking a sip of coffee. If only she could go back to La Folie! And be near Paul...

John cleared his throat. 'Shall we look at our next move with regard to the Blakes? I've been chatting to the guys on the case and made a suggestion, which they're considering. But it does involve you two so you have to be happy with the idea,' he said, shifting on his chair.

Louisa looked from one to the other. 'Sounds ominous. Does that mean that it's dangerous?' Her pulse raced at the thought.

'Not really, it's a bit...unorthodox. The idea is that Edward's brought in for questioning about the burglary on the basis that there's a witness. He'll assume it's you. His DNA will be taken to make him think they're trying to match it with something from the scene. My mates aren't expecting a confession, but want to put the wind up him. Get him rattled.'

'Okay so far: what happens next?' Malcolm asked, leaning forward.

'You'd be wired and follow Edward home, arriving at the same time. He'll be in a state and need to share it with his father. You say you're an old friend of Archie's and insist on coming in. He can't really refuse and you confront Archie about what happened to Roland. Edward will be angry that his father lied to him and we're hoping there will be a big bust-up and that Edward talks about what *he* did. The police will be in an unmarked car outside, listening in to the recording. If Edward does confess, they can come in and arrest him,' John said, leaning back in his chair.

For a moment there was silence as Louisa and Malcolm mulled over John's plan.

'I'm up for it,' Malcolm said, 'I'd love the chance to confront the pair of them, particularly Archie. But there's no guarantee that Edward will confess, is there? Then what do we do?'

John fiddled with his mug. 'Well, I thought of that. If we wire-up Louisa and she was to turn up–'

'No way! I don't want her in any danger! He's already responsible for Susan's death. I'll go alone and–'

Louisa cried out, 'I *want* to go. He's a coward and been used to Archie telling him what to do. If I suddenly appear it might just be the tipping point that makes him confess. And if we're both wired then the police could rush in if there was any hint of violence.' She stared at her father. 'I need to do this. For Mum.'

Malcolm's jaw was clenched and looked as if he was struggling to control himself. Then he let out a long breath and muttered, 'Okay.'

John gave her a hug, saying, 'Thanks, Louisa. You're a brave girl. But I'll make sure nothing happens to you, I promise. I'll be outside too and the coppers will be armed. We'll be more than a match for that scum, you'll see.'

chapter 25

A couple of days later, John phoned to say that the police would take Edward in for questioning the following morning; his day off from work. Malcolm and Louisa were to join him at the station and would be able to watch the interview unobserved.

'Are you absolutely sure you want to go ahead, my dear? I'm quite happy to do this on my own,' Malcolm said after the call.

'Yes, of course. I'm prepared to do anything to bring Edward to justice. But, I might not be needed and you'll end up the hero of the hour,' Louisa said, trying to make light of it. Underneath she *was* scared, but determined to help if needed. Even Charlotte had tried to talk her out of it. They had met up at Charlotte's house the previous day after Louisa had phoned to say she was in London. In need of a break from the tension of the past few days she looked forward to seeing her friend.

Charlotte lived in Bloomsbury, round the corner from the British Museum. Louisa's eyes widened as she approached her friend's house in the small garden square. A three-storey, double fronted Georgian terrace built in plain brick and with the original small-paned sash windows, it looked exquisite. And expensive. She had guessed that Charlotte was wealthy, but not this wealthy. The door was opened by a middle-aged woman dressed in dark grey. At least there was no butler, Louisa thought to herself, grinning. She followed the housekeeper upstairs and was ushered into a sunny drawing room with the words, 'Miss

Canning, Madam. I'll be back shortly with the refreshments.'

Louisa found it hard not to giggle and Charlotte, rising from behind a writing table covered in papers, must have seen her struggle and laughed.

'I know, it's all terribly upper class, isn't it? But I couldn't possibly manage on my own–'

'Hey, it's fine. And I'm *so* glad to see you: a lot's happened in the past few days.'

They hugged before sitting down on the pale blue, linen covered sofa.

'I wasn't expecting to find you living in such…such–'

'Grandeur?' Charlotte cut in, with a rueful grin. 'It's not something I like to talk about, although I'd guess most of the guests at La Folie are equally well-heeled. The problem is, if people know you have money, you are never sure if that's why they want to be your friend.' She waved her arm as Louisa tried to protest. 'Oh, I don't mean you, silly. You looked almost as lost as I was and obviously genuine.'

There was a muted knock at the door and the housekeeper brought in a tray loaded with a tea pot, fine bone china cups and saucers and a plate of muffins. Louisa raised her eyebrows at the cakes and, after the woman had left, Charlotte explained that Chef had given her a low calorie recipe for the muffins. 'So, we can eat and enjoy without putting on an ounce,' she declared, pouring the tea.

'I inherited the house from my father so, thankfully, my ex-husband can't get his sticky fingers on it. I'll show you around after you've told me what's been happening. I'm all agog!' Charlotte settled back on the sofa, cup neatly balanced on the saucer, giving Louisa an expectant look. She obliged willingly, leaving nothing out. Charlotte's face registered a gamut of emotions as Louisa described how they had waited for Edward to leave his house in order for her to see him in the flesh. And when Louisa laid out the plan to corner Archie and Edward in their flat, she became agitated.

'Oh, Louisa! You mustn't be involved. Malcolm can take care of himself but what if this Edward turned on you? You're a witness and without you there wouldn't be a case against him. By all means sit outside in the police car and listen in but–'

Louisa shook her head. 'Malcolm would look out for me and he's bigger and stronger than Edward, in spite of his age. And remember the police could rush in at a moment's notice. It's not as if the man's armed and dangerous!' She finished her tea, carefully replacing the cup on the tray.

'But he killed your mother!' Charlotte cried, clutching her arm.

Louisa paled. 'I know. But this is different. Ideally, he'll admit to Malcolm what he did and I won't need to go in.' She took a deep breath before adding, 'I want this man punished for what he did. And if that means I have to be there, then so be it.'

Charlotte nodded. 'Then I'll keep my fingers crossed that you won't need to.'

★

An unmarked police car picked them up at the agreed time and John sat beside the driver, who introduced himself as Detective Sergeant Dickens. Malcolm ushered Louisa into the back seat before settling beside her. After a brief exchange of greetings, John informed them that Edward was on his way to the police station and would arrive shortly after themselves. No-one seemed inclined to chat and Malcolm was content to stare out of the window as the car travelled the short distance to Tolpuddle Street station. It seemed strange that, after all these years, he might shortly be face to face with his father's killer: Roland's nephew and his own cousin. In the meantime he and his daughter would be party to the police interview of the man responsible for Susan's death: his second cousin. *What a family! I hope to God I can bring an end to this horror and justice prevails.* Glancing at Louisa, his heart lifted at the sight of the one good thing that had come out of the sorry mess. His daughter. He was proud of her and sent up a silent prayer that she would be kept safe from harm. Louisa must have felt his eyes on her and turned towards him with a smile. He gripped her hand and she nodded as the car pulled into the back of the police station.

The sergeant led Malcolm and John into a room with a desk and chairs, asking them to sit in front of the glimmering computer screen. Louisa was taken to another room to wait for them. It had been explained to her that, as a potential witness, she could not see Edward being interviewed.

'I'll be in there,' the sergeant said, nodding at the picture of an empty interview room on the screen, 'with Detective Inspector Wallace. You'll be able to watch what happens and I'll come back for you when the suspect's ready to leave.' He nodded briefly at John and left.

'I suppose this was all in a day's work for you, John?

'When I was based in the Met, yes. But there wasn't much call for this sort of interview in Guernsey. We dealt mainly with petty crime rather than violent. Although I did lead an investigation into the mysterious death of a couple at sea...' He stopped talking as three men arrived in the other room; Dickens, Edward Blake and a man who Malcolm presumed was Detective Inspector Wallace. The detectives sat on one side of a table and Blake on the other. Malcolm leaned forward, keen to hear every word. Blake looked terrified: his eyes darted around the room as if looking for escape, and he kept twisting his hands together. *Good! He's rattled. That's what we want.*

DI Wallace explained to Blake why he was there and at the mention of the address and the circumstances, he clenched his hands tight as if to stop them shaking.

'Can you tell us where you were that evening, Mr Blake?'

'At 'ome with me dad. He's not well, see, and I 'ave to be there in the evening after I finish work. Don't get out much at all,' Blake said, looking from one detective to the other.

'And your father will verify this?'

'Yes, o' course.' A thought seemed to occur to him as he added, 'But what made you want to question me? And after all this time?'

DI Wallace tapped his fingers on the table before looking Blake in the eye.

'We've had a witness come forward, giving a description of a man resembling you, leaving the property that evening.'

Blake visibly paled under his grey stubble. Malcolm wondered if he would now own up and save them all a lot of trouble. He was disappointed.

'They must 'ave been mistaken. Anyways, how would a description lead you to me? I've not got a record or anything. Must be lots of men look like me,' he said, sitting straighter in his chair.

'Ah, but how many work for London Underground, Mr Blake? The man they saw wore a top bearing the Undergound logo.' Wallace smiled grimly as Blake squirmed in his chair.

Dickens, apparently playing "good cop", chipped in, 'But if your father can provide you with an alibi for that evening, Mr Blake, then we may not need to trouble you further. In the meantime we need to take a sample of your DNA to eliminate you from our enquiries. Okay with that?'

Edward nodded and the sergeant took a swab from his mouth.

DI Wallace went on, 'Is it all right if someone calls round tomorrow morning to take your father's statement?'

Blake's head bobbed up and down. 'Yes, suppose so.' He looked at Wallace, asking, 'Does this mean I can go?'

'Yes. I'm afraid we don't have any spare cars; can you make your own way home?'

Standing up quickly, as if afraid they might change their minds, he said he could and shot out of the door.

Wallace turned to face the video camera and gave the thumbs up. It was time to put the trap into operation.

Malcolm and Louisa had their wires fitted by Dickens and, together with John, piled into the unmarked car. Edward was being tailed on his Tube journey home by plain clothed officers and they expected to arrive at his house before he would. Dickens told them that the surveillance vehicle, an unmarked van, was already in place.

The sergeant parked a few yards up the street and they had to wait about twenty minutes before the call came through that Edward was approaching. Malcolm shot out of the car in readiness. As Edward arrived at the front door, Malcolm came up behind him, calling, 'Mr Blake?'

Edward jumped. As he turned round Malcolm saw the terror in his eyes.

'Who are you? What you want wi' me?' Edward's voice shook as he looked up and down the street.

'The name's Roget. I'm an old friend of your father's. I was told he lived here with you and, as I haven't seen him for years and heard he's not well…' Malcolm spread out his hands.

Edward hesitated, clearly trying to think of a reason to refuse, but Malcolm edged forward, placing his foot firmly over the top step.

'I've come a very long way, Mr Blake, and I'm sure your father will be only too happy to see me.'

'Uh, all right then. But you can't stay long, he's in a bad way and has to rest a lot.' Edward turned and limped off down a narrow hallway before opening a door on the left.

'Someone to see you, Dad. Says he's an old friend. Name of Roget.' He turned to Malcolm and gestured for him to enter.

Malcolm walked into the stuffy room, trying not to gag. The air was heavy with the smell of stale urine and unwashed clothes. The small room was filled with a hospital bed, raised so that its occupant could sit up and see the old fashioned television propped on a table near its foot. Green threadbare curtains were closed against the sun and Edward flicked a switch, bringing to life the single bulb hanging from the ceiling. Malcolm blinked, staring at the small wizened body dwarfed by the bed and huddled in unsavoury-looking bedclothes. On the bedside table stood a couple of empty beer bottles, a glass and packets of pills. Two dim eyes peered up at him from a skeletal head.

Edward moved as if to leave the room but Malcolm asked him to stay, adding, 'I think you'll be interested to hear what your father and I have to talk about.'

He looked surprised and his head switched from his father to Malcolm. Shrugging, he perched on the end of the bed while Malcolm, feeling nauseous from the smell and the sight of the man who had caused his mother so much pain, moved round to the side so he could be seen clearly.

'Who are you? Don't recognise you. You're no friend o' mine.' A thin raspy voice emerged from the bony head covered in white wispy hair.

Edward jumped off the bed. ''Ere, you said you

were–'

'I know. It's sort of true. Just shut up and listen,' Malcolm glared at him and Edward, looking even more scared, did as he was told.

Malcolm addressed Archie. 'I'm Malcolm Roget, Betty and Roland's son. And I know you killed my father.'

Edward gasped, his eyes wide with horror, while Archie blinked.

'I don't know what you're talking about. Don't know any Rogets.'

'My mother changed her name after we left for Canada. She didn't want you finding us. You knew her as Betty Le Cras and my father was Roland Blake, your uncle. You killed him at his home in Guernsey and stole his money and jewels before burying him. Then you forced my mother to flee to England with you, saying you'd tell the police *she* had killed him.' Malcolm felt the anger bubbling up inside as he pictured the scene described by his mother many years ago. His fists clenched, itching to hit the bag of bones on the bed.

'Wha...what's he on about, Dad? You told me your uncle died of a heart attack after he changed 'is will. Leaving you out of it, you said.' Edward's eyes were wild as they darted between Archie and Malcolm. 'And who's this Betty? You never mentioned 'er.'

'Don't believe anything he says, son. It's a bunch of lies–'

Malcolm faced Edward. 'Betty was my father's housekeeper and they became engaged when she fell pregnant with me. This was in 1939 and war had just been declared. My father planned for them to leave for Canada once they were married. But before they had a chance to do this your *father*,' he spat out the word, 'killed Roland by hitting him over the head after he told Archie he'd never been, and never would be, his heir.'

Edward turned a greenish colour. 'Tell me that's not true, Dad. You always said them jewels were rightfully ours and they was stolen from you.'

Archie's breathing rattled in his chest as he struggled to answer.

'He's lying, I tell you! He's just trying to get his own hands on what's mine – and yours.'

'You mean this?' Malcolm said, pulling out one of the earrings from his pocket. In spite of the poor light, it dazzled. Edward's mouth fell open and he reached as if to touch it but Malcolm slapped him away. Archie groaned, his white claw-like hands twisting on the sheet.

'Liar! You can't prove anything! You weren't even born then! It's all lies–'

'But my mother saw what happened. And we recently found my father's body, with this ring on his finger...'

Archie gasped as Malcolm held up Roland's ring.

'It...it was an accident...I didn't mean to kill him. I was angry about the...the will–'

Edward leapt up and started shouting. 'You bastard! You've lied to me all these years, telling me we was robbed of our inheritance but that one day we'd get it back if I...' He appeared to realise what he was saying and stopped, glaring at Archie who had shrunk further into the bed. Then they both started shouting at each other. Malcolm was trying to think of a way to encourage Edward to confess when the doorbell rang. 'I'll go,' he said, rushing out of the room. It was Louisa.

'What are you doing here? I can manage–'

'We think I could be the final straw,' she said, heading for the open door and the raised voices.

Edward spun round as they entered.

'Who's this?' he shouted.

'I'm Louisa Canning and my mother was Susan Canning. You...you killed her when you forced your way

231

into her house.' Malcolm admired his daughter's calmness as she stood, unflinching, near the bed.

'Oh shit! We're finished! The fuzz already suspect me.' His face suffused with purple as he turned to Archie. 'It's all your fault! You crazy, stupid old man. Because o' you I'll be blamed for that woman's death. And for nothing! Those damn jewels were never ours. God, I could kill you!' And with a sudden lunge he picked up a beer bottle, aiming it at Archie's head. Malcolm and Louisa both moved to stop him but she was closer. She tried to grab his arm and Edward twisted round violently to shake her off. The bottle caught the side of her head and she cried out. Malcolm could only watch in horror as his daughter slumped to the floor, blood oozing from her forehead, shards of glass flying around her.

chapter 26

'I…I didn't mean to hurt her!' cried Edward, looking ashen as Malcolm cradled Louisa in his arms.

'Damn you! She's my daughter and you'd better pray that she recovers or–'

The door burst open and three uniformed police officers pushed into the room, while the two detectives and an anxious looking John Ferguson stood outside – there being no space for all of them. Edward was grabbed and handcuffed before being led away by two policemen and the sergeant. Louisa was unconscious and Malcolm dabbed at the head wound with his handkerchief, willing for her to open her eyes. Wallace knelt beside him as the room cleared, with John hovering behind him.

'I've radioed for an ambulance. What happened? We heard Louisa cry out and realised something was wrong.'

Malcolm told him while continuing to cradle Louisa.

John groaned. 'I never meant for this to happen. I should have refused to let her come in. But she was adamant…'

Malcolm frowned. 'I bear as much responsibility, if not more, as her father. But it did the trick. We got Edward to confess. Did you get that on tape?' he asked, looking at Wallace.

'Yes. Everything's pretty clear and we're arresting him on suspicion of the manslaughter of Susan Canning and will be charged. We'll add the assault of your daughter too.' He stood up as a policeman asked him what they were to do with the old man.

Malcolm had forgotten about Archie in his concern for Louisa. Now he became aware of a weird noise coming from the bed.

'What's going to happen to me? Where have you taken my son? I can't cope on me own…lost everything…ain't fair, should have been provided for…' Archie tossed about on the bed, emitting a thin mewling sound like a baby. Malcolm gritted his teeth, still feeling the urge to hit the man. Archie deserved all that he got. And more. His one consolation was hearing him confess to killing his father.

Malcolm heard Wallace arrange for Social Services to be contacted, asking someone to call round as a matter of urgency. Minutes later an ambulance arrived and Louisa was placed gently on a stretcher and taken on board. Malcolm went with her while John followed in a police car.

For Malcolm the next two hours were the longest in his life. He had never liked hospitals, not since he had watched his mother deteriorate rapidly in those last days of her life. He could not bear the thought of losing Louisa and hated seeing her being wheeled off for scans and various tests. John kept him company but neither seemed willing to talk, taking it in turns to go in search of what passed for coffee in hospitals.

Eventually a doctor came up to announce that were no any signs of serious brain injury, and Louisa was now fully conscious. Malcolm's body sagged with relief. The doctor added that she was suffering from concussion and would need to spend the night in hospital.

'Can I see her?'

'Of course. She's in a private room as you requested, and you can sit with her as long as you like. But please don't tire her, she needs to rest. If you'd like to follow me?'

The two men followed the doctor to a room off the main trauma ward. Malcolm's stomach twisted at the sight of Louisa's white face bearing a padded dressing on her forehead. As they entered she opened her eyes.

'Did we do it? Has Edward been arrested?' she said, looking anxious.

'Yes we did. Thanks to you, darling. But you shouldn't have–'

'It's okay. I'm glad I was able to help. Just wish I'd been there to see him arrested,' she said, wincing as she tried to sit up. Malcolm eased her up gently, propping the pillows behind her.

John cleared his throat. 'Well done, Louisa. Mission accomplished. I just wanted to check you were all right before going back to my digs. I'll leave you two alone and catch up with you tomorrow.' He gave Louisa a peck on the cheek, careful to avoid the violet bruise close to her eye. A quick handshake with Malcolm and he left.

'Well, this seems a bit déjà vu, don't you think? Only last time it was me in the hospital bed!' joked Malcolm, holding onto her hand.

She grinned weakly. 'And then you were the one with the almighty headache! I've been told I can go home tomorrow as long as I'm not nauseous or see flashing lights.'

'That's good. The doctor said you needed to rest so perhaps I'd better leave you alone. Is there anything I can get you from home or the hospital shop?'

'I'm all right, thanks. I've been given what I need for tonight.' She yawned. 'If you don't mind…'

'Of course. I'll ring in the morning to find out what time I can collect you. Sleep well.' He dropped a kiss on her cheek and left.

★

235

Louisa woke the next morning with a splitting headache. For a moment she wondered where she was and then the memories flooded in. Even the pain could not dampen her pleasure of what she and Malcolm had achieved – with a little help from John and the police, of course. She was grateful she had only spent a short time in that awful room in the flat. It had taken all her self-control not to let the sickly smell force her out again. And that old man! It made her shudder to picture him; little more than a skeleton, with a face covered in liver spots and wrinkles and talking in that weedy voice. It had been instinctive to shield him from Edward's attack, but not because she felt he had a right to live. He and his son were poor specimens of humanity in her book. But it was clear to her he wasn't long for this world and she was happy for nature to take its course. As for Edward, he would be going to prison, as he richly deserved.

While the thoughts tumbled around, a knock on the door announced the arrival of a nurse bearing a breakfast tray. Not having eaten for twenty-four hours she was starving and soon tucked into the porridge and toast, washed down with a cup of tea. The nurse returned later to say that the doctor would be around shortly to decide if she was ready to go home. After checking her temperature and blood pressure, she suggested that Louisa try to walk to her bathroom for a shower unaided. This she managed, albeit slowly, and the nurse, looking satisfied, left.

Feeling much better after her shower, Louisa dressed quickly in yesterday's clothes. Her T-shirt bore a couple of blood stains and she could not wait to get home and change. The top she planned to throw away, not wanting any reminders of what had happened in that room. Provided with a basic toiletry kit, she carefully pulled a comb through her tangled, unwashed hair, wincing at the pain from her wound and the bump the size of an egg. The nurse had said to wait a few days before washing her hair, to allow the wound to heal. She tried to pull her hair over the ugly purple bruise but it still stood out against her pale face. Even her freckles were bleached of colour.

Louisa picked up a glossy magazine from a selection on a side table and settled in the easy chair to read, but nothing registered other than pictures of exotic places. She just wanted to go home and get back to normal. She sighed. Could life ever be normal after what she had experienced the past few months? She turned a page absentmindedly and was transfixed by a familiar sight. It was a photo of La Folie, the focus of an article highlighting spas and retreats. There was also a picture of Paul, leading a yoga class. She squeezed her eyes tight, ignoring the pain. *Oh, Paul! I need you, I miss you. Can we find a way to make it work between us?* The memory of their kiss caused her pulse to quicken, bringing warmth to her cheeks.

A knock at the door interrupted her reverie.

The doctor came in and smiled broadly as he saw her.

'Good morning. I'm pleased to see you're looking much better, more colour in your cheeks. How do you feel?' he asked, sitting on the bed beside her.

Louisa smiled inwardly. If only he knew where the colour came from! 'Better, thanks. Still have a headache but managed to have a quick shower.'

'Good. I'll give you a prescription for pain killers, but I'd expect you not to need them for much longer.' He reached for the chart at the end of the bed and glanced through it. 'All looks fine. I think we can let you go home, unless you'd rather stay and enjoy our hospitality longer?' he teased.

Louisa grinned. 'I'm happy to go home, thanks. Will someone let my…my father know?' She still found it strange to say "my father". But it felt good.

The doctor stood up, and shook her hand. 'Yes, we'll do that now. Look after yourself and try and stay away from people wielding bottles!' he said, with a wink.

After he left, she turned back to the article on La Folie, and her daydreams.

Once back at home, Louisa went upstairs to change. Feeling cleaner and more like her old self, she made a couple of phone calls. The first to Margaret, to find out how she was and to tell her of the latest developments.

Margaret's cough as she answered the phone told her that she was not much better. Not wanting her aunt to worry, she decided not to mention her head wound, focusing instead on Edward's arrest.

'Oh, Louisa, that's wonderful news! I'm so glad. You must be feeling relieved that it's all over,' Margaret croaked.

'Yes, although it's not over until after the trial. I'll have to be a witness and I'm not looking forward to that but…'

'Well, he might plead guilty and save you the trouble. Either way, my dear, I think you can be proud of what you and Malcolm have done. For…for Susan,' Margaret said, her voice breaking.

There was a pause as the women remembered their lost loved one and Louisa's eyes welled up. Dabbing them with a tissue, she needed to clear her throat before telling her aunt she hoped she would be better soon and would call again in a few days. She poured herself a glass of water before making the next call.

'Hi Charlotte, it's me.'

'Louisa! Thank goodness, I've been so worried about you. Now, tell me everything,' her friend said, relief in her voice.

Moments later, after hearing what had happened, Charlotte insisted on coming round to see for herself that Louisa was all right.

'I can be there in an hour; I just need to re-schedule a meeting. Take care, bye.'

Louisa went downstairs to tell Malcolm about Charlotte's impending visit. He was in the kitchen, checking their food supply.

'Good,' he said, looking up from his shopping list. 'We're low on a few items and I thought I'd pop round to the grocery store. You're in no fit state to eat out so I thought I'd include some ready prepared meals to put in the oven. I can manage that,' he said, smiling. 'You girls will want to chat without my hovering around so I'll go once Charlotte arrives. The doctor doesn't want you to be on your own in case you feel unwell.'

'Thanks. Shall I double-check what we need?'

Between them they finished the list and then Louisa mentioned she had spoken to her aunt, who was still too unwell to travel.

'That's a pity. I'd hoped to meet the lady while I'm here. Your mother always spoke so warmly of her. I gathered they were pretty close,' Malcolm said, leaning on the kitchen table.

'Yes, they were. Mum had her here to stay after Charles, her husband, died last year. I think Mum was trying to persuade Margaret to move down to London, but she's a country girl and wasn't keen.' She sighed. 'Perhaps it's as well she didn't come after…' she fell silent, chewing her lips. God, when would she stop wanting to burst into tears? She was so strung out emotionally…

Malcolm gripped her hand and they shared a moment of reflection.

The sound of the doorbell broke the silence and Louisa went to welcome her friend. The look of horror on

Charlotte's face was quickly replaced by a forced smile and a bear hug.

'You poor thing! Are you sure you shouldn't be in bed? I don't want to cause a relapse or something,' said Charlotte, hovering near the front door.

'It's not as bad as it looks. Come and say hi to Malcolm before he disappears.' She led the way to the kitchen where he was gathering up his list together with a few carrier bags.

'Hello, Malcolm. You're not going on my account, are you?'

He chuckled. 'No, my dear. Just buying supplies. I'll see you later.'

Louisa put the kettle on for coffee. Smiling, she said, 'Sorry I can't offer you calorie free cakes–'

'No problem,' said Charlotte, placing a Harrods shopping bag on the table. 'I thought you might want something to cheer yourself up and brought some goodies from home. Luckily, Mrs Thomas has been baking so...' she pulled out containers filled with muffins and biscuits and a bottle of Krug champagne. Louisa opened her mouth to protest, but Charlotte continued, 'I realise you can't drink alcohol at the moment, but it's for when you can. We'll just have to make do with coffee now,' she said, smiling. Louisa hugged her friend, overcome with her generosity and thoughtfulness. After loading up a tray, they went through to the garden, where the sun was shining as if nothing untoward had happened in the past twenty-four hours.

Charlotte looked around. 'I must say, you have a lovely garden. And, from what I've seen so far, a beautiful house. And a lot more manageable than mine!'

'Which is just as well, as not all of us can afford a housekeeper,' Louisa said, grinning at her friend. While they drank their coffee and nibbled the still-warm muffins,

Charlotte asked for more details of what had occurred at the Blakes' home. She listened intently, nodding or asking questions as Louisa described what Malcolm had told her and what she had heard from the listening device.

'God! Sounds like something one would watch on television. You know, those gritty detective dramas that are so addictive.' Charlotte frowned, 'Not that I'm saying–'

Louisa laughed. 'Don't worry, I know what you mean. I find it hard to believe myself that it's actually happened.' She touched her face. 'Until I look in the mirror and know it did.'

Charlotte leaned forward. 'You…you won't be scarred, will you?' Her voice was gentle.

'No, the doctor said it should heal cleanly. Luckily when the bottle broke on my head, I was only cut by one piece of glass. Although I was told it bled a lot, it wasn't that deep and the doctor sealed it with some special glue instead of stitches. I'm just glad it missed my eye.' She shuddered.

Charlotte nodded in agreement. 'Mm, by the way, have you heard from Paul? Does he know what's happened?'

'He's not rung and I've no idea if he knows. I suppose it's possible that Malcolm's told him but…' she shrugged, the mention of Paul reminding her of the article she had read that morning. And the feelings it evoked.

'I'm sure he'll get in touch once he knows. Now,' she said briskly, putting down her mug, 'I simply must tell you about this group I've joined…'

Louisa listened attentively, pleased by the change of subject. It turned out that Charlotte had signed up for a creative writing course, having attended the first session the previous evening.

'I couldn't actually use my real name in case someone recognised it, so I'm using a *nom de plume* which will also be my author name – if and when I write a novel that's

241

published.' She paused and Louisa cocked her head in anticipation.

'So? What *is* your name?'

'Louisa Krug.'

They stared at each other before erupting into a fit of giggling.

'You don't mind do you? It does have a certain *je ne sais quoi*, don't you agree?'

Louisa nodded. 'I think it's brilliant – and so *you*. But won't it upset the real Krugs?'

Charlotte waved her hands. 'Oh, that's not a problem. Daddy's grandmother was a Krug. That's why I adore their bubbly!' She laughed, setting off Louisa again. They were still laughing when Malcolm arrived at the kitchen door.

'I'm glad to see you girls are enjoying yourselves. And where did that bottle of Krug come from?'

This prompted more giggles and Malcolm, looking bemused, turned back into the kitchen to unpack the groceries.

Eventually calming down, they piled everything onto the tray and returned inside. Malcolm had put away the fresh food in the fridge, leaving various packets and bottles on the side. He grinned as they walked in.

'Care to share the joke?' he said.

Charlotte explained about her *nom de plume* and he whistled.

'What a great name! You're bound to be a success with a name like that. And you say you're related to the Krug family? Well, well. I do have some real classy guests at my little retreat, don't I?'

Louisa began putting away the remaining items from the shopping when Charlotte, glancing at her watch, groaned.

'I have to run. There's an important editorial meeting I simply cannot miss. Louisa, I'll ring later, see how you are.' She gave her a hug before saying to Malcolm, 'Care to show me out? There's something I want to ask...' Leaving the kitchen they headed for the front door and a few moments later, Louisa heard it open and the sound of muted voices. Then the door closed and her father walked into the kitchen.

'I hope you two weren't talking about me behind my back,' Louisa said, mock serious.

'She was only offering to help if needed. You've made a great friend there. Now, what do you fancy for lunch? There's...' he reeled off the choices and they started the preparations.

Over lunch in the garden, Malcolm told her that DI Wallace would be round later to take her statement. And that John would be with him.

She nodded, chewing on her salad. *Good, now they'll find out what had happened to the Blakes.*

Malcolm put down his knife and fork on the empty plate.

'Enjoyed that. Now, I need to make a few calls, if you'll excuse me,' he said, standing up. He looked down at her. 'You all right? Not feeling dizzy or nauseous? You would tell me, wouldn't you?'

She grinned at him. 'I'm absolutely fine, don't worry about me. And of course I'd say if I wasn't well, I'm no masochist!'

Looking reassured he carried his own plate into the kitchen, leaving her to finish the last few mouthfuls. She *was* all right, physically anyway. Her head still ached and the wound was sore and itchy, but she could cope with that. It was the pain in her heart she found hard to deal with. Talking to Margaret had stirred up the barely-buried hurt of losing her mother. And seeing and talking to Charlotte had reminded her of the other person missing from her life. Paul.

chapter 27

'Good afternoon, Louisa. How are you feeling?' asked Detective Inspector Wallace, standing on the doorstep, accompanied by his sergeant and John Ferguson.

Opening the door wide, she replied, 'Better, thanks. Please come in.'

She led them to the sitting room, where Malcolm was waiting. Greetings were exchanged. After everyone was seated, Louisa asked the question uppermost in her mind.

'What's happened to the Blakes?'

DI Wallace smiled grimly. 'Edward was remanded in custody after coming up before the magistrate this morning. We opposed bail and he'll be on remand until the case comes to court. Which will be weeks, if not months, from now. He's been charged with the manslaughter of your mother and assault against yourself.' He leaned forward. 'Are you happy to press charges against him for hitting you?'

Louisa nodded.

'Good. We'll be using your statement, as well as your father's, as evidence. Now, with regards Archie,' he pulled a face, 'he's been taken into hospital. The old bugger's had a relapse and not expected to live for more than a day or two.' He gave Malcolm a sympathetic look. 'The doctors reckon it was the shock of coming face to face with you and what you told Edward. Seems he had convinced himself his version of events was the real one and you turning up put paid to that. As you know, we hadn't intended to charge him with your father's death anyway, but it looks like he's about to get his just deserts. If that's any consolation.'

'It sure is. I hadn't expected him to be still alive, let alone confess what he'd done. So, I'm happy,' Malcolm said, nodding at the detective.

'Right. Now, Louisa, if you'd like to give us your statement, the sergeant will write it down and when it's typed up, perhaps you can come in and sign it?'

Once the detectives left, Louisa, Malcolm and John relaxed in the garden with cold drinks. The days were warming up as summer made its steady approach. Now late April, it was only a few weeks away.

'Well, John, I can't thank you enough for your help. Not sure if we'd have achieved what we did without you. So, here's to you, my friend.' Malcolm raised his glass of beer in salute, followed by Louisa with her glass of juice.

John shifted in his chair. 'Thank you. But I was only doing my job. It's what you pay me for,' he grinned at Malcolm.

'I know, but we're both more than pleased with the outcome. I'd like to think we can be friends and keep in touch when I'm back in Guernsey. Are you going home now?'

'Tomorrow. Having a last get-together with the lads tonight. Then it's back to the missus and snooping on adulterers!' he sighed.

Malcolm laughed. 'I'm planning to return to Guernsey in the next couple of days. We must go out to dinner...' The two men started to discuss the merits or otherwise of various local restaurants while Louisa felt numb, shocked that her father was abandoning her so soon. Not that she needed him, exactly, but it felt good to have him around and he'd become the one constant in her life of late. With Malcolm back in Guernsey, what should she do? Her aunt was being looked after by a neighbour and, besides, she couldn't go up there looking as she did now.

Margaret would have a fit. Anyway, she was to return to the hospital for a check-up the following week so had to stay in London. Thank goodness Charlotte was around! Her friend was great company and perhaps they could spend more time together once Malcolm had left. The thought was cheering but did not stop the nagging idea that she was becoming needy, something she had vowed never to become. Muttering, 'Excuse me,' she picked up her empty glass and went to the kitchen.

After pouring a refill, she stayed there, watching the men through the window. The two of them got on so well, she thought, pleased for her father. He had found a mate to talk to and she knew he would keep his word about dinner with John. From what he had told her, his life had been that of a loner, but that was changing. Which was good. Though it brought home to her that she had to make changes in her own life. But what? At that moment, the thought of looking for another job was distinctly unappealing. Even if she could find one in a lovely natural health centre like La Folie…She gulped. That was the crux of the problem. She really wanted to work there. With Paul. But then they couldn't be a couple…*Oh, damn it! What the hell am I going to do?*

After John's departure Louisa, pleading a headache, went upstairs to rest. The headache was real enough and she swallowed some pain killers before curling up on her bed. The events of the past couple of days were catching up with her and she was soon fast asleep. However, it was far from restful. The confrontation at the Blakes' flat formed part of a weird dream; one minute she was there, facing Edward and Archie, the next she was seeing Edward leaning over her mother, holding a bottle, about to smash it onto her head. She rushed forward to stop him, and he turned, morphing into Archie holding a paperweight which he brought down on her own head. She woke, covered in sweat, her heart beating so fast that she thought it would burst. Gulping lungfuls of air, she struggled into a sitting position, relieved to find she was in her own bed and still alive. The images stayed imprinted on her mind for what seemed like ages, but was actually only a moment or two. Crawling to her kitchenette she filled a glass with water and drank greedily. Her head throbbed but, on checking her watch, she saw it was only two hours since taking the painkillers. Re-filling her glass, she slumped into an armchair in her sitting room. Slowly, the throbbing eased and she felt ready to re-join Malcolm downstairs.

They shared a subdued supper in the kitchen that evening. They could have eaten in the dining room but, as it was last used for her mother's funeral, Louisa could not face eating there. Not yet. Malcolm had remarked on her pale face and she admitted she had had a bad dream, but did not elaborate.

'By the way, I've been thinking about those darned jewels. I can't go on keeping them locked in a safe forever. Strictly speaking they should be yours, being passed down to the women of the family. My great-grandfather gave them to his bride on their wedding day and, according to my mother, my father planned to do the same on theirs. Would you like them?' He gave her a quizzical look.

Louisa was stunned. Millions of pounds worth of jewels! And they could be hers. But...

'Thanks for the offer, but I think they've caused enough problems for all concerned. There's no way I'd be comfortable wearing them. As they were stolen originally, would it be better to return them to the rightful owner? The Government or whoever?'

He smiled. 'I'd hoped you say that. Queen Victoria would have been the original beneficiary, and may well have donated the jewels to the V&A along with other various artefacts from India. So, how about we do that? Donate them to the V&A Museum? I'm sure they'd be delighted.'

'What a great idea! Then at least the jewels would be seen by thousands of people and not locked away.' She was struck by a thought. 'You wouldn't be in trouble with the authorities for possession, would you?'

He laughed. 'No, these things happen all the time. I'll make some enquiries once I'm home.'

Malcolm was helping her clear away the dishes when the phone rang. Louisa was relieved to find it was Charlotte. As they started chatting, Malcolm indicated he would finish off and Louisa moved to the sitting room.

'You're sounding a bit down. Is anything wrong?' Charlotte asked.

Louisa told her about Malcolm leaving and the bad dream.

'Oh, I'm sorry to hear that. But I'm sure Malcolm won't leave if you need him.'

Louisa sighed. 'That's the point. I shouldn't need him. I'm a grown woman–'

'Yes, a grown woman who's had some shitty things happen recently. No wonder you're feeling vulnerable.' Charlotte seemed to be thinking, before adding, 'Once your father leaves you would be very welcome to come here. There's bags of room as you well know!'

Louisa was touched. 'That's very sweet of you, but I must learn to be less needy. I figure my emotions are all over the place at the moment, which is why I get upset over nothing–'

'Nothing! I hardly think being nearly killed by the man who killed your mother is nothing! Which reminds me, have you heard from the police yet?'

Louisa told her friend about their visit, adding that she was going to the station tomorrow to sign her statement.

'I'm so pleased that this horrible business is nearly behind you. How about coming round here after you've been to the station? I'm working from home for the day and I'll ask Mrs Thomas to make some more of her delicious muffins. How are you getting there?'

'The police will pick me up.'

'Good. Ask them to drop you round here and afterwards you can get a taxi home. Sorted.' Her voice softened, 'Hope you have a good night's sleep and I'll see you tomorrow. Night.'

Louisa could not help but smile at her friend's taking control. At least it showed she cared, which was more than could be said for some, she thought ruefully, thinking of Paul.

After breakfast the next day, Malcolm announced he had booked a flight for the following morning.

'As long as you're feeling okay and can manage without me,' he added, patting her arm. 'There's things needing my attention in Guernsey, but I can postpone if necessary.'

'I'll be fine. I've got Charlotte and, in fact she's invited me to stay with her, but I said no.'

Malcolm's eyebrows lifted. 'Did she? That was kind of her. Why did you refuse?'

'Well, she has a company to run. She hasn't time to nursemaid me! I can potter around the garden here, there's loads to do. The weeding for a start. And I can plant some bulbs and replenish the pots.' She managed a smile. Although she did intend to do all those things, her heart wasn't in it. But her mother would turn in her grave if she saw her garden being neglected.

Malcolm frowned. 'Mm. You will come over to Guernsey soon won't you? Once you've been given the all clear from the doctor.' He coughed. 'I...I shall miss you.'

'Oh. I guess I could. For a few days, perhaps. Before I start looking for a job,' she said, knowing she would miss him too. Would it be awkward seeing Paul if he were around when she visited Malcolm? She would have to cope with that if and when it happened.

When Louisa came downstairs the next morning Malcolm's case was sitting by the front door. Although still not happy about his leaving, she was feeling much better in herself. A good night's sleep had helped and her head no longer hurt except when she combed her still unwashed hair. She had resorted to using a dry shampoo to keep it looking, and smelling, clean. Putting on a cheerful smile, she walked into the kitchen and came face to face with Paul.

chapter 28

'Hello, Louisa. How are you?' Paul strode across the floor and embraced her before kissing her cheek. His eyes were clouded with concern.

'I…I'm okay, thanks. This…this is a surprise!' She felt her legs wobble and sat down on the nearest chair. What on earth? Did her father set this up? Her eyes swivelled towards Malcolm, who was making a fuss of filling the kettle. Catching her eye, he smiled.

'Paul wanted to see for himself that you were okay, so we thought he could take a couple of days break over here, while I shoot back to Guernsey.' He nodded at Paul. 'I'm fixing breakfast for us before I leave. Paul caught the red-eye so I'm sure he's famished.'

He had set the table with plates and bowls and now fetched the box of muesli from the larder and the juice from the fridge.

Louisa was in shock. She felt the heat in her cheeks from Paul's kiss and embrace. Not sure what it all meant, she decided that it had to be good if he cared enough to take time off. And Malcolm had obviously approved it…

'Louisa? I asked if you want some toast,' Malcolm's voice cut in.

She nodded and the men joined her at the table.

'How…how much do you know about what happened?' she asked Paul, who sat opposite.

He looked sombre. 'Malc told me everything. I'm so sorry you got hurt, but glad that you found those men and you'll have justice for your mother. That's what you wanted, wasn't it?' His voice was gentle.

Gripping her mug of coffee in front of her as if it was a shield, she nodded. 'Yes,' she whispered.

Conversation was sparse during the meal, the air heavy with the words unsaid. Louisa struggled to chew the food in front of her and her stomach was so knotted she worried she would be sick.

At last they all finished and Malcolm, after checking the time, said that his car would be arriving any minute. Pushing back his chair he came round the table to pull Louisa to her feet, enveloping her in a bear hug.

'You take care of yourself, you hear? Any problems just give me a ring. I want you to know I'm always there for you. And I hope to see you soon.' He stood back and she saw a twinkle in his eyes. *Did he know something?* She smiled and kissed his cheek as the doorbell rang.

'You take care too. And thanks for everything.'

He shook hands with Paul before walking with her to the front door. She stood on the threshold while he got into the waiting limo, waving as it pulled away. Taking a deep breath she returned to the kitchen and Paul.

'Okay. What's going on? You and Malcolm have cooked this up between you and–'

He stopped her with a kiss. A kiss that went on and on until she felt she was running out of air and pulled back a little. His eyes were so close she could see the warmth and desire reflected in their depths and she gasped.

'Malc has taken on the role of matchmaker,' he said, grinning. 'Or it might be more accurate to say that Charlotte has.'

'How come…?'

'She told Malc that you…care for me and that you had heard I care about you, too. But that there'd been a misunderstanding so neither of us had said anything. Is it true? Do you feel something more than friendship for me?' His eyes held hers as they remained in a locked embrace.

'Yes,' she whispered.

His face broke into a broad smile. 'That's what I hoped to hear.' He gently pushed her hair back from her face, his fingers stroking her yellowing bruise. His voice husky, he went on, looking more serious, 'I'd really like to make love to you but I don't know if you're ready. Your head…'

Her heart sang with joy. 'You don't have to worry about that. Anyway, I heard sex is good for headaches!' She giggled. His face cleared and she took his hand, leading him upstairs to her bedroom.

Opening her eyes, the first thing she was aware of was that she wasn't alone. Turning her head on the pillow she saw Paul's beloved face, his eyes closed in sleep. Knowing he had been awake since dawn, she did not want to disturb him. Anyway, she wanted to continue drinking him in while re-living their sensuous love-making. She still tingled with the after-glow and her limbs felt as light as air. Her head no longer throbbed and she grinned at the thought of no longer needing painkillers. Being loved in such a way was soooo much better! Paul had brought her to heights she didn't know were possible and their bodies felt so right together. The joining of yin and yang energies, as Paul would say. As he slept his arm lay across her body and she felt secure as well as loved. She sent up a silent prayer of thanks to Charlotte and Malcolm for making this possible.

Paul's eyes fluttered open and he smiled.

'Hi, gorgeous,' he said, stroking her face. 'That was wonderful! Do you fancy a repeat performance?' Before she could reply, his lips connected with hers and his hand began to stroke her thighs. She didn't resist.

By the time they finally made it downstairs, it was lunchtime. And for some reason they were both starving.

Malcolm had stocked the fridge with a great choice, and they were soon in the garden sharing a prawn salad.

'So, when exactly did my father phone you?'

He looked up and grinned. 'A couple of days ago. Apparently Charlotte had convinced him he should suggest I come over. But she told him before she left Guernsey that she knew we both cared for each other.'

Louisa chewed this over. 'The problem was you offered me a job, and then later that evening implied that we couldn't have a relationship if I *did* work at La Folie. It was confusing, to put it mildly. I'd thought there was something between us.'

He squirmed in his chair. 'Yeh, that was stupid of me, wasn't it? I didn't think it through. I offered you the job so that we could spend time together; later realising that both the staff and Malc might not be too keen on the idea.' He stroked the back of her hand. 'Malc's made it clear he's totally for you joining the team and he'll make sure no-one's unhappy. We have a friendly bunch of therapists, as you know,' Louisa nodded in agreement, 'and they all like you. And adore Malc, so it's not a problem.'

'Does that mean that the offer's still open?'

'What do you think?' he said, leaning over to brush her lips with his own.

She felt herself melt inside. God, how was she going to cope, working with this man who had this devastating effect on her?

'Okay, if I do accept, where am I supposed to live? It's too soon for us to shack up together.'

He nodded. 'Absolutely. I – we – thought you might prefer to rent your own place. Keep some independence.'

She laughed. 'You two have got it all worked out, haven't you? And what if I'd said no?' she teased, tilting her head.

'Oh, that was never likely to happen, was it? Not with my...powers of persuasion.' He kissed her palm before going further up her bare arm.

'Behave yourself! I'm hungry – for food! But seriously, we'll have to be more circumspect when working together. And that might prove difficult if you keep looking at me like that.'

'Don't worry, I'm the consummate professional, as I'm sure so are you. I think the only thing that bothers Malc is the chance that we might fall out and one of us would have to leave.' His eyes clouded at the thought and for a moment Louisa imagined the awfulness of that occurring.

'Hey, we'll just have to make sure that doesn't happen, won't we? As long as you continue making love to me like you did this morning, there'll be no problem,' she said. Then added, with a cheeky grin, 'Failing that, just remember who's the boss's daughter!'

He aimed a bread roll at her, bringing on a fit of the giggles. They finished their meal happy that plans were advancing for their future together.

Later that evening, while Paul was preparing dinner at his own suggestion, Louisa curled up in the sitting room to phone Margaret and Charlotte. Her aunt was stunned at her news, never having heard Paul mentioned until now. Louisa explained how their relationship had developed and that her father had given them his blessing. Margaret, still fighting her cough, said she hoped to meet both men as soon as she was fit. Louisa invited her to stay with her in Guernsey as soon as she had found a place to rent. Paul had already hinted that Malcolm was planning to check the availability of open market flats: not being a "local" she was, like him, restricted in where she lived. Her aunt, seemingly mollified, wished her well. Breathing a sigh of relief, Louisa then called Charlotte.

'He's here!' she burst out as Charlotte answered the phone.

'He? Who…Oh, Paul! Paul's arrived at your house? Well, well, well. Tell me everything. And I mean *everything.*'

Charlotte's husky laugh echoed down the line several times as Louisa brought her up to speed. She was clearly delighted that her chats to Malcolm had brought results.

'So, where's the lovely man now?'

'In the kitchen cooking supper, so I can't talk much longer. And…and it looks like I'll be moving to Guernsey as soon as I find somewhere to rent. You will come and visit, won't you?'

'Will be delighted. I'm booked into La Folie in September, so will see you then if not before. It'll seem strange you being a therapist and not a guest. You might be too busy to talk to me.'

'I'll find time. Paul's assured me that I won't be working silly hours, probably four days a week at most. He's taking on another yoga teacher too, so that he can spend more time as the manager. As long as he works out the schedules so that we get time off together, it should be fine.'

They chatted for a couple more minutes before Paul popped his head round the door to announce supper was ready. Louisa quickly arranged to meet with her friend once Paul returned to Guernsey in a couple of days.

Before he left, Paul accompanied Louisa to the hospital for her check-up and they were both relieved when the doctor passed her fit. The dressing was removed and the wound had healed cleanly: although there was a scar, the doctor assured her it would be invisible within a few weeks. He also advised her against high-impact sports for a while, but as none figured in her life, it was not an issue. As soon as they arrived home she headed for the shower and Paul joined her, tenderly washing her hair so that she became both soothed and turned on by his fingers massaging her head. They dried each other off before falling onto the bed. After some quick, but satisfying lovemaking, they dressed ready to go to the airport.

Malcolm had generously organised a car, giving them more time to relax together. During the journey they sat, hands clasped, making plans for when Louisa would join Paul. She had to find a tenant for her house first: not wanting to sell yet, if at all. It would be a good investment, bringing in a substantial income if she kept it. And she had to resolve the issue of what to do with the business. Malcolm had already emailed agents' details of apartments to rent in Guernsey and Louisa looked forward to sifting through them.

As they stood entwined outside the terminal, they shared a last, lingering kiss before reluctantly drawing apart, conscious that the chauffeur was keeping the engine running. With a final wave, Paul turned and went through the glass doors. Louisa, already bereft, huddled onto the vast rear seat, lost in the expanse of leather. The driver glanced at her through the rear-view mirror and smiled sympathetically before pulling out from the kerb and driving her home.

chapter 29

Over the next few days Louisa barely had time to think. Which was a blessing; whenever she had a breathing space, her thoughts turned to Paul and how much she missed him. They kept in touch by phone and hearing his voice proved a powerful incentive to work through her lengthy to-do list as quickly as possible. Charlotte recommended a top agency to handle a lease on the house, but the hard part was accepting the need to pack up her mother's precious furniture and personal possessions, such as books, paintings and ornaments. The task seemed overwhelming and again Charlotte came to the rescue. She suggested that a friend of hers, normally hired to de-clutter a home, be asked to help. Louisa thought it a brilliant idea and, once a tenant was found, planned to use her services. In the meantime, she had to discuss the future of the travel agency with Glenn, the manager. She had just put the phone down after arranging a meeting with him for that afternoon, when it rang.

'Louisa Canning.'

'Morning, Louisa. It's Detective Inspector Wallace, I've got some news for you.' His voice was sombre.

Her immediate reaction was that something was wrong. That Edward had somehow escaped and was on the run. Coming after her…Taking a deep breath, she managed to say, 'Right. Has something happened?'

'Yes. Archie Blake died last night. Thought you might like to know.'

The relief was immense. That horrible old man was dead! Good riddance to bad rubbish, as her grandmother used to say.

'Thanks for telling me, I appreciate that. I'll let my father know, I'm sure he'll be…pleased. Will Edward be allowed to attend the funeral?'

'I should think so, if he wants to. But I got the impression there was no love lost between them after he learned the truth. Be assured, if he does attend, he'll be hand-cuffed and guarded at all times.' He coughed, as if acknowledging his part in allowing Louisa to risk her life by meeting Edward. 'Oh, and speaking of Edward, we have a date for the trial: the second week of July. Just got in before the summer recess.'

'That's good. When will I know if I have to appear?'

'Not until his plea is taken, I'm afraid. Although he confessed, he could retract and plead not guilty. Personally, I doubt it, but we have to assume the worst and arrange background reports as well as collate the evidence.' She heard an exasperated sigh. 'All a load of bureaucratic nonsense, if you ask me, but…' Louisa imagined him shrugging.

'Okay. I'll pencil it in my diary and keep my fingers crossed. Thanks for phoning, Inspector.'

After phoning Malcolm with the detective's news, she pushed the unpleasant thought of the impending trial to the back of her mind and switched on her laptop. Her father had said he had emailed details of a new rental property and she was keen to take a look. So far she had not seen anything appealing: mainly apartments in the busy town centre, but she really wanted something with outside space. The rental costs approached those of London and she despaired of finding something she liked at a reasonable price. Opening Malcolm's link she was pleased to see the property was a 1930s semi in a small close within walking distance of the town centre. It had plenty of off-street parking and a pretty, sheltered garden. And available at the end of May – only a month away. It was perfect! She phoned the agent to arrange a viewing and was told that a let had been agreed within the past hour. Disappointed, she asked to go on the mailing list, explaining her preference for parking and outside space.

Glancing at her watch and seeing it was time to see Glenn, she left the house to walk the few hundred yards to the office. One of a little row of bijou shops and cafés, not far from Angel station, the agency's windows bore none of the garish travel posters favoured by the giant travel companies. "Voyages" was started by her mother to cater to the wealthy: those who wanted tailor-made itineraries and absolute attention to detail. Nothing was too much trouble; the clients' needs were paramount. At the time the business had begun, there were few offering such a service and Susan quickly cornered the market. Nowadays, there was fierce competition from bigger companies, but the regular clientele stayed loyal. Thanks to the internet, most of their clients now contacted them via email rather than in person. Susan's death had not, according to Glenn, affected business – a reflection on the high quality of the staff and their training.

The office looked more like a small, intimate club than a travel agency. Comfortable leather chairs were set round low tables spread with the crème de la crème of travel brochures. A couple of clients were in deep conversation with assistants who, with rapt attention, wrote copious notes of their requirements. Louisa smiled at the girls before going through to Glenn's office. It had been Susan's and she still found it hard not to see her mother sitting behind the antique desk, smiling a greeting.

Glenn looked up from a pile of what appeared to be bank statements. He came round the desk to give her a warm hug.

'How are you? When you told me what that monster had done to you I was ready to go out and kill him!' he cried.

Louisa grinned. Glenn was, as ever, a tad theatrical, but he knew his job backwards and the clients adored him almost as much as they had her mother.

'It's fortunate he's locked away out of reach, then. I wouldn't want my favourite manager to end up in jail, too,' she said, sinking into a chair.

Glenn chuckled before returning to his seat.

Then, looking more serious, he said, 'You wanted to talk about the future of "Voyages"? I can assure you it's still doing well…'

'I know. I've seen the figures.' She hesitated, wondering how to broach the subject. 'The thing is, Glenn, I'm planning to leave London and move to Guernsey and…and I don't want the responsibility of the business any more. You're doing a brilliant job, but…well, I need a fresh start.' She hardly dared look at him, afraid of his reaction.

But, surprisingly, he was smiling. 'I've been expecting this. Particularly after you told me about your father.' Glenn picked up a sheaf of papers and pushed them across to her. 'I've been giving it a great deal of thought and would like to buy the business from you. Here's my proposal.'

Louisa felt a weight lifting from her shoulders. It would be the perfect solution but she knew the business was worth a tidy sum and doubted if Glenn could afford it.

'I know what you're thinking and I have a plan. I propose to pay you a lump sum now and the rest monthly over the next three years. As long as you were happy with that, of course,' he said, looking less confident.

'Let me look at the figures first.'

The proposed offer was based on the valuation produced for probate and the figures looked reasonable. The initial lump sum was about half of the valuation and Louisa was happy for the rest to be paid over time. She knew she could sell to one of the bigger companies; indeed the sharks had been circling since her mother's death, but she wanted the business to remain as it was. And Glenn was the ideal man to ensure it did.

'Well, this looks fine. I'm happy to accept the terms. As long as you haven't had to mortgage the wife and kids to raise the money!' she joked.

Glenn beamed. 'As you well know, Louisa, that's not at all likely! Oh, come on, let's have a hug to celebrate.' They embraced, laughing, before Glenn disappeared into the kitchen to make a celebratory cup of tea.

'It should be something stronger but you know the rule, no alcohol on the premises. Your mum was right, but it would have been appropriate for once.'

'Tell you what, let's go to the pub for a drink once you close the office. The girls can come and we'll have a proper celebration. I haven't been able to drink because of this,' she said, pointing to her head, 'but am allowed to now. And you've just made my day.'

'And you mine! We'll meet you there in,' he glanced at his watch, 'twenty minutes? I'll tell the girls.'

Finishing her tea, Louisa left and took her time walking to the pub, enjoying some window-shopping on the way. The happiness she felt at Glenn taking on the business more than made up for losing the house in Guernsey. She would just have to keep looking…

A couple of days later the agent handling her house called Louisa to say she had someone wanting to view. They agreed a time for later that day and in the meantime she rushed around tidying up. As most of the rooms were not being used, it did not take too long, but it affected her emotionally. It brought home that her life was about to undergo a major change and, although it was what she wanted and longed for, it was scary. Having already effectively sold her mother's business, she was about to rent out her beloved house to strangers. *Oh, Mum, please don't be cross! Glenn will make a great owner of the agency and I'll be careful who I choose to live here. And I know you would have adored Paul! I really want it to work for us and so does Malcolm. Oh, I wish you were here, Mum.* She had to force back the tears as she gathered up the cleaning bits and pieces and returned them to the kitchen cupboard. It was at times like this that she wished her mother had been buried, not cremated. She would have loved to take flowers to the grave and have a chat. But Margaret, ever practical and forced to organise everything, had opted for a cremation. As she had for Charles. Louisa accepted it was the more eco option, but it still did not feel right.

Dead on time, the agent rang the doorbell and Louisa made herself smile welcomingly at the couple accompanying her. Introduced as Mr and Mrs Saunders and in their late thirties, she guessed, they seemed nice enough. They needed a home for themselves and their children while the husband took up a new twelve-month contract in London. At the moment they lived in Manchester and would rent out their own house until they returned. Louisa let the agent show them around while she weeded some garden pots.

They followed her outside after touring the house and Louisa could see how impressed they were. As they should, she thought. She heard them mention her little flat as being ideal for the nanny. Twenty minutes later she showed everyone out and the agent promised to be in touch. Louisa made herself a much-needed cup of coffee and took it outside. About an hour later the agent rang to say the couple loved the house and wanted to take the lease for the twelve months.

'That's...that's great. I thought they seemed keen. When do they want to move in?'

There was a cough on the end of the line.

'Ah, well. I do hope that this will not be a problem, but they want to move in a month from now. Or they will withdraw their offer.'

chapter 30

Louisa panicked and phoned Charlotte. Her friend dispensed her usual words of wisdom.

'It can be done. With a lot of help, naturally. When do you have to let them know?'

'First thing tomorrow. They're due to fly back to Manchester in the afternoon. Apparently they had agreed on a house but the owner changed their mind at the last minute, deciding to sell instead. So, they're pretty desperate. But so am I! I haven't anywhere to live.'

'Calm down, I'm sure there's somewhere you could stay. You can come here if you can't find something in Guernsey. But I'm sure Malcolm would put you up until you found a place. Either way, it's not an issue. I think you're panicking because you realise it's time to move on. And sooner than you thought.' Charlotte's voice was gentle, sounding sympathetic.

Louisa knew she was right. She had been facing up to moving on since selling the business. It was just happening so fast...

'So, what are you going to do?'

'Accept, I guess. They seem ideal tenants and have glowing references, so the agent said. And they would be happy for me to leave some of the furniture as their own house is smaller. We'd have to agree on which bits, but that should be okay. I'm looking for something small in Guernsey so won't need to take all that much.'

'Good girl. I'll give Fiona a ring and tell her to expect your call when you've finalised the details. She'll be a big help, I promise. Several friends have used her to de-clutter their homes. Something I'm not in need of at the moment!' she laughed.

It was too early to phone Paul, working until seven that night, so she rang Malcolm to get his viewpoint.

'That's great news, my dear. Can't say I'm surprised it's gone so quickly, it really is a beautiful house.'

'It would have been even better if I hadn't missed that house you sent me details of. Apparently it went that morning and would have been ideal for me.'

'Something will turn up, it always does. Once you've got the ball rolling over there, why don't you come over for a couple of days and look around for yourself? You'll get a much better feel for the properties in the flesh, as it were. Stay with me and I'll drive you around. Afraid we're full at La Folie.'

'Thanks, I'd like that. I should look for myself. Oh, and I've sold the business...' She went on to explain the deal with Glenn and he sounded delighted. He had met Glenn when he went in to tell him about Louisa's injury and she knew he had liked him.

'That man's got great people skills and is ideal to take over. That way there's no outward change to the ownership, which is good. I've been thinking I should talk to him about a cross-promotion with La Folie. He could make all the booking and travel arrangements for guests. What do you think?'

They talked for a while longer before leaving it that Louisa would let him know when she could come over. She felt much more positive after the call so that by the time she phoned Paul, she had convinced herself that moving out of her home in a month's time was a minor challenge rather than a disaster.

'Hi, it's me. I've got something exciting to tell you...'

The agent sounded pleased when Louisa phoned to accept the couple's conditions. Louisa wasn't surprised; the agency had earned a fat commission for very little work. The wife had asked, if the deal was on, if she could call round to discuss the furniture. Louisa was happy to agree and an hour later a beaming Mrs Saunders arrived. They walked round, each with their notepads, conferring on what could be left behind. It was all very amicable and an hour later they shook hands on what they had agreed. From Louisa's point of view it had worked well, she would be saved either storing or selling furniture she might not yet need, but may want in the future. It was time to phone Fiona, the "de-clutter" lady.

Fiona turned out to be very similar to Charlotte, and Louisa was not at all surprised to learn they had been at school together. Like her friend, she was warm and friendly, if slightly bossy, and sympathetic to Louisa's plight. It transpired that it was not the first time she had helped someone clear a house following a death. They went through each room methodically, making various lists: 'To keep', 'To throw away', 'To sell', 'To store', 'Charity shop'. The worst part was going through her mother's clothes and intimate possessions. Soon after Susan's death, Margaret had chosen, with Louisa's approval, a few pieces as mementoes of her beloved sister. At the time Louisa had not felt able to face a proper sort-out. Fiona was at her kindest, helping to fill black bin liners with clothes destined for charity shops; setting aside those to be sold at dress agencies. Fiona had all the requisite contacts and promised to arrange for collections. Going through the house took a whole day and by the end Louisa was as wrung out as a rag. After Fiona left, she crawled onto the sofa clutching her mother's photo, and howled.

The next morning, after enjoying the sleep of the exhausted, Louisa woke determined to crack on and complete the necessary arrangements for her move. Although painful, the sifting through the house and its memories had been cathartic. Feeling ready to face the world, albeit with puffy eyes and a still-bruised face, she leapt out of bed, her to-do list running through her brain. After breakfast she phoned the removal firm recommended by Fiona and was promised a visit after lunch. The man she spoke to confirmed they could arrange to have her moved by the agreed date and provided a full packing service. She would only need to finish filling bin liners with items to be thrown away, and pack her personal stuff. Until she knew she had a place of her own, everything would go into storage.

The morning was spent focusing on the rubbish and the bin bags piled up alarmingly. She planned to ferry them to the local tip a car-full at a time. Fiona must have made the promised calls, as Louisa was phoned by the charity and the dress agency to organise collections. She arranged for that to happen the next morning, then phoned Glenn to ask him to book a flight to Guernsey for the following afternoon.

After the meeting with the removal man, Louisa began the trips to the tip. It was late afternoon before she returned from the final one and felt absolutely filthy. She was having supper at Charlotte's that evening and jumped in the shower to wash away the grime before changing into an outfit befitting the occasion.

Sitting back in her seat as the plane took off, Louisa could not help comparing the difference between how she felt now and the first time she had flown to Guernsey. Then, she had been anxious about meeting her father. Always assuming she *would* meet him. And how he would react to learning he had a daughter. Now, she was not only on her way to stay with Malcolm, but was also looking forward to being re-united with the man she loved. Thinking about it, she had been lucky enough to gain not one, but *two* loving men in her life, and found herself grinning with pleasure.

Malcolm was waiting at the airport and they were soon driving away into St Peter Port.

'I've arranged for us to see a property this afternoon. If it doesn't suit, we can look at others tomorrow. Oh, and I've booked a table at La Fregate for the three of us tonight. If that's okay?' he said, with a broad smile.

'Fine by me. Have you got the property details with you?' She hoped it would tick the right boxes.

'No, the agent will bring them along. But I'm sure you'll like it. Now, tell me how the plans for the removal are progressing.'

Louisa did not know St Peter Port well and when Malcolm pulled off The Grange, one of the main roads leading into the town, she was lost. He drove along a one-way street until, after turning right into a close, he pulled into a drive which looked familiar.

'But…isn't this the house that's been let? The one I really liked,' she said, puzzled.

'Yes it is, but don't worry about that. It's available if you like it.' Getting out of the car, she followed him up the drive to the front door, where a young woman waited, a folder tucked under her arm.

'Mr Roget, good to see you again. And you must be Miss Canning. How do you do? Please, come on in.' She opened the door, signalling them to follow. 'I'll wait here until you've looked around and will be happy to answer any questions you may have then.'   Before Louisa could say anything, Malcolm marched through the kitchen and into the garden. She had no choice but to follow, getting a quick glimpse at the modern kitchen, before joining him. The garden was just as pretty as it looked in the details.

'What do you think? Would you like to live here? I know you've not seen it all yet, but–'

The penny dropped. 'You've been here before, haven't you? And you agreed to rent it?' She didn't know whether to be pleased or annoyed that he had made the decision without asking her.

'Well, I didn't want to risk you losing it. The agent already had more viewings lined up. So I asked Paul to come with me and we both thought it was perfect. But if you really don't like it we can cancel the deal,' he said, his face registering uncertainty.

'Let me see the rest and I'll tell you.' Keeping her expression neutral, she went inside for a detailed tour, leaving Malcolm outside. When she returned to the garden she was grinning. 'I love it, thanks. But why didn't either of you let me know? I've been totally worried I wouldn't find somewhere in time.'

He looked relieved. 'I wanted to surprise you. And, to be honest, hadn't realised how disappointed you were when it was let.' They shared a conciliatory hug before going in search of the agent. Louisa had a couple of questions to ask and, satisfied with the answers, asked when she had to sign the lease.

The young woman, frowning, looked between her and Malcolm. 'But–'

'It's all right, Jane, I'll explain to my daughter. Thanks for showing us around. I'll be in touch.'

They said their goodbyes and got back into Malcolm's car.

'Okay, what is it you have to explain? Seems you've kept something else from me,' Louisa said, turning to face him. Holding her hand, he said, 'Knowing you won't be earning a lot at the centre, I wanted to help with the cost of your accommodation. So the lease is in my name because I'm paying the rent.'

On the way to his apartment, Louisa tried to persuade Malcolm to change his mind, but he was adamant. It was his way of making up for the "lost years" as he called them. This brought a lump to her throat and she gave in. At least he hadn't gone and bought her a house, she consoled herself. If she and Paul looked as if they would stay together, then she would sell her London house and buy here. But for now, this arrangement suited her perfectly.

Before Paul was due to arrive, Malcolm said he wanted to say something important.

'The reason I've poked my nose in between you and Paul is that I didn't want you both making the same mistake that I did with your mother.'

Louisa leaned forward on the sofa, wondering where this was going.

'I was too pig-headed to admit I loved Susan and we…we lost each other. Missing out on years of what I'm sure would have been a wonderful time together. Raising our daughter,' he said, gripping her hand. She felt a lump in her throat. 'No-one can guarantee that you two will have a long and loving life together, but at least now you can give it a shot.'

'I…I don't know what to say,' she said, smiling. He had more than made up for those "lost years". She could draw a line under the past and its sorrows and look forward to a future containing not only a new love, but her father.

Kissing his cheek, she murmured, 'Thanks, Dad. For everything.'

COMING NEXT

The Family Divided
– The Guernsey Novels (Book 4)

Edmund Batiste is killed during the German Occupation of Guernsey. Labelled a collaborator, it was assumed he was punished by the local resistance. But was he? Years later, his grandson, Andy, seeks to find the truth of what really happened, and why his pregnant grandmother was forced to flee from the island after it was liberated. The wealthy Batiste family has remained divided ever since: Edmund's brother is now the head of the family and enjoying the wealth that would have been Edmund's. Andy not only wants to clear the family's name, but to restore his father's rightful inheritance.

Charlotte Townsend was left by her husband and found healing at La Folie, the natural health centre in Guernsey. Returning for another retreat, she meets Andy and together they embark on a search for the truth.

Lightning Source UK Ltd.
Milton Keynes UK
UKOW04f1355041217
313844UK00001B/140/P